Candy

Other titles by Sarra Manning:

Guitar Girl
Pretty Things
Diary of a Crush: French Kiss
Diary of a Crush: Kiss and Make Up
Diary of a Crush: Sealed With a Kiss
Let's Get Lost

Look out for:

Fashionistas: Laura
Fashionistas: Hadley
Fashionistas: Irina

Sarra Manning

Fashionistas

Candy

Hodder Children's Books

A DIVISION OF HACHETTE CHILDREN'S BOOKS

Text copyright © 2008 Sarra Manning

First published in Great Britain in 2008
by Hodder Children's Books

1

A Catalogue record for this book is available from the British Library

ISBN-13: 978 0 340 93223 0

Typeset in Bembo by Avon DataSet Ltd, Bidford on Avon, Warwickshire

Printed and bound in China by Imago

The paper and board used in this paperback by Hodder Children's Books
are natural recyclable products made from wood grown in sustainable
forests. The manufacturing processes conform to the environmental
regulations of the country of origin.

Hodder Children's Books
a division of Hachette Children's Books
338 Euston Road, London NW1 3BH
An Hachette Livre UK company

YA

Dedicated to the memory of Kate Jones

Acknowledgements

Thanks to all at my agency, ICM Books. Props as well to my editor Emily Thomas and all at Hachette Children's Books.

And may I finally say, watching *Project Runway* helped this shoddy seamstress understand the proper way to make pretty frocks!

http://sarramanning.blogspot.com

BOOK FOUR:
Candy

'You're so sheer, you're so chic
Teenage rebel of the week . . .'
– Virginia Plain by Roxy Music

Previously on

Laura, Irina, Hadley and Candy – all signed to global talent agency, Fierce – move into a flat together in London… Pretty, girl-next door Laura gets a rude awakening when she's told to lose her attitude and her excess weight to make it in modelling. But does that mean losing her devoted boyfriend Tom, too? Read all about it in

Laura

All-American, former child star, Hadley Harlow comes to London to re-launch her failed career. But can Hadley handle fame the second time around – or the attentions of notorious modeliser, Reed? Read all about it in

Hadley

Nothing is going to stop former shoplifter, Irina Kerchenko, from becoming a supermodel. Will Irina lose her head as well as her heart when she hooks up with gorgeous photographer, Javier? Read all about it in

Irina

Prologue

'I'm moving to London and that's all there is to it,' Candy informed her mother, who was clipping coupons.

'Is this about that boy who tried to do the kiss and tell, sweetie?' Bette cooed, putting a fifty-cent coupon for cupcakes in the 'yes' pile. 'I know that you've had your heart broken but what has London got that New York hasn't?'

'It doesn't have you in it,' Candy wanted to say, but she stuck to the lines she'd rehearsed in her head. 'It's got nothing to do with that ass-wipe,' she bit out, which was only half true. 'I'm fed up with taking part in this freaking freakshow. God, I just want to be halfway normal for a little bit!'

'If I ran off to London every time life let me down, I'd have dual nationality by now,' Bette breathed. 'C'mon, Candy Cane . . .'

'I've told you not to call me that . . .'

'. . . you're not a quitter. Stay in New York and we'll buy new shoes, go to the Waverly for brunch, anything you want, you'll soon be sunny smiles again.'

'I've never been sunny smiles in my life,' Candy snarled, because Bette was the most infuriating woman in the world when she was purposely not getting a clue. Actually, scratch that. She was the most infuriating woman in the world. Period. Candy glared at her half-brother, Reed, who was here under duress and hadn't made eye contact with Bette yet. He really needed to get over the whole my-mother-left-me-and-my-father-when-I-was-five-to-run-off-with-a-degenerate-punk-icon thing.

Reed sighed. 'I don't think this is the best place for Candy to be right now,' he said, gesturing at the cluttered apartment, his gaze resting on one of the cats licking milk from Candy's half-finished bowl of cereal. 'And I'll be in London to keep an eye on her.' He sounded far too big brother-ish for Candy's liking. Like he wasn't just saying it to get her mom off her back but as if he was planning all sorts of fun things like curfews and rules.

'But you're just so young, baby girl,' Bette breathed, eyes wide.

'I'm sixteen and when you were my age, you were gallivanting around the world and being all modelly and shit,' Candy pointed out.

'And look how well that turned out,' Reed muttered, *sotto voce*, but Candy wasn't done.

'I'm old enough to take care of myself,' she burst out, her voice rising to a pitch that had Conceptua bustling in with a handful of laundry.

'She go to London, she miss school,' Conceptua intoned darkly with her heavy Portuguese accent. 'Then she stay out all night, start with the drinking, then the drugs. She be dead before twenty.' Conceptua was a big fan of the worst-case scenario. 'I light a candle to pray for your immortal soul.'

Candy rolled her eyes. Reed stared at his nails.

Conceptua shooed the cats off the laundry and Bette carried on clipping coupons that she was never going to use. She'd just put them on one of the many piles of crap in the apartment and they'd stay there for ever.

'God, I can't bear to live in this dump any longer,' Candy snapped and she was halfway to flouncing out of the room when her father headed her off at the pass.

'Can't sleep with all this yelling,' he mumbled, scratching his spiky black hair. He paused to pick up one of the cats and wrap a long, skinny arm around Candy, as Conceptua shot him a dark look.

'Is five in the afternoon. You should not be sleeping,' she announced censoriously and speeded up with the folding; her gnarled fingers making light work of Candy's polka-dot bed linen.

David Careless yawned. 'Yeah, well, power nap,' he said vaguely before his heavy-lidded eyes rested on his only child. 'What's bugging you, baby?'

There was no short answer to that question and just as Candy was trying to come up with a reply that wouldn't take several hours and about a hundred swear words, Bette beat her to it.

'Oh, Candy's having a hissy fit,' she said lightly. 'She wants to move to London to mend her broken heart.'

'My heart is *not*—'

'Baby, that's so Henry James,' David smirked. 'Can't remember which book it was, but they shipped the girl with the ruined rep back to the motherland. Or was it Edith Wharton?'

'I'm going to London,' Candy said forcefully. 'I am and that's all there is to it. If you're all down with the goddamn dead novelists, then you should be happy that Reed'll be there to act as a chaperone.'

'Don't take the Lord's name in vain,' Conceptua said automatically as Bette actually put down her scissors and looked at her estranged son in consternation.

'Reed, I can't believe that you put this idea in her head.' Bette probably thought that she sounded all reproachful and dignified, but it actually came out really whiny.

'She came up with it all by herself.' Reed shrugged and still managed not to make eye contact with his mother. 'And if Candy's mind is made up, then short of calling out the National Guard there's nothing any of us can do about it.'

Candy wriggled off David's lap because he was trying to tickle her and giggling wasn't very effective when she was meant to be laying down the law.

Bette had this look that Candy recognized. A look that meant she needed a large vodka and tonic to get through the next five minutes. Like a shark scenting blood in the water, Candy moved in for the kill.

'If you don't let me go to London, I'll . . . I'll . . .' Her voice rose perilously high as she weighed up the countless threats she had good to go. And then it hit her. She smiled triumphantly. 'I'll get a lawyer and I'll divorce you and become a legally emancipated adult and then I can go where I like, do what I like and there'll be fuck all you can do about it!' Candy hadn't paused for breath once and as

4

she stood there panting, enjoying the shocked expressions on Bette's, Conceptua's and even David's face, there was a cough from the corner.

'That was great, guys,' said the director of *At Home With The Careless*. 'But we need another take – we're not happy with the lighting in this scene.'

Candy looked up to where the old wall of the kitchen had been until the TV production company had bought the apartments on either side and knocked through so they'd have room for their cameras and the gazillion people that needed to mill about with cups of coffee and clipboards.

'So much for fly-on-the-wall reality TV,' Reed noted sagely.

'*At Home With The Careless* is not reality TV,' Bethany, the assistant director, hissed. 'It's a genre-defining, *reality-based* dramedy, actually.'

Reed didn't look at all chastened. 'I'm out of here,' he said. 'I'm meeting some finance guys at the Gramercy Park Hotel in half an hour.'

'But we haven't wrapped the scene yet,' Bette protested, but Reed was already heading for the door with a terse, 'Not my problem.'

'I thought we told you to make him sign a contract,' one of the producers said, but the director clapped his hands.

'On your marks, people. Scene five, take seven, action!'

Chapter One

Three weeks later, Candy was in the back of a black London taxi cab with a removal van following behind containing her matching skull-and-crossbones luggage. She was beyond ready for a fresh start.

That's what Candy kept telling herself, but deep down she knew she was carrying more chips on her shoulder than a Doritos delivery truck.

She was moving into a Fierce Management flat in Camden, London, with three other girls who had their own careers. Proper careers. Candy was just a girl with a big mouth from a reality show, famous for having all her monologues beeped out due to excessive swearing. Which was why, as Candy hauled herself up two flights of stairs, her knees were knocking and her skin was clammy at the prospect of meeting her three flatmates. Two of them were models, which made Candy shudder with horror as she imagined two teenage Bettes, oozing self-obsession from every pore. And then there was former child star, Hadley Harlow, who was totes over, but at least she'd had a successful career before she'd washed up on the shores of the C-list. The only plan of attack Candy could come up was to call dibs on the biggest room, which would establish her as the quasi leader of the household. It was a lame plan but it had been all that Candy could come up with.

The front door was open so Candy tiptoed inside, caught a glimpse of a tall girl stuffing her face in the kitchen, but stealthily crept down the hall, pushing open doors until she found the largest room. It was still unoccupied so Candy flung her coat on the bed, sidled back to the front door and sent it crashing on its hinges, as if she was making a grand entrance.

'Hello! Anyone home?' The really tall girl poked her head round the kitchen door. Living in New York, Candy liked to think that she was immune to beauty because every time she stopped at the corner deli for a Snapple, she'd pass five women who'd spent thousands of dollars on their looks. But there was something about this girl's heart-shaped face, the absolute perfect symmetry of her wide-spaced green eyes, delicately arched brows and pouty lips that almost made her do a double take. Almost, because Candy was way too cool to do that. She also looked strangely familiar. Candy knew she'd seen her somewhere before but she just couldn't . . . That was it! She'd won a British TV model search that Candy and Bette had watched on cable. Bette had been a guest judge on the American version so she'd wanted to check up on the competition, and Candy never tired of mocking the girls as they'd cried about having to be photographed in their underwear. It was as close to mother/daughter bonding as Candy would ever allow.

As far as Candy could recall, Laura had won the public vote because she'd torn into one of the judges for daring to criticize her glittery lipgloss. She couldn't have won for any other reason because although she was beautiful enough to stop traffic, she was *way* too fat to be a model. Whatever.

They stared at each other for a second until Candy remembered that she had the relevant details on a piece of paper. 'Laura Parker,' she said, then wished she hadn't because way to state the obvious.

But it didn't matter that Candy had blown her cool because this other girl didn't have any cool to blow. She was staring at Candy like she was having a religious vision.

'Oh goodness, you're Candy Careless,' she breathed, her tone both incredulous and humble, which was just how Candy liked it.

Laura, who didn't actually seem like the brightest bulb in the box (she'd been a hell of a lot peppier on *Make Me A Model*), wanted to bond over their shared reality TV appearances, and Candy had to put her right on that. *At Home With The Careless* might not have been high art but it was several million steps above some grubby model search. Thankfully just as Candy heard herself spit out the words, 'a genre-defining, *reality-based* dramedy', the removal men finally finished dragging her luggage up the stairs.

It was only when Candy followed them down the hall with her ancient Singer sewing machine with the wonky needle (which was, like, fifty per cent of the reason that she was here in London) that she realized that someone was in her room. Someone tall and fugly enough that she could only be the other model: the Russian girl. She was bony and angular with deep-set eyes, lips like tyres and horrible brown splotches all over her face. Candy could just imagine that face on the cover of *Vogue*. So she put her shoulders back and prepared to do battle. Because Candy knew about models from way back. She lived with a superannuated one after all and she'd spent most of her childhood trailing behind Bette at fashion shows and designer ateliers and vintage auctions. In Candy's experience you treated models like feral dogs; they had to know who was the boss. Models were pack animals and they respected hierarchy. Candy had even seen one girl insist that her former best friend enter the room behind her after she'd opened the Marc Jacobs show. So it was important that she established a pecking order, and anyway she'd already put her coat in that room and just who did this fricking Tsarina think she was to just come in and start making herself at home?

'Hey! *Hey!* What the hell do you think you're doing? This is my room!' Candy made sure to use simple words and pointed at herself so this girl couldn't plead the language barrier. Funny how models never ever pleaded the language barrier when it came to being first in line for the designer freebies at the end of a shoot.

The other girl didn't say anything at first, just gave Candy a look that should have had a warning sticker slapped on it. 'Get out!' Candy shouted because she was going to start as she meant to go on – not taking crap from anyone just because they were a foot taller than her and thought they could out-attitude Candy. She'd had enough of that at school and in the hipster clubs of the Lower East Side.

'I not understand,' the Russian girl said, but there was a really annoying smirk playing about her lips that seemed to indicate that she understood only too well. 'Is my room.'

She obviously didn't regard Candy as a threat because she sprawled on the bed in her goddamn hideous tracksuit and stupid naff sneakers and had the audacity to knock Candy's coat to the floor, with no respect for its vintage status. Candy couldn't stay in the room a second longer without doing something with her fists and that smug face.

'It's my room,' she heard herself shriek because the girl, the stupid, bony girl with the comedy Russian accent, had decided to follow her back into the lounge. 'It's so obvious it was my room.'

'Tough sheet,' the girl drawled and started talking to Laura like Candy didn't warrant any more attention. And if there was one thing Candy hated worse than being walked over, it was being ignored. Neither of them ignored her though, when she picked up her smallest case and threw it at the wall where it collided with some revolting picture of a kissy couple, which fell to the floor with a crash.

It was when Candy heard herself railing against her new living arrangements while Irina and Laura and even the removal men stared at her like she'd crash-landed from another planet, that Candy realized that she'd gone too far and that she needed to lock herself in the bathroom on a self-imposed time out.

The bathroom didn't even have a shower, which sucked too. Candy climbed into the tub and hugged her knees and made herself a solemn vow that she was going to pretend that the last fifteen minutes had never happened, and also she was going to make an extra special effort not to be a brat. And to stop making snap judgements about people, even if they were practically begging her to. And to stop being an ugly American and looking down on people just because they'd grown up without Tivo and Old Navy and US citizenship. Well, Candy pledged to *try* at least.

She emerged from the bathroom and followed the sounds of conversation to the kitchen, where Laura was making tea. Candy would have much preferred a caramel macchiato from the nearest Starbucks, but she asked for a cup too to show willing, before asking the Russian girl her name. It came out rather aggressively, but the Russian girl was still giving her these looks, which were an unfriendly mixture of contempt and amusement.

'Irina, Candy. Candy, Irina,' Laura supplied in the end, giving both of them a wary smile.

Irina didn't say anything, but now she was giving Laura the evil eye too. 'You on TV,' she stated accusingly. She turned her gimlet stare back to Candy. 'You too. Weird.'

And as if there was nothing else to say on the subject, she grabbed a mug of tea and a handful of flapjack and sauntered out.

Laura giggled nervously and it made Candy feel better. Like, she wasn't the only one who was scared and freaked out about the whole moving-away-from-home thing. Not that that it would do Laura any good if she wanted to be a model. 'You were cool on that show,' Candy said and she managed to sound sincere, so yay for her.

There was a bit more desultory chit chat until Candy couldn't think of anything else to say. Before the conversation could come grinding to an embarrassing halt and Laura would tell everyone that actually, Candy Careless was really boring, Candy gave a theatrical shrug. 'Well, I guess I'd better get on with my unpacking,' she said. 'I wish Conceptua was here to help me out.'

It was a relief to disappear into the largest room and shut the door behind her. First, Candy checked that her sewing machine hadn't got damaged in transit. Then she checked to make sure that Bette's vintage dresses had remained undiscovered in Candy's suitcases and not been spirited away – it was the only thing that Bette got really mad about. Candy fingered the dull jet sheen of a satin Patou dress before arranging it on one of her padded hangers. Soon all her clothes were hanging up; her cashmere beaded cardigans, her huge collection of little black dresses and the motley collection of clothes she'd started to make herself from vintage patterns she'd bought on eBay. They weren't very good; lots of crooked seams and ragged hems, and she still couldn't get the hang of sleeves, but she'd figure it out. People used to make all their own clothes in the olden days so how hard could it be? But Candy'd rather not figure it out with a camera shoved in her face, thank you very much. Trying to make your dreams come true was hard enough, without all your mistakes and bad decisions being recorded for posterity.

Candy's reverie was interrupted by the doorbell. It was

a whole 'nother dilemma and she was getting really sick of them. Irina probably didn't even know what a doorbell was and Laura was too chicken to go and answer it, which left Candy padding out into the hall and hoping that it was Reed because she really needed to see a friendly face. Stat.

And Candy did get a friendly face when she opened the door – plus an armful of vanilla-scented, skinny Californian blonde: Hadley Harlow in the fake-tanned, almost-size-zero flesh, yelping in her ear. 'Oh! My! God! I am so psyched to be here!'

Candy wriggled free and shook herself like a cat that had just had an unexpected bath. 'Hadley,' she said, trying to inject a little enthusiasm into her voice. Hadley was sort of a friend. Well, not exactly, but they knew each other. Well, again not exactly. They'd sat next to each other at some shows during LA Fashion Week and they'd hung out a bit at the MTV Movie Awards and once they'd bumped into each other at a photo studio. But the last time Candy had seen Hadley had been that morning on one of the entertainment channels, standing on a courtroom steps giving a statement about how her father had totally stolen all the money she'd made when she'd been the world's most famous child star. Candy had been amazed when she'd seen Hadley's name on the tenant list that the agency had emailed over half an hour later. Obviously she was trying to make it big in London because her career back in LA had flat-lined.

'I'm an actress and a singer and I do a lot of charity work . . .' Hadley was already in the lounge and giving

Laura a quick rundown of her résumé as the other girl stared dumbstruck at the former star of the super unfunny *Hadley's House* sitcom and the equally lame *Little Girl Lost* film franchise. Or maybe it was because Hadley was wearing a teeny tiny mini-skirt, five-inch heels and a big-ass pair of shades, either way Laura didn't seem to realize she was in the presence of Hollywood royalty.

'Hadley, she doesn't know who you are,' Candy said gently, because otherwise Hadley would rattle on for hours. 'Isn't that why you're in London? To re-launch your career?'

'Hey, my career does not need re-launching!' Hadley snapped. Except it was hard to snap when you talked in a girlish, breathy giggle all the time. Candy had forgotten how Hadley sounded. Or how freaking irritating it was, especially as Hadley was back to reciting the highlights of her fifteen minutes of fame.

'I'm going to put the kettle on,' Laura said helplessly, and it was true – the British really did drink tea all the time. But then, Laura went over to the dark side, before Candy could even shout out a warning. 'You were in *Hadley's House*,' she exclaimed excitedly. 'I wanted to be you when I was a kid.'

'Don't encourage her,' Candy warned, but Hadley had already gone into this fifth-rate Norma Desmond impersonation about the pressures of celebrity, and it was so obvious that it was a lie and that really Hadley was aching to throw herself back into the arms of that bitch called fame. It was why Candy had left New York before she got sucked into the empty, meaningless existence of being just another celebrity in a world that had far too many of them. If she was going to be remembered it was because she was going to make something of herself.

Candy stood back with her arms folded and took stock. Laura seemed OK. At least she was malleable. Hadley didn't have two functioning brain cells and Candy would easily be able to shut her down if she started getting upitty. Only Irina looked like she was going to be an uncomfortably bony pain in the ass, but she was fresh off the plane so again, Candy had the advantage.

Candy allowed herself a small triumphant smile. First she'd rule her room-mates and then she'd take on the rest of London.

Chapter Two

Eighteen months later

Candy huddled on the sofa and tried to see the TV over the mound of boxes that were in the way. She groped for the remote control in vain as the sounds of *yet* another argument floated down the hall.

'You not even here!' Irina was yelling in a belligerent manner that did not suit the new face of the latest Chanel fragrance. 'Is not your business if I want your room as an overspill wardrobe.'

'I am here and I pay rent,' Laura snapped back, because she'd lost tons of excess weight and grown a pair in the process. 'I'm just storing some of my stuff at the new place but I can't move in until the builders have finished the kitchen.'

'You have more money than sense,' Irina said in that lofty way that made all three of them want to smack her. 'Is stupid to pay rent here when you own other property.'

'Yeah, whatever. Thanks for that lesson, Donald Trump.' Yeah, now that Laura had racked up a few ad campaigns and front covers too, she wasn't so malleable any more. Pity, that.

There were a couple of loud thumps followed by some anguished yelps and Candy hunted desperately for the channel clicker as she heard Hadley enter the fray.

'Don't just stand there, Reed! I can't move my boxes with you blocking the hall!'

Candy gritted her teeth until she remembered that her dentist had told her to stop doing that otherwise she'd have to wear a mouth-guard at night. OK, Laura wasn't her friend any more – she could deal with that, even though she still didn't understand the reasoning behind Laura's ass-hat decision to become BFF with Hadley and live the cliché by dating a footballer. And Irina and Candy had made a pact to, more or less, tolerate each other. But Hadley . . .

Candy had never hated anyone as much as she hated Hadley fucking Harlow, former child star, former has-been and current indie movie darling, cult TV presenter and Reed's *girlfriend*. Candy ground down hard on her back molars; it was either that or start scratching her own skin off. Christ on a crutch! She hated everything about Hadley from her stupid baby voice to her stupid fake blonde hair to her stupid *everything*.

'Reed, be careful with that box. I've got my third tier shoes in there,' Hadley trilled, and Candy knew that she should be pleased that Hadley was moving out as she'd already told Irina that she had first dibs on Hadley's room, but Candy wasn't pleased. She was bereft. Devastated. Absolutely goddamn gutted.

Because Hadley was moving in with Reed, like he wasn't pussy-whipped enough. Candy scowled as Reed himself walked through the door and collapsed next to her on the sofa with a slightly anxious glance out into the hall, in case Hadley forced him to do a little more hauling for her.

'What's up?' he enquired idly, as he unearthed the remote control from under a pile of magazines and changed the channel.

'I was watching that!' Candy growled, even though she'd been staring mindlessly at a programme about loft conversions.

'No, you weren't,' Reed replied imperturbably, muting the TV. 'Anyway, I want to have a chat with you.'

Candy narrowed her eyes as Hadley's door opened again. 'Reed? I need you to help me.'

Reed didn't seem that bothered. 'Yeah, be there in a minute,' he called, but sprawled out on the sofa like he had no intention of moving. 'So, how long are you going to stay pissed with me then, Cands? It's getting on for three months now.'

Had it been that long? It seemed like only weeks ago that Candy and Reed were tight in the way that only sibs (well, half-sibs if you were going to get technical about it) were when they'd spent sixteen years apart. Bette was always deliberately vague when it came to the bits of her life that didn't include modelling or being married to David, but Candy knew all about her first husband. Well, she knew that they'd dated in high school, until Bette had run off to Europe to become a supermodel. Then on a visit home she'd paid a trip to her old boyfriend because he was now a doctor and she'd had an allergic reaction to some

19

shellfish. After a whirlwind courtship of two weeks, they were married. Candy didn't know diddly squat about the next five years, all she knew about was the moment that David and Bette had first locked eyes in a coffee shop in the Village and they'd been glued at the hip ever since.

Sometimes Candy had wondered what it would be like to have an older brother, but mostly it had involved pounding the shit out of the kids at school who picked on her for being the tiniest in her year, *every* year. And for having parents who forgot to come and pick her up, or when they did her dad would be wearing pyjamas and Bette would have a 1920s couture gown on even though Candy qualified for free school lunches. And when Candy had got a bit older, she'd thought that having an older brother would mean a passport to a world of foxy friends of the big brother who'd dote on his little sister and sneak her into rock shows.

The reality hadn't even come close. Candy, by now a genuine celebrity as the show's first season had just aired, had been in some tacky midtown club having a ferocious argument with Jacob, the guitarist in a shit band that she'd lost her virginity to three weeks before.

'You were going to sell your story!' she'd been screaming at Jacob in the club vestibule. 'My publicist got a call this afternoon.'

Jacob had shrugged her hand off his arm and tried to stare her down with his limpid green eyes. 'Get me on the show and I'll keep my mouth shut,' he'd said baldly, and not even making an attempt to deny it. He'd been way more charming when he was talking Candy out of her pants. 'I mean, why else would I have spent weeks getting you into bed?'

Candy had lost it big time. She'd tried to take a swing at him and, when she'd missed, she'd burst into tears and started hurling insult after insult at Jacob while he'd stood there with a shit-eating grin on his face because a paparazzi video crew were trying to film them from behind the velvet rope.

And then someone had punched the smug smile right off Jacob's stupid face and the same someone had grabbed Candy by the arm and before she could even process what was going on, she'd been hustled through the club and out on to the street. And when she'd blinked up at her mystery benefactor, into eyes the exact same shade of blue as her own, he'd said, 'I'm Reed, your half-brother, and what the hell do you think you're doing out so late on a school night?'

It had been the beginning of a beautiful friendship. But it was more than that – because Candy and Reed shared the same blood and DNA and shit. It meant that nothing could come between them. That was the deal with brothers and sisters, or so Candy had thought. And those first few months in London had been great because she'd hung out with Reed every day and for the first time in her life there was someone to look out for her and nag her for not eating enough vegetables and swearing too much. OK, Conceptua had done that too, but she was paid help so it didn't really count.

But something had come between them. While they were still catching up on the sixteen years they'd both missed out on. Or rather *someone* had come between them. Hadley. So Candy stuck out her chin and gave Reed a mutinous look.

'Are you planning on dumping *her* any time soon?' she asked in her most snotty voice.

Reed didn't even flinch. 'Hadley's moving in with me so, no, I don't really see a dumping scenario happening.'

'Well, then I'm still pissed at you,' Candy gritted.

'There's no reason to be such a brat,' Reed told her tiredly, like he was sick of talking about it already. 'I thought you and Hadley used to be friends.'

'We were never friends,' Candy pointed out. 'And I'm sick of you and Hadley being the couple version of a buy one, get one free offer. We never do stuff, just the two of us any more.'

'I've been busy with my movie,' Reed said doggedly, which was true, but he always managed to make time in his busy schedule to be bossed about by Hadley.

'Yeah, busy sucking face with your leading lady,' Candy supplied sourly. 'God, she's so banal. And how can you stand to be around her without industrial-strength ear plugs?'

'You know, Candy, coming to London was this great opportunity for you to get away from all the shit in New York and start over,' he said flatly. 'Guess you got bored with that.'

Candy hadn't got bored with anything except being treated like last season's bubble skirts. 'Like you even care,' she sniffed petulantly in a way that was guaranteed to get Reed's eyes flashing, except there was a cry from the hall.

'Reed! Where are you?' Hadley whimpered, like she was in great pain instead of just having a packing crisis. 'I need you!'

Reed's heavy sigh made Candy feel slightly better as it suggested that he wasn't completely down with being at the beck and call of Sadley, but he was still levering himself off the couch. 'We're not done here,' he warned Candy. 'This is just a raincheck. We're going to have this out at a later date.'

'I can't wait,' she sniped, picking up the remote control. 'Better run along before your girlfriend breaks a nail.'

Reed muttered something under his breath as he hurried out of the room to be fallen on with excited cries by Hadley. But before Candy could start dry-heaving when the cries turned into kissing sounds, Laura and Irina started arguing again, Hadley's rat-dog Mr Chow-Chow started yipping, and she had no choice but to up the volume on the TV until she couldn't hear anything but some DIY geek going on about loft insulation.

Chapter Three

It was a relief to fly back to New York. Not just because New York was home and always would be, but because now that the flat was empty of everything but boxes waiting to be collected, Candy found the silence too loud. And the flat, which had always been a poky shithole when the three of them were falling over each other and fighting to get into the bathroom, was now this huge empty space which she couldn't quite fill up all by herself.

Irina and Laura got all awestruck about New York because they were such a pair of tourists, but it was different when you were a native. Growing up in New York was like being raised by a pack of wolves. Candy could hail a bright yellow taxi cab before she could even walk. Her first complete sentence had been, 'Get the hell out of my way, asshole,' and when she still used to brown bag it to school, her sandwiches were made by Eduardo at the deli on the corner of their block because Bette wasn't really the packed lunch kind of Mom.

After school, Courtney, Candy's babysitter, (now the female lead on TV's hottest show that wasn't about people with superpowers) would take her to MOMA to see the Warhols. Or they'd go to Central Park to feed the ducks gluten-free blueberry muffins, and sometimes they'd take the A-train out to Brooklyn to sell test pressings of early

Careless records so they could afford life's necessities: pizza, guava juice and, oh yeah, the rent. Eat your heart out, Holden Caulfield. Candy made a note on her iPhone to call Courtney and waited for Ignacio, Conceptua's nephew and her regular driver, to get her bags.

'I think Bette and David might still be in LA,' Ignacio said as Candy scowled at a lurking photographer. They never got tired of hanging around outside their grubby front door waiting for a member of the Careless clan to emerge. 'And Conceptua's gone to see her sister on Staten Island.'

Candy was already on the phone to Kris, her New York assistant, to see what guest lists he could get her on for tonight. It was bad enough that she was friendless in London, no way was she kicking it solo in New York too. 'Get me on the guest list for Socialista and is anyone playing the Bowery or the Highline tonight?' Candy demanded. 'Also half my clothes are in London. Can you phone Betsey Johnson and get them to courier over some outfits?'

Kris didn't sound too hopeful. 'They said they wouldn't lend to you again after you sent the last lot back covered in cat hair,' he reminded Candy. 'I could try Zac Posen?'

Candy clamped the phone under her ear as she shouldered open the door of her room. Well, it used to be her room – now it was merely a TV set of her room with a missing fourth wall that doubled up as *At Home With The Careless*'s sound editing suite. She'd sleep next door. 'His stuff doesn't fit properly,' she grumbled. 'Come and pick me up at nine and we'll go to dinner. Get us a table at the Waverly.'

'Candy, it's a bit short notice . . .' Kris began and then Candy heard him shut his mouth with an audible snap. It was bad enough that she had to ask her assistant to be her plus one for the evening, but it was even worse when he expected her to beg for the privilege.

'Kris,' she sighed. 'I'm only in New York every few weeks. It's not like I ask you to do this all the time and, by the way, thanks for making me feel like a total social retard.'

'Fine, can I bring some friends? They're in fashion. You'll love them,' Kris promised then rang off before Candy could make a decision one way or the other.

Candy didn't love Kris's friends and, big surprise, they didn't love her. They were all older than her, taller than her, more sceney than her and after the initial air kisses and 'love you on *At Home With The Careless*', they all ignored her as they ordered chicken Caesar salads (turned out that Atkins was back in vogue) and expected her to pick up the tab.

It was the same story once they got to the Highline Ballroom to see the latest emo darlings fresh off the bus from Austin, Texas. The audience was too cool to actually approach her because they might lose some indie cred points, but as she stood at the edge of Kris's crowd trying to look animated and not deathly bored, she was aware of the sidelong glances, the whispers, the sniggers. Candy could never escape the feeling that, on some level, she was still in fifth grade. Then one aggressive-looking girl in a weird leggings and playsuit combo detached herself from the throng and made a beeline for Candy.

Maybe Candy knew her. She had the look of someone who worked on a trendy magazine with a readership of about ten people. 'Can I interview you for my blog?' she shouted at Candy over the screeching set from the DJ, and Candy immediately stiffened.

'You need to speak to my publicist,' she said brusquely. 'He handles all my press requests.'

The girl thinned her already really thin lips. 'I thought I could spend a night hanging out with you and do this live blogging feed,' she explained as if Candy hadn't spoken.

Like that would be a riveting read. Candy tried to shoot Kris an imploring look but he had his tongue shoved down his boyfriend's throat. 'Put something in an email,' she said vaguely, wondering why anyone would wear an outfit that was so relentlessly unflattering.

'You know, you're pretty arrogant for someone who's famous just for being famous,' the girl informed her. 'Like, your dad was cool back in analogue times but you and your mom have just squeezed out all his genius.'

Candy turned on her furiously. 'Well, if I'm so crap, how come you want me to be in your shitty little blog?'

The girl stood there like she was made out of some incredibly dense material. 'It's part of a series I'm doing on the notion of celebrity in post 9/11 New York and how we're living in these spiritually and morally bankrupt times. I'm hoping to get a book deal out of it.'

'Fuck off,' Candy spat because she was neither morally or spiritually bankrupt and it wasn't her fault that Bette had signed their lives away and not even consulted her.

The girl folded her arms. 'Y'know, this is great material you're giving me.'

'What part of "fuck off" did you not understand? KRIS!' The PA was no match for the full force of Candy's lung power. Kris disentangled himself from his boyfriend so he could push his way between Candy and the blogging bitch from hell.

'If you don't move away from her right now, I'm having you thrown out,' he growled and Candy didn't delude herself that his icy glare was out of concern for her. More like his $5,000 a month retainer.

'You can't throw me out. I'm on the list,' the girl said snottily, but she was taking a step backwards as Kris raised his hand and looked around for one of the security guards. 'Right, whatever. I'm still going to blog about you and you're not going to like it.'

She turned on her platform heel and stalked off as Candy blinked back tears. Fame was meant to be more fun than this, otherwise why did everyone chase it so hard?

'I'm out of here,' she told Kris, who tried to look like her announcement was causing him pain.

'Are you sure? My friend Lewis has just turned up and he's dying to meet you.'

Candy angled a glance over at Kris's friends. The newest addition had floppy blond hair and a MC5 T-shirt. He was also the third most beautiful boy Candy had ever seen in real life. And he smiled shyly at Candy, like he wasn't worthy to get down on his knees and kiss the hem of her borrowed Zac Posen dress. Candy wasn't buying what he was selling for a second. But then again . . . Damn! He was so cute!

'Well, OK, then,' she grudgingly conceded, like she was doing Kris a huge favour. Then she let him lead her over to Lewis, who shook her hand and started whispering sweet nothings in her ear.

They really were sweet nothings because Lewis was a standard issue MAW – a model/actor/whatever. And it was as if God had been so busy making his outside stuff spectacular that there'd been no time to work on the inside stuff, like brain cells. Fame had many benefits, but Candy could never work out if being fawned over by hot guys who wouldn't even have deigned to notice her before was a good thing. Maybe she should just learn to love it for what it was.

'You're so tiny,' Lewis breathed with wide eyes. 'Like a Blythe doll come to life.'

Candy decided that Lewis would be better if he wasn't talking. She batted her glittery false lashes. 'Wanna come to the VIP room with me?'

Lewis's brow scrunched up in consternation. 'Don't you want to see the band?'

'Nah, they'll just be generic mope-rock with a few pretentious lyrics thrown over the top to satisfy their emo fanbase,' Candy said scathingly.

Lewis's brow was starting to look painful. 'Huh?'

God, why did they always have to be so stupid? 'Let's go to the VIP room and make out,' Candy clarified.

'OK! Yeah!' Lewis nodded eagerly and let Candy lead

him up the stairs to a roped-off balcony. It was pretty deserted, but just to be on the safe side, Candy pulled Lewis to an empty corner.

'You want to get a drink?' Lewis asked as they sat down.

'Maybe later,' Candy hedged and then she snuggled in close to Lewis, who obligingly lifted his arm so Candy could press against him and purse her lips.

Thankfully, Lewis didn't have to ask for directions. He just cupped Candy's face in his hands and started kissing her.

His kisses were OK. They were definitely above average. Lewis didn't just stick his tongue in and swirl it around but did some of the teasy weasy stuff first. Like nibbling on Candy's lips as if they were the appetizer and playing with the ragged ends of her choppy bob at the sensitive spot on the back of her neck. *Then* he stuck his tongue in and swirled it all around.

It shouldn't have felt as good as it did, but Candy had long come to terms with the fact that she was a total kiss slut. It wasn't something she was proud of, but after the fallout from Jacob she wasn't ever going to have sex again. Not until she was twenty-five and her lawyer made the other party sign a sworn affidavit first that he wouldn't attempt to sell the gory details to *US Weekly* when it all turned sour. Because it *always* turned sour.

So, for now, Candy had to make do with kissing. And if beautiful boys were lining up to kiss her because she was on primetime TV, then it was just her personal cross to bear. Actually, the kissing cute boys didn't suck at the time.

It was just the way she felt after the event – slightly grubby because she'd been kissing under false pretences. Kissing just for the sake of kissing. Kissing without all the cuddles and dates and having an 'our song'. That was probably the thing she most resented Laura, Irina and Hadley for – that they'd all landed boyfriends who appeared to be besotted with them. Especially Irina and Hadley, who had far more personality defects than Candy had.

'Oh, no!' One of Lewis's beautiful hands (he did hand modelling occasionally, so he'd told her) suddenly clamped itself around one of Candy's breasts. Technically, that was second base. And Candy didn't do second base. Candy wriggled and wriggled until there were several inches of space between her and Lewis. 'OK, I need a breather,' she gasped, tracing a finger over kiss-sore lips. 'Be a sweetie and go and get me a drink. A Mojito would be great.'

If he asked her for the money to pay for it, Candy would kill him. But no, Lewis was nodding eagerly again and levering himself upright. Really, he'd make a wonderful house-pet. 'Don't go anywhere,' he purred. 'I'd really love to get your advice about finding a new agent.'

Candy's instincts had been totes right. He wasn't wowed by her bitching outfit or her stunning repartee, just by her address book. The moment that Lewis turned the corner towards the bar, Candy grabbed her bag and hurried down the backstairs. A minute later she was getting into a cab. There had to be some microwave popcorn at home and she'd Tivoed the entire series of *Project Runway*, which was going to be a far more fulfilling way to spend a few hours.

Chapter Four

'Candy, I'm a cool mom. I let you drink and smoke and swear and the word "curfew" isn't even in my vocabulary, but I won't have you stealing my dresses and then cutting them up!' Bette sounded as angry as she ever got. She drew in breath between words as she surveyed the Halston dress that Candy had taken up a few inches. Not like she ever wore it.

'I didn't cut it, I *altered* it and you can't get into it since you had your boobs done,' Candy sniffed.

'That's not the point. Halston's due for a revival and I promised I'd lend my collection when the V&A do their retrospective.'

Candy looked up from her prone position on her knees in front of Bette's closet, where she'd been caught red-handed. 'You have no respect for your clothes. You used to wear them on stage with The Careless and your sweat rotted out all the armpits.'

Yeah, Bette was definitely ticked now. She was even trying to scrunch up her forehead, though the Botox was getting in the way. 'Horses sweat, men perspire, women merely glow.'

'Yeah, well you *glowed* buckets,' Candy said triumphantly and then she heard the steady hum of thousands of dollars worth of recording equipment. 'You're not meant to be filming this,' she protested at the crew, who'd crept in while she was snarking. 'We're getting ready for our next scene.'

'But this is so much better than anything we drafted,' the assistant director said smoothly. 'Can you hold up some of the dresses with the rotted armpits?'

'No,' Candy and Bette both snapped in unison, which had to be a first, and this look swept over Bette's face for one unguarded moment, this 'what have I done?' look, before it was replaced with that bright, hollow smile that she always did so well.

Candy wondered if Bette had really known what she was signing up for when she'd fallen under the sway of the TV channel's commissioning director, who convinced her that the Carelesses could be America's alternative First Family.

To be fair, before *At Home With The Careless*, it had been a really tough year. Although all their years were tough ones. The Careless had been dropped by their record company after their manager was jailed for tax evasion. David had only just come out of rehab and was too fragile even to do a short tour. Money had been really tight. Candy could remember going into Bette's purse to steal five dollars to buy smokes and there'd been nothing in there but a credit note from Miu Miu and a couple of dimes.

Being broke was a constant theme of Candy's childhood. The Careless were one of those bands that everyone namedropped but no one really listened to. A long, long time ago, David and two guys he'd met at

Juilliard released these edgy, symphonic albums that married breakbeats with feedbacking guitars and Sixties melodies that were so ahead of their time that they confused both the critics and the record-buying public. Candy had found some of their old live performances on YouTube and it was a revelation to see David hunched over his guitar, spitting out words like he had fire in his belly. Even after Bette joined the band, they still had something; her girlish backing vocals and strange swaying to the music giving the band this ethereal quality that was at odds with all the grungy bands coming up and stealing their thunder. But by the time Candy was on the scene, skinny young men in stadium bands would call round for an audience so they could tell David what a huge influence he'd been on their music, even though The Careless were lucky if they could get a gig on the college circuit. Besides, being a huge influence didn't pay the bills, and even though Bette had a lot of annoying fashion friends who always wanted her advice on volume and hemlines, they only ever paid her in clothes.

The night, the famous night, that there'd been nothing to eat because David had fallen off the wagon and taken their last $50 to go out and score, had led to the moment when Bette had sold them all out. Candy had been lying on her bed not doing her Social Studies homework when Bette had appeared in the doorway, hesitated for a second and then burst into tears.

Then she'd crawled on to the bed and proceeded to get mascara streaks all over Candy's homework. Candy wasn't a girl who did much in the way of hugs, but she found herself cuddling Bette and murmuring soothing words about how everything would be all right. Except everything was so far from all right that it was hard to know how to fix it.

'There might be a way,' Bette had hiccupped when she'd finally stopped crying. And then she laid it on Candy; the secret meetings with the commissioning editor. The $50,000 they'd get for a short mid-season run of six episodes of a fly-on-the-wall reality series, as long as they promised not to swear and David agreed to weekly drug testing. How could they have known that the show would take off like a greased pig at a county fair?

'So, what do you think, hon?' Bette had asked. 'I'd understand if you said no, but it's either this or food stamps again.'

Candy had shrugged and not thought about it too hard, other than to wonder if she'd get to skip school. 'I guess it'll be OK,' she'd grunted. 'It's only six episodes.'

But three years, fifty episodes, two Christmas specials and a Careless stadium tour later and their lives weren't much better off. OK, she got to fly regularly to far-flung corners of the globe to open some tacky nightclub or awards ceremony for vast sums of money which meant that she'd never live on food stamps again. But Candy also knew that most of the world viewed her as a fairly ridiculous character whose fifteen minutes should have been up ages ago. It left Candy feeling like she'd sold her soul in some Faustian pact. A girl needed a little mystery and hers had become yet another commodity to be traded.

Which was why she now had a plan for the future. The next afternoon, Candy patted the folder in front of her as she and Bette sat waiting for Mimi, their agent and Candy's godmother, at their usual table in Soho House, New York.

Bette was purring into her phone at someone called 'Darling'. Lots of people Bette knew were called 'Darling' because she could never remember their names. Candy rolled her eyes and watched as Mimi weaved through the tables to get to them, stopping every now and again to greet someone with a gracious smile and a regal nod, as befitted the fifth most powerful woman in the entertainment business according to *The New York Times*.

'Bette, Candy,' Mimi murmured as she finally reached their table, bending down to brush her preternaturally smooth cheek against their faces in turn. Sometimes Candy thought that if Mimi had anything else lifted the whole lot would collapse. Today she didn't take off her dark glasses, just shook out her trademark glossy bob and sat down. There weren't many people that Candy was frightened of but Mimi was right at the top of the shortlist. She had this way of looking at Candy, even with her shades on, especially when Candy was shooting her mouth off, that made her feel like a stupid little kid with dirty fingernails.

'I've got some very exciting news,' she murmured, not

sounding very excited at all as she beckoned the waiter for her usual order of shredded arugula leaves with lemon juice and a mineral water.

Candy patted her folder again like it was a protective talisman and ordered a burger and fries, mostly because it made Mimi and Bette flinch at the prospect of so many calories and fat units. They'd both been in the fashion business too long. In fact, Mimi had been Bette's booker when she first started modelling and, for some strange reason that Candy couldn't even begin to fathom out, had stuck with Bette through the years, even though she now ran Fierce Management with an iron fist and a steely disposition.

It took Mimi half an hour to fill them in on the latest fee negotiations with the network for the new series. The ratings were still up, despite Candy's decamping to London, mainly because of weeks like this when she came back and shot scene after scene for fourteen hours a day. Then there were the offers she wanted them to consider. A mother/daughter modelling campaign for a skincare line. ('Hell, no.') Becoming the spokesmodel for a range of sneakers that Candy wouldn't be seen dead in. ('Again, hell no.') And hosting some music awards in Helsinki. ('Yes, but they have to fly me out first class, provide my own chef and I want $200,000.') Candy had learnt from bitter experience that it was better to do one-off gigs in different continents for hellacious sums of money than anything where she was expected to turn up regularly and frequently. She did perk up when

Mimi talked about a possible book deal: *The Candy Careless Guide To Getting What You Want. Exactly When You Want It* but it turned out that she'd simply have to turn up for the cover shoot while some junior editor at *Teen Vogue* actually wrote it.

Finally, Mimi was done and looking significantly at her watch. 'Well, if that's everything, I should leave you two . . .'

'Actually I have some stuff to tell you,' Candy piped up, wishing her palms weren't sweating. She surreptitiously wiped them on the tablecloth and took a deep breath as Mimi focussed her dark-glassy stare on her. 'I've been thinking about the future.'

'Your future is being very carefully looked after,' Mimi said dismissively. 'We're investing eighty per cent of everything you earn. You're never going to have to worry about money, Candy, we've talked about this before.'

They had. At great length. Which was why Candy did the gruelling, red-eye flights to do guest appearances, because this was her window to make as much money as she possibly could. But . . . 'I want my future to involve more than counting my wads of cash,' she said, then reined herself in. Mimi got really snippy if she thought Candy was being flippant. 'I want to have a career. A proper career that isn't just about being some celebutante—'

'I hate that word,' Bette interrupted, so Candy knew that she had actually been listening.

'I want to make something of myself,' Candy continued, glaring at Bette in a shut-the-hell-up sort of way. 'I want to make something, clothes to be precise. I've decided that

I'm going to become a fashion designer.'

There was a moment's silence. Neither Mimi or Bette were laughing their heads off or, well, responding in any particular way at all.

'You know that the only thing I inherited from you is the fashion thing,' Candy told her mother. 'And I've been teaching myself to sew from scratch, not just customizing any more, and I have all these ideas . . .'

Mimi decided that this was serious enough to warrant putting down her BlackBerry. 'Why don't I get in touch with some retailers and tell them that you're interested in putting your face to your own little capsule collection? Like Kate Moss for TopShop but probably with cheaper price points because your fanbase is getting very tweeny, sweetie? Or maybe we could do an accessories and back-to-school line with someone like Walmart? Pencil cases with skulls on them, that kind of thing.'

Why did everything have to have a product endorsement and a photo opportunity attached to it? 'No,' Candy stated, feeling her eyebrows pull together in a tight, angry line. 'I want to do this properly. Like, go to college and learn how to pattern cut and do the business thing.'

'You're still only seventeen, there's time enough for that later on,' Mimi said crisply. 'If you still want to.' It was obvious from her tone of voice that she thought this was some silly whim, like the time Candy had taken drumming lessons until she realized that she had absolutely no sense of rhythm. Which it *so* wasn't.

'But it will take me three years to get my degree

and then I'd have to do some placements at different fashion companies and design studios,' Candy protested. 'And I'll be twenty, almost twenty-one by then. So now is the right time.'

'Now is *not* the right time,' Mimi insisted. 'You're over-extended enough as it is. I'm sure you barely have a minute to yourself right now.'

Which was wrong because Candy had way too many minutes to herself to do nothing but contemplate what a stupid, friendless loser she still was. 'I'll make time,' she said fiercely, but Mimi was signalling the waiter for the bill.

'You do this and how will you find time to fly back and shoot your episodes?' she asked. 'I don't think any fashion college is going to take kindly to you disappearing for weeks on end. And how are you going to get into fashion college? You haven't even graduated high school.'

'I'll take my high school equivalency exam,' Candy offered magnanimously. 'And I've been getting a portfolio together . . .'

'Candy Cane, this is so silly,' Bette breathed. 'It's like the time that you wanted to be a burlesque dancer . . .'

'I was thirteen . . .'

'You promised,' Bette said, her voice throbbing. 'We made a deal that we'd jump on the train and keep riding it until the money dried up. You can't jump off now.' She patted Candy's hand gently. 'I do understand the call of fashion, baby. Tell you what, I'll get you another runway slot in a charity fashion show. You'd like that, wouldn't you?'

Candy would rather have her eyeballs pickled while they were still in their sockets. 'But . . .'

'Well, I could make a couple of phone calls,' Mimi said, signing her name on the credit card slip. 'But really I'd prefer to see how you feel about this in six months' time, Candy.'

'I'll still feel exactly the same then,' Candy choked out, and Mimi nodded regally then started packing away her papers. Which wasn't the same as a yes or no answer. It was absolutely infuriating. 'I'm moving out of the Fierce apartment in London and getting my own place!' The words burst forth from her mouth in a huge sticky mass like congealed pasta.

'Candy, babes, what has gotten into you today? You're being so weird.' Bette shot her an anxious look. 'What's going on? You can tell me, we're best friends.'

'No, we are not. You're the woman who gave birth to me – there's a big diff.'

Mimi stood up. 'You're not moving out of there until you're eighteen,' she said firmly. 'I want you in that apartment where I can keep an eye on you and that's non-negotiable. Bette, I'll call you about the Nordstroms ads.' She was gone in a waft of Fracas before Candy could start spitting out protests.

Bette pulled her chair nearer so she could place a consoling hand on Candy's arm, until she shook it off in irritation. 'Come on, baby, don't be like that,' Bette pleaded, leaning back slightly as if she was waiting for a major explosion. She didn't have to wait long.

'Jesus, it's amazing that I'm old enough to have to deal with a whole bunch of crap, but the moment it's something I want to do then you pull the under-age card. It's not fucking fair!' Candy made no effort to lower her voice and the stupid bitch on the next table could glare all she wanted – no one had asked her to listen in.

'Sweetie, Mimi and I are just looking out for you. I'm sure the fashion thing would be lovely, but it seems like an awful lot of hard work. Most designers go bust in their first two years,' Bette said gently and she kind of did know what she was talking about, which just made it even more annoying. 'And you used to love that apartment. What's changed?'

'Everything!' Candy spat, squirming in her chair with frustration. 'The other girls are all moving out and they hate me anyway and Reed's never there because he's shacking up with that retard Hadley—'

'Oh, Hadley's a doll . . .' Bette interjected and then wished she hadn't when Candy's face went so red that it was a perfect match for her Ruby Woo lipstick.

'Oh, well you got that right. She's a fricking Barbie doll. She's completely fake and plastic, but I s'pose you like that. You'd rather have someone like Sadley as a daughter so you can dress up in matching outfits and agree about everything.'

Bette did what she always did when confronted with Candy being difficult. She fluttered her hands and eyelashes and smiled like the brave little trouper she always was. 'Do you want to go shopping?' she asked hopefully, because of course a new handbag would solve all of Candy's problems. 'My treat.'

'No, I don't want to go shopping. I don't want to go anywhere with *you*.' Candy knew she was being a bitch. She knew that technically none of this was Bette's fault, which had to be a first, but she was the only one around to bear the brunt of her assault, so she'd have to do.

And if Candy had to suffer the hurt look on Bette's face then whatever, she could deal.

Chapter Five

Once she was back in London, Candy started to doubt the wisdom of confiding in Mimi and Bette. Their total and utter non-enthusiasm had left her feeling as if she was doomed to fail. She dreamt about the dresses teamed with darling little shoe boots that would make up her first runway collection, the way other girls dreamt about sucking face with soccer players. But what if Mimi and Bette were right and it was just a stupid whim because Candy would never be able to get the hang of seam allowances or pin tucks? Or maybe she should have kept her mouth shut and presented them with a *fait accompli* once she'd actually managed to sweet talk her way into a fashion college that didn't want her to have completed high school first.

'Ninety-nine per cent of all fashion designers go bust in their first year of business,' Mimi reminded Candy the next time she phoned and that was all she had to say on the subject, because she put her assistant on the line to give Candy details of a charity fashion show that she was hosting later on in the week.

Normally Candy loved a good fashion show; from agonizing over what she was going to wear, to turning up at some bizarre venue like a circus tent or a disused fire station. She loved queuing up in the bony scrum of fashion editors and buyers to get to her seat, which was always in the front row these days. She loved delving into the goodie bag that had been left on her chair and scoping out what other people were wearing and what they were talking about.

'I hear he's going to do colour this season.'

'Apparently the whole collection was inspired by *Grey Gardens*, so expect lots of turbans and upside-down skirts.'

'You didn't hear it from me but the girl who was meant to open the show checked into rehab this morning, that's why they're running so late.'

And the shows never started on time so it could be hours before the house lights dimmed, the music started and the first impossibly tall, impossibly thin, impossibly beautiful girl stepped out on to the runway in some outlandish costume that made her look like a fairytale princess or an astronaut or a singer in a Sixties garage punk band depending on who the designer was. Fashion shows were adrenalin-charged theatre and Candy loved every fraught second of them.

The charity fashion show was a completely different beast. They were always held in the ballroom of some fancy hotel or a members-only nightclub. The models were always B-list celebrities or horsey-faced posh girls crammed into dresses borrowed from some designer who everyone had stopped paying attention to sometime in the mid-Nineties.

But it was always for a good cause. This time it was for some sick little kids who'd benefit from the dresses being auctioned off to anorexic, rich socialites. Candy gave the invitation a cursory glance as she packed one of her own black dresses into a garment bag. They were meant to be clothing her but Candy knew that whatever she was given wouldn't fit. Fierce always faxed over her measurements. But fashion designers expected everyone to be at least five foot nine and a size six, and even with heels and body-shaping underwear on, Candy couldn't fake that.

'You ready?' Irina enquired from the doorway. 'They send the car.'

Candy pinned back her hair with a couple of Kirby grips and grabbed her make-up case. They never had the right shade of red lipstick either. 'You're going to the cancer thing?' she checked, because it really didn't seem like Irina's bag.

From the scowl on Irina's face, it really wasn't. 'Ted tell me I have to walk for free,' she glowered. 'Is not my problem if they have cancer.'

Candy gaped at her. 'Jeez, Irina, that's pretty harsh, even for you.'

Irina shrugged nonchalantly. 'I not believe in charity. In Russia, the State provides proper medicine and sheet.'

'Yeah, but this is to give their parents financial help and pay to take them on holiday and . . .'

There was no point in continuing in the face of Irina's most stony-faced look. 'We go now,' she said implacably. 'Then we come home. I set the Sky+ box because there are gazelles on the nature channel.'

Some misguided fool had recently told Irina that

she had a gazelle-like grace, so she was obsessed with anything to do with them. Candy shook her head. Irina was so weird. But she was also fast approaching the rank of top model; one of those girls who was only known by her first name and her uncompromising looks. Maybe this fashion show wouldn't be the awesome suck Candy had thought it would be.

Backstage though, it was the same old story. A gaggle of braying posh girls clutching glasses of champagne were meant to be organizing things but were just getting in everyone's way.

It was left to Candy to find a stray make-up artist and a spare workstation and start getting ready. They had a brief tussle over some red eyeshadow that would have made Candy look like she had impetigo, but as she was the host rather than one of the clothes-horses, she could pretty much kick it freestyle when it came to how she looked. Which was the usual liquid eyeliner, red lipstick and just a smidgeon of glitter on her cheekbones.

A harried-looking woman suddenly pulled up a chair and started briefing Candy on the collection and the names of the models appearing. It was like a *Who's Who* of the last five years of *Vogue* cover stars and Candy perked up a little as she ran down the list of names. The show wasn't as low rent as she'd feared.

'We didn't have time to prepare a script,' the woman confessed apologetically. 'But your agent said you'd done auctions before and you know how to ad lib.' She jumped in her chair as someone squealed loudly behind her. 'Do you think you'll be OK?'

'It's cool, just tell me how much money you're expecting to make and I'll rack up the bids. I've done this a gazillion times,' she assured the woman, who looked like she was seconds away from a complete breakdown. 'I'll be ready in five minutes. I just need to change into the dress I brought.'

'Oh, but we have a dress for you,' the woman said, and Candy's heart sank right to the bottom of her tatty Converses. 'Nico Lonsdale designed it especially.'

Nico Lonsdale was one of the brightest names on the London fashion scene, famous for sending real girls down the runway in tight but fluid clothes that seemed to shimmy over their curves like liquid. He'd also made headlines when he'd turned down a job at Chanel after his first collection had seen copies of his 'Venus' dress hit every high street in the country. 'I couldn't learn anything from Karl Lagerfeld,' he'd sneered. 'He should be learning from me.'

'It will probably be too long,' Candy said wistfully, but she was already getting up and racing over to the rail that the woman had pointed out, and practically tearing through the dust cover to get to the dress. It was so pretty; a cotton black dress with puff sleeves and a slightly boned bodice with a skirt made from layers and layers of red and black taffeta. It was something that Rebecca from Sunnybrook Farm might have worn if she'd ever fallen in with a gang of Goths. If it didn't fit then Candy was prepared to have a hissy fit of monumental proportions.

But it went on like it had been made for her. Well,

actually it had. Candy kicked off her Converses and slid her feet into red velvet heels which nipped her toes so badly that she decided it was sneakers or bare feet. She was going to be standing behind the auctioneer's podium, so it wasn't like anyone was going to see them.

Candy did a quick twirl in front of the mirror and pronounced herself pleased with the overall effect. She was never going to be beautiful. Not like Laura. And she wasn't easy on the eye like Hadley. Candy thought that her looks were more like Irina. Not that she was blessed with cheekbones and silver eyes, but Candy didn't look quite normal; big eyes that dwarfed everything else on her elfin face, which was why Candy never went out in public without a slash of deep red lipstick on what Bette called her 'bee-stung lips'. It was also a face that looked goddamn awful if caught from the wrong angle by a camera lens so that Candy resembled a pufferfish. So, remembering to keep her chin tilted slightly down, she stepped out on to the stage when she heard her name being announced.

Some people were terrified of public speaking but Candy liked it. Even though it was majorly dorky, she'd been on the debate team at high school, because public speaking was like her superhero skill. She never had to think about it too hard; she'd just open her mouth and words would come out that got laughs and she always remembered to catch the eye of people in the audience for a count of three. Candy was a public-speaking ninja.

Like now, Candy started off with a topical joke about someone mistaking her Primark boots for Prada, and reeled off a list of cancer stats that she'd quickly memorized before she went on stage. Then she welcomed some of the kids on stage who'd been helped by the charity, picking the cutest one and asking her about her favourite dress.

'My pink one with the ribbons,' she lisped to the obligatory 'aw's from the audience, and now that they were nicely tenderized, Candy called the first model out on stage.

It was a lot of fun to make funny remarks about each girl to see if they'd crack a smile (though none of them did) and comment on the dresses. When Irina stalked out last in a daringly-cut, flesh-toned dress that made her look almost naked, Candy grinned. 'And this is Irina Kerchenko, the face of Chanel Bonne perfume and my room-mate. She looks pretty hot right now but two hours ago, she was cutting her toenails in our front room and eating doughnuts.'

There was a guffaw of laughter from the floor, but Irina didn't react apart from a little tightening of her jaw that warned Candy she was in trouble.

After that there was a brief interlude so the audience could eat their £200-a-plate dinner and listen to the lyrical song stylings of a platinum-selling artist. Then it was time to start the bidding.

Candy despaired of the idle rich. They bid thousands of pounds on the glittery, slit-up-to-the-neck gowns but the edgier designs weren't doing too well. And it was for sick kids too. Officially, she'd had enough. She unclipped her mic from its stand and descended from the stage into the audience.

'Hello,' she chirped at some greasy guy who was with a

woman wearing so many diamonds that Candy was temporarily blinded. 'You look very rich, why aren't you bidding?'

The man looked momentarily dumbfounded, then he beckoned Candy closer so he could reach the microphone. 'If I write you a cheque for an obscene amount of money, will you leave me alone?' he drawled.

Candy continued to work the room like no room had ever been worked before, even stopping to sit on the lap of a singer she knew slightly and begging him to buy a dress for his girlfriend, who hugged Candy, to loud applause, when he paid £5,000 for a dress that wasn't even worth a tenth of that.

The final dress was a Nico Lonsdale number in dull grey satin that Candy would have bought in an instant if there was a procedure where she could have herself stretched by about eight inches. 'If no one bids on this to my satisfaction, then things are going to get ugly,' she announced. 'We're starting the bidding at £1,000.'

She looked around the room, gratified when someone's hand shot up. '£1,500 to the woman in green. Love your hair, darling.'

But the bidding was sluggish and Candy had no choice but to pad over to Irina's table with an evil smile. 'Hey roomie,' she called brightly.

Irina opened her mouth, probably to tell Candy to piss off, but she was sitting next to her booker, Ted, who must have kicked her under the table because she just swallowed hard and glared.

'Irina, you'd look so beautiful in this dress,' Candy cajoled. 'And remember when we were getting ready and you said how you felt so sorry for any poor, defenceless child that had a life-threatening disease?'

Christ, Irina was made from breeze block. She just sat there, eyes flashing. 'Is bad when a kid gets sick,' she said finally, like it was right up there with the times when she couldn't find the TV remote.

'So you should bid on this bee-yoo-ti-ful frock,' Candy insisted. 'I mean, how much are Chanel paying you? Two mill, isn't it?'

Ted was hissing frantically at Irina, who finally roused herself. 'OK, I bid £10,000. Now, go away, Candy, before I smack you.'

Candy didn't need to be told twice, she was already edging away and looking to see if anyone else was bidding. They weren't. 'The gorgeous Nico Lonsdale dress is sold to my fast-food-scoffing roomie for ten grand and I'm going to match that and pay the same amount for the Nico Lonsdale dress I'm wearing right now,' Candy said, climbing back on stage. 'You've been a really generous crowd, so on behalf of the organizers and Cancer Cares, I'd just like to thank you . . .'

Irina was out for Candy's blood the second she came off stage. She looked close to tears. '£10,000 for a dress? I never pay for clothes,' she cried. Parting with money always made Irina extra emotional.

Candy collapsed on the nearest chair. 'It was for a good cause and no one will ever know that beneath your stony exterior lies more stone.'

'They better not,' Irina said grimly. She nudged Candy's shoulder with one bony hip. 'You good up there,' she said, as if the admission had been dragged out of her with rusty pliers and electrodes. 'I guess having the big mouth works out for you sometimes.' And with one last put-upon sniff she flounced off.

Candy's on-stage high slowly evaporated in the time it took for one of the Park Lane princesses to coo, 'You really are funny, Candy. A little too brash, maybe, but it went down well in the cheap seats.'

Then she saw Dean Speed from The Hormones and got totally blanked by him. Worse, he walked over to Irina, made a big show of looking pleased to see her, then they sat whispering in the corner and shooting evil glances in Candy's direction. If Irina was telling him that Candy, on one solitary occasion, may have planted a lipstick kiss on a picture of Dean that was pinned on the kitchen noticeboard, then there was going to be extreme hell to pay. Dean was hot, sinfully, undeniably hot, in a skinny emo way that made Candy weak of knee and short of breath, but in person he'd been a major disappointment.

Whenever Candy talked to him, his eyes flickered in every direction, like he couldn't wait to get away from her. Then he'd asked Laura out on a disastrous date – and Laura hadn't even liked The Hormones until she heard Candy playing them. *And* she'd arrived with Dean and left with Danny. But the thing that had killed Candy's crush on Dean Speed once and for all was the awful day he'd said in an interview that she was the one person in the world that he'd least like to be trapped in an elevator with. 'She's the worst kind of publicity whore,' he'd said. 'And she obviously wasn't slapped enough as a kid.' After that little character assassination, Candy had thrown out all her Hormones CDs and told Irina that if he ever came round to the flat, she was going to throw boiling water over him.

Once again, Candy found herself wondering if this was actually the time of her life and, instead of skulking and having a self-pity party for one, she should be making the most of it. Or at least going to find George, Hadley's ex-fake boyfriend and one of the few people that Candy could actually stand to be around. He was very shallow but at least he owned it.

'I think I owe you a glass of champagne at the very least,' a voice said in her ear, and Candy turned round to see the slightly podgy face of Nico Lonsdale beaming at her. 'Come and meet my boyfriend, he's also my business manager. He wants you to autograph something for his mum.'

Candy let herself be pulled across the room. She had a huge gay fanbase — they did love their small, self-dramatizing girls, whether it was Judy Garland, Kylie Minogue or Candy Careless. 'Why are you called Nico when you have a Welsh accent?'

'Because I was born and brought up in Llanelli and christened Griff,' Nico said silkily, leading Candy to a table where a beautiful boy with black hair and sleepy blue eyes was lounging. 'This is Christian. He thinks you're the funniest girl in the world.'

'Which would be my cue to not think of a single funny thing to say,' Candy drawled, leaning over so Christian could kiss first one cheek, then the other.

'You're small,' Christian noted wisely. 'Nico, she's tiny. Like a little pocket Venus. Can we take her home? Can we keep her?'

'I don't know,' Nico said, joining the game as Candy sat down between the pair of them. 'I don't think she's housetrained.'

'I'm not,' Candy said, showing all her teeth. 'So, how did you get started in the fashion business?'

Nico, né Griff, began his career sewing dresses for his sister's Barbie dolls, did his fashion degree at Central St Martin's, spent two years in Paris under the tutelage of a legendary and tyrannical designer, and then started his own label with private backing from the wife of a hedge-fund manager.

'Of course, the only way to really make money is to do handbags,' Nico sighed. 'So I'm designing a capsule bag collection for next season and getting my PR to place them with celebrities in the vain hope that one of them becomes the new It bag.'

Candy said nothing, just nodded her head because nothing Nico was saying was a surprise. 'And what qualifications did you need to get into St Martin's?' she asked, wondering if she should whip out her iPhone and start taking notes.

Nico paused. 'You're not just making polite conversation, are you?'

'I never make polite conversation,' Candy gasped indignantly. And she was meant to be better trained than this. After all, Mimi had sent her to a media handler before *At Home With The Careless* aired, but Nico put a warm hand on her knee and Christian dropped the louche act and it was all spilling out. Well, not *all* of it. But the part where her fashion dreams had been cruelly thwarted and Candy felt the closest she'd ever come to being a fashion designer would be putting her name to a garish collection of plastic accessories adorned with skulls and crossbones.

Candy squinched up her face as she got to the end of her impassioned rant. 'I'm not saying that I'm the new Coco Chanel or anything but I just want a chance to see if I have any talent. I'm not afraid of a little hard work.' She'd never actually done anything that qualified as proper work, but she'd racked up plenty of jet-lag as a globe-trotting celebrity and that had to count for something.

'How do you feel about making coffee and photo-copying?' Nico asked with a sidelong glance at Christian, who shrugged and smiled.

It wasn't right up there on her list of favourite things in the world. 'Well, they fill a need,' Candy hedged. 'Why?'

'Because if you came to work for me as an unpaid intern you'd be doing a lot of that,' Nico said, mistaking Candy's mouth falling open as outrage. 'But you'd also learn all the technical aspects of design and I could get one of my team to mentor you. How does that sound?'

It sounded heavenly. So heavenly that Candy wanted to check that she hadn't just died and been fast-tracked upstairs. 'I don't know what to say,' she panted, which was officially a Candy Careless first.

Nico mistook Candy's non-wordiness for reticence because he started a hard sell. 'I know you have a really busy schedule but we can fit in around that and I'll give you some free frocks, make you an ambassadress for the brand. Even give you a rag-picker's commission if you find some good vintage stuff on your travels that I can rip off for the runway.'

It was just getting better and better. Learning on the job was far more practical than toiling away doing homework and course assignments. And Mimi would totally freak, which was an added bonus. 'That sounds fine,' Candy said eagerly. 'Shall we swap deets?'

Chapter Six

Candy wasn't the kind of girl to have fashion crises. She sneered in the face of appropriate daywear. As far as she was concerned, if she wanted to wear a gold lamé ballgown to a lunch meeting, then she damn well would.

But her first day as a fashion industry professional had her standing in front of her full-to-bursting closet and scratching her head. She needed to show that she was on trend but she didn't want to look like she was trying too hard.

In the end, Candy went for vintage. A black-and-white polka-dot sundress that she'd chopped to just above the knee and trimmed with green rickrack, teamed with a little cashmere cardie in the same shade of green, woolly tights and a pair of biker boots. It was an outfit that said: 'I know what's hot, I know what's not and I can customize with the best of them, thank you very much'.

Even though it was cold and the number of her car service was on speed dial, Candy decided to kick it like a normal girl. Well, she walked to the top of Bayham Street and hailed a black cab to Hackney. There was nothing wrong with taking the bus, but she couldn't deal with the whole fare thing, and there was *always* some asshole who recognized her and decided that she needed taking down a peg or two.

Soon she was being dropped off in front of a distinctly seedy-looking building in the bit of Hackney that hadn't been made cool yet. There wasn't even a Starbucks, so Candy had to get her morning jolt of caffeine in a workmen's café full of builders, before she gingerly pressed the intercom. This place looked like it was a sweatshop rather than a fashion studio.

She was buzzed in, and made her way to the fifth floor in an old freight elevator that creaked and shuddered and gave the impression that it would send Candy hurtling to her death if she made any sudden moves. Finally, it ground to a halt and she struggled to slide back the heavy metal door.

Waiting for her was a tall, blonde girl who looked like she could have been a model if only her features weren't off by just a few degrees. Her eyes were a fraction too small, her nose ever so slightly crooked and her lips were a little too thin – although that could just have been because she was frowning at Candy. If she smiled, she might have been a knockout. She was wearing a tight pencil skirt, a fitted Forties blouse and the kind of pointy heels that gave Candy blisters just looking at them.

'Hey,' Candy said breezily. 'I'm Nico's new intern.'

She didn't bother to introduce herself because, unless you'd been living at the bottom of the ocean for the last three years, you knew who Candy Careless was.

'Nico's in Milan,' the girl said shortly and Candy revoked the smiling theory. This girl didn't have an ounce of joy in her. 'You'd better come through here.'

She hefted open another heavy metal door and Candy stepped into a minimalist reception area: white walls with framed prints of models wearing Nico's designs and pop art furniture painted gold and silver. It was completely at odds with the Third World conditions outside.

'This way,' the girl ordered, and Candy scurried to keep up as the girl poked her head through various doorways.

'Kitchen, coffee maker, kettle. Make sure we don't run out of milk. Petty cash is with Jeanne on Reception.'

She threw open another door. 'Fabric room.' Candy barely had time to take in the bolts and bolts of silk, satin and velvet in a rainbow of different colours before they were off again.

'This is Nico's office.' Candy peered over her shoulder at a messy room littered with books and magazines and scraps of material before she was whisked away.

'Fitting room for the models on the left, bathroom's on the right, the offices are just down the hall,' the girl chanted as they reached a flight of stairs. 'And up here is where the design team work.' She folded her arms. 'Any questions?'

Candy had a million of those, starting with, 'What the hell is your problem?' but she reined it in. 'What's your name?'

'Sophie,' she said, leaning against the banister. 'Normally our interns have fashion degrees. Do you even know how to cut patterns?'

'Well, not exactly,' Candy admitted. 'I'm here in an unofficial capacity.'

Sophie sniffed. 'There are to be no camera crews

61

without Christian's express permission. You're not to get in anyone's way. And you're not to bother Nico unless he asks you to.'

'Cool,' Candy agreed equably, though every instinct she possessed was telling her to take this bitch out. 'So, where do I start?'

Sophie opened her mouth, then shut it again. She had this mottled red rash rising up from under her collar. 'You know . . .' she began, then stopped. 'OK, I'm just going to say it. Some of us are here because we had to slog our guts out and beg for bank loans on top of our already colossal student debts. We don't have the connections to just swan in here for a couple of weeks because we thought that being a fashion designer might be, like, the best fun ever.'

'Good to know,' Candy drawled, but no way was she going to take shit from anyone. Let alone some uptight ex-student who had her hate on just because Candy was getting a free pass for once in her life. 'Just so we're clear, I can't cut patterns but I've been hanging out in designers' ateliers since I was in my stroller, so I don't need any lessons in etiquette from you. And I'm planning to stick around for the long haul so if you have a problem with that, then I suggest you take it up with Nico, who's a close personal friend of mine.' It was on a par with playing the my-dad's-more-famous-than-your-dad card that she'd seen the young Hollywood kids pull out at parties, but it worked. Sophie was edging backwards but hadn't managed to lose the look of loathing. 'And just who the hell do you think you are anyway?' Candy asked.

Sophie drew herself up, because when all was said and done, she still had the advantage of height over Candy. 'I'm Nico's intern.' She smiled with absolutely no humour. 'What I meant to say was that I'm Nico's *other* intern and if you screw this opportunity up for me I will shut you down.'

'Fine,' Candy said, resting her coffee on one of the stairs in case Sophie wanted to bring the smackdown right there and then. 'I'll make a deal with you. You stay out of my way and I'll stay out of yours.'

There was a faint look of disappointment on Sophie's face, like she'd expected Candy to back down like a little pussy. Which was never going to happen. She pursed her lips while she gave Candy's generous offer serious consideration. And it was a totes generous offer because Candy could easily have her fired.

'Staying out of your way would be my absolute pleasure,' she hissed. 'Now, wait for Alfie to come and get you – you're going to shadow him.' She turned to leave but couldn't resist one last parting shot. 'You look *much* taller on TV.'

Candy stuck her tongue out at Sophie's stiff back, then looked around expectantly for Alfie. She hoped that he wasn't copping as much attitude as Sophie.

But whether he was or not remained a mystery because Alfie continued to be a no-show. Candy wondered if she should just head to the studio, but she didn't want to incur any more unwarranted wrath. So she sat on the stairs and drank her cooling coffee, which took all of two minutes.

It took one minute to re-apply her lipstick. Another minute to tap a reminder into her iPhone to send Mimi some flowers because she was fuming almost as much as Sophie about Candy's new internship. And then Candy was rapidly approaching her boredom threshold.

And enough was enough. She was going into that design studio because she wasn't some scared little muppet who shied away from difficult situations. Hell, no. Candy stood up with renewed purpose, foofed out her skirt, and looked up to see a man in a suit peering quizzically down at her from the top of the stairs.

'Are you the new girl?' he asked. 'I'm Alfie. I forgot you were coming in. It's Cindy, isn't it?'

Was he for real? 'Candy, actually.' Like, he didn't know *exactly* who she was.

Candy headed up the steps towards the man who wasn't actually a man. He was a tall, thin boy who was looking at her with a perplexed expression. 'You're the girl from that show,' he remarked. 'How odd. Hmm, maybe Nico mentioned it. I'll have to Google you. What college did you go to?'

'I didn't,' Candy said, following him through a set of glass doors – and finally she was in the studio. Actually she was in Paradise. It was a long, open-plan room with huge workstations for the designers, who each had a sewing machine, a computer and a mood board to work from. 'I'm just here to get a feel for it.'

Alfie didn't seem particularly perturbed by that bombshell. He was walking rapidly down the length of the room, throwing random names and titles over his shoulder at Candy. 'Jacques, Clare: accessory designers.' Pause. 'Ivy, Lola: pattern cutters.' Pause. 'Sit.'

At first Candy thought it was someone's name, possibly someone from Scandinavia, but Alfie was pulling over a stool and watching as Candy tried to clamber on to it and not lose any cool points. Alfie's workspace was spartan. There wasn't a single piece of paper to be seen. His magazines were neatly stacked on a shelf and on his mood board there was one solitary picture of two rapier thin models in tweed suits talking animatedly to each other. 'Avedon,' Candy noted and Alfie stopped staring at her and shook his head as if he was coming out of a trance.

'Avedon,' he agreed gravely, sitting down on his own chair. 'Your rickrack's slightly untethered.'

Candy looked down at her skirt to see that the green trim was beginning to hang loose. She covered it with her hand and wished that Alfie would stop staring at her like she was a freak.

In fact, he kind of looked like a freak. He was wearing a suit for one thing. The kind of slim suit men wore in old black-and-white movies like *La Dolce Vita*. It was charcoal-grey, and cut to perfection so Alfie could show precisely one inch of snowy white cuff from his jacket sleeves. He even had a matching handkerchief folded into a perfect triangle in his breast pocket. His glossy black hair was cut short, short-back-and-sides short, the top long enough to be pushed back by an impatient hand as he blinked big blue eyes, framed with sooty lashes.

65

Candy couldn't work him out. Was he a gigantic poseur or just a sharp dresser? Why did he have blue eyes when his skin was the colour of the cup of coffee she'd just drunk? And was he gay, because she doubted very much if a straight boy would go to all the trouble of finding a tie that exactly matched the shade of his eyes?

She realized that Alfie was talking as he straightened his collection of colour pencils to his obviously exacting standards. 'I do a lot of the tailoring and the finishing,' he was saying. 'It's all about the fit and the detail. So . . .'

'So?' Candy prompted. 'I'm meant to be shadowing you.'

Alfie gulped as if he had something lodged in his throat. 'But I don't do anything,' he said in a slightly peevish tone. 'I just sit here and sew.'

'Oh, there's loads of stuff I could do to help you. I could collect your pieces from the pattern cutters . . .'

'I do my own cutting,' Alfie informed a tad snootily. 'And I collect my own fabrics and trims too. I'm sure some people in this room don't wash their hands properly.'

He wasn't the only one who was going to be doing some cutting if he kept bringing the haughty, Candy thought. Being on her best behaviour was starting to become a strain. 'Well, I can sharpen your pencils to optimum pointiness . . .'

'But I prefer them to be slightly blunted.' The peevish tone was upgrading to an aggrieved whimper. 'You can just sit there and watch me and ask questions,' Alfie decided magnanimously. 'But don't touch anything.'

Candy gave him a look that said far more than words

66

ever could, but Alfie was already walking towards his dress form so it was wasted on him. Which was a pity because it was a really good look.

Alfie drew up another stool, plucked a box of pins from a freakishly tidy drawer and began making lightning quick adjustments to the muslin that was draped on the form.

'What comes first?' Candy asked, pulling out her new notebook and selecting a shiny red pencil from Alfie's selection. 'The draping or the pattern?'

Alfie stopped pinning long enough to glare. 'I told you not to touch anything!' he snapped. 'And I'm trying to concentrate.' Then he realized that as mentors went, he was a very crap one. 'You can ask me questions when I've finished. Now put my pencil back exactly where you found it.'

Pouting so furiously that Candy thought she might have sprained her lower lip, she shoved the pencil back accompanied by Alfie's anguished moan.

'Line them up again!' he ordered. 'They're all crooked.'

It was going to be a very long day.

Chapter Seven

By the end of her first week as an intern, Candy knew for certain that she loved working in fashion. Well, not the actual working part, because so far Alfie had only trusted her to go on coffee runs for the rest of the team.

She'd offered to get him a coffee and he'd handed her a mocha-coloured square from a Pantone book. 'Make sure it matches that precisely,' he'd said, like it was the most reasonable request in the world and he wasn't as crazy as a barrel-load of monkeys. And then he'd had the nerve to snatch it back. 'On second thoughts, I'll get it myself.'

So being Alfie's little shadow, who wasn't allowed to speak, touch stuff or breathe too loudly, was distinctly unfun, but the rest of the design team were cool. So far, Candy had been sent to a fabric wholesaler's to buy spools and spools of ribbon in every different shade of white, off-white, cream, ivory and oyster that she could find. And she'd archived fifty years' worth of *Vogue Italia* that Christian had bought at auction. But mostly she gossiped.

Gossip in the fashion industry was hard currency, and Candy was rolling in it. From Bette, Laura and Irina, she had scurrilous scandals of models and their eating disorders, drug habits and dodgy boyfriends. From David, she had tales of rock 'n' roll excess. Reed and Hadley used to be a great source of Hollywood horror stories. And Candy had picked up a few priceless pieces of dirt on her travels.

'Not boys,' she told Lola, one of the pattern cutters. 'Girls, two at a time.'

Lola shook her dyed red bob in disbelief. She was French and incredibly sophisticated. 'Oh, Candy, your gossip is beyond compare.'

Candy smiled modestly and angled a glance at Alfie, who was bent over his sketchpad. He'd been particularly taciturn that morning and had already told her off for dropping a box of pins on the floor. 'What's Alfie's story? He's not on prescription medication by any chance?'

'He's a little intense, yes?' Lola shot Alfie's back a fond smile. 'A true English eccentric.'

'Well, that's one word for it,' Candy muttered. 'There has to be a reason why he's like, well, *that.*'

'He got headhunted by Versace after his graduate show,' Lola revealed casually. 'Flew off to Milan and was back in London after a week because he say that he can't work under those conditions.'

'What conditions?' Candy breathed, leaning on the cutting table.

'No one knows,' said Ivy, the other pattern cutter, as she started unfolding a bolt of cloth. 'And last summer the air conditioning broke and it was the first time that Alfie ever took his jacket off.'

Oh my God, he was such a freak! 'For real?' Candy squeaked. 'And when he took it off did he have a tail?'

'Don't be silly,' Ivy scoffed, deftly handling the billowing swathes of fabric. Candy never tired of watching Nico's

70

team do their thing, their hands swift and sure as they worked. 'Alfie's a sweetheart, he's just a little bit of a perfectionist.'

Candy was saved from having to issue a denial by Alfie himself. 'Candy, can you wash your hands like I showed you and then come and hold this muslin for me?'

Candy rolled her eyes as Ivy and Lola grinned, then hurried to do Alfie's bidding. Today he was wearing a black suit and, in honour of the fact that it was completely freezing, was wearing a V-neck sweater under it, his shirt collar and tie just visible. Candy bet he starched and ironed his shirts every night, when he wasn't poring over copies of old fashion magazines with a magnifying glass and surgical gloves so he wouldn't sully the pages.

The mental image made her snigger loudly enough that Alfie gave her an odd look. Or that could be because she was wearing a little black dress demure enough to do for tea at Buckingham Palace but she'd accessorized it with purple woolly tights and greying sneakers.

But he didn't say anything, just coughed pointedly and held out a piece of muslin. Despite Candy's carping, it was fascinating watching Alfie work and seeing how the piece of muslin slowly transformed itself into a dress, pieces of tape delineating the different panels, carefully pinned nips and darts giving it shape. When they were done, Alfie took six steps back, folded his arms and stared at the dress form. And stared. And stared. And stared a little bit more.

Candy wasn't exactly sure what he was looking at. But occasionally he'd 'Hmmm,' and then take a step to the side so he could start the same process from a different angle. She shuffled uncomfortably because she was getting a cramp, and Alfie finally noticed that she was still there. He smiled and it was like the sun coming out after a week of storm clouds. It completely transformed the tight, stiff lines of his face, which were usually pinched in concentration, and he almost looked like a real, live boy.

'Tell you what,' he said conspiratorially. 'After lunch, I'll let you make a bodice all by yourself.'

Candy didn't have the heart to tell Alfie that she'd been making her own clothes unsupervised for the last two years. Not when he was smiling at her like that.

Fortified with an all-day breakfast from the café next door, Candy was raring to go on the bodice-making project. She'd even begged the ends of a roll of velvet from Lola. Alfie was nowhere to be seen (probably eating peas individually with a knife and fork somewhere) so Candy, remembering what she'd seen that morning, started draping the fabric across the form.

She was thinking about ruching, because she was that kind of girl, so she started adding pins, though her fingers weren't as agile as Alfie's and the nap of the velvet was starting to look a little grubby from where she kept jabbing and pulling at it. Still, everyone had to start somewhere. Eventually the velvet was hanging to Candy's satisfaction.

What had Alfie done then? Walked around it for hours like he was taking inventory. Candy did a quick three hundred and sixty, decided that the bodice met with her approval, and picked up the pinking shears.

Her heart always dipped when she first cut into the fabric. One false move and everything could go horribly wrong. But soon she was snipping away happily, trimming away all the excess material and so excited by the crunching noise of the scissors that she didn't hear footsteps behind her.

'What the *hell* do you think you're doing?' OK, she definitely heard that because Alfie was yelling. Candy didn't know he could achieve anything louder than a pained whimper.

'Why am I doing what?' she asked, making short work of the ragged ends, until Alfie's hand closed over hers and he started prising her fingers away from the shears' handles. 'What are *you* doing?'

'I told you to make a bodice!' Alfie was still shouting. 'That meant making a pattern, then working on muslin. Look what you've done to the velvet. You've destroyed it!'

People were looking. Soon they would start pointing and smirking. 'It was the ends of a roll – it's not like it could have been used for anything else,' Candy pointed out, but she could feel her blood pressure rising and that itch in her skin that made her want to start shouting and swearing and really, really flouncing.

'That's not the point!' Alfie protested, finally succeeding in wrestling the shears away from Candy with sheer brute force. 'How can you hope to work in fashion if you have no respect for the process?'

Candy sucked into her mouth the finger that Alfie had practically bent backwards and tried to kill him by making red–hot lasers shoot from her eyes. It didn't work. 'My hand,' she hissed, waving it in Alfie's face so he could see the damage he'd done. Well, technically it was just a little red, but that wasn't the point. 'How dare you maul me?!'

'You mauled the velvet,' Alfie huffed, stroking his hand over the form. 'You did more than maul it, you butchered it. You've completely destroyed the nap. I just cannot work in these conditions.'

'Yeah, well I'm not working with some jumped-up little grunt who has to get his kicks from staring at a dress form for hours because he's completely lacking in social skills,' Candy burst out. And it was too late. Her blood had risen and there wasn't a damn thing she could do but shout at Alfie a bit more. 'Do you know who I am?'

It was the singularly most lame thing to say, especially if you were a bit of a celebrity. And Alfie was all good to go with a retort. 'A little brat who doesn't know how to behave in public,' he suggested scathingly.

From somewhere behind her, Candy heard a snicker. She bet it was Sophie, who'd kept out of her way as promised but sniffed contemptuously every time they were in the same room. 'If I'm a brat then you're a suit-wearing jerk with a stick so far up your ass that—'

'Children! Am I going to have to send you both to separate corners?' Nico suddenly popped out of nowhere and planted himself firmly between them. 'What's the problem?'

Where to start? 'He's fucking impossible . . .' Candy spat. 'He's a goddamn control freak and I'm this close to garrotting him with his stupid tie.'

Alfie spread his hands imploringly. 'Really, Nico, do you see what I have to put up with?' He sighed, then he actually took out his neatly folded pocket square and mopped his forehead with it.

Candy could only stare at him in amazement. 'Dude, it's the twenty-first century, why can't you use a tissue like everyone else?'

Alfie shut his eyes as if he was in great pain. 'Nico, please,' he whispered. 'This is expecting far too much of me.'

Before Candy could insist that she'd been the epitome of restraint all week, Nico was curving an arm round her shoulder. 'I've got some bag samples with me from the factory in Milan, I'd really like to get your opinion on them,' he said soothingly. Normally talking about handbags would have perked Candy up no end, but she was still mad.

'Aren't you going to check that I've washed my hands, like, a gazillion times before you let me handle expensive leather goods?' she pouted, but let Nico lead her down the stairs and into the soothing red space of his inner sanctum.

There was coffee and sticky buns that Sophie had to get from the bakery in the next road. Nico didn't even call Candy on her temper tantrum, but spent half an hour explaining what a special little flower Alfie was.

'I don't use the term "genius" lightly, my darling, but that boy can do things with organza satin and a sewing machine that would make the angels weep,' he said, his Welsh accent getting more pronounced. "I know he's got some strange ways about him, but that's just our Alfie.'

'By strange ways, do you mean that he should be put in a straitjacket and carted off to the nearest funny farm?' Candy asked.

'He's a perfectionist,' Nico insisted. 'And being a little odd goes with the territory. Look at Karl Lagerfeld . . .'

Candy had sat next to Karl Lagerfeld at a dinner once. He'd turned up two hours late, spent the rest of the time fluttering a lace fan in front of his face and then offered to make Candy a dress for the MTV Awards after she'd told him a really filthy joke about a chicken and an egg. 'Karl just plays up for the press,' she said knowingly. 'Really, he's a total sweetheart.'

'So is Alfie. He's just super high maintenance,' Nico said, snagging the last bun. 'Now, let's talk handbags.'

Chapter Eight

Candy flew to Tokyo that weekend to do promotion for the release of the *At Home With The Careless* Season Two DVD.

As usual, her shopping and sleeping time was sacrificed so Candy could do as much work in forty-eight hours as possible. She'd looked at her itinerary on the plane and blanched, but the actual reality of it was just a succession of cars, conference rooms and studios; an endless blur of faces and names being thrown at her as she smiled politely and bowed her head.

It was ironic that she was famous for being a loud-mouthed beeyatch on TV, because when she was doing promo, Candy prided herself on being a consummate professional. The maths was simple. The more DVDs she helped to flog, or sneakers she agreed to model in a lucrative endorsement deal, the more dollars appeared in her bank account. Candy wasn't sure that she ever wanted children, especially if they turned out like her, but if she did, then they sure as hell weren't going to spend their formative years eating peanut butter and jelly sandwiches because there was no money for anything else.

And if a little ritual humiliation was needed to earn the paycheck, Candy could deal, which was why she agreed to dress up as a goddamn Sumo wrestler in a fat suit for some weird-ass TV show at the end of her trip. Hopefully it wouldn't end up on YouTube, Candy thought as she waited in the green room for her cue. She couldn't actually sit down because the padding was getting in the way, but she propped herself up against a wall and watched the show on a monitor. Wai, Candy's translator, whispered a running commentary as members of the audience were selected at random and lowered into a gigantic tank of water, but Candy still didn't have a freaking clue what was going on.

Then she waddled on stage to present some prizes, did a quick interview with the over-excitable host and saw them to the final credits by reading some phonetically translated Japanese from the autocue. Candy was in the car on the way to the airport before the adverts even started, cleaning the make-up off her face with a baby wipe as she did a quick phone interview with some US teen magazine.

'And are you seeing anyone?' the journalist wanted to know, after Candy had finished a poignant diatribe about how much she missed Little Debbie Triple Fudge Brownies, which weren't sold anywhere in Europe.

Candy looked at her watch. It was time to wrap this up. 'Not at the moment,' she admitted shortly.

There was a pause and she heard the journalist rustle her list of questions. 'You don't seem to have dated at all since Jacob Bruckner,' the girl ventured. 'You know, from The A-Trains?' Like, Candy might have forgotten the name of his band.

'And your point is?' Candy demanded, though really

she should have just said her goodbyes and put the phone down.

'Well, just that you seem to have it all going for you: you're cute and famous and our readers really aspire to be like you rather than some anorexic celeb. You're real, y'know. But why don't you date?'

Because, apart from Jacob and he *really* didn't count, no boy had ever asked Candy out. 'I've given it up for Lent,' Candy sassed back. 'Seriously, I'd much rather hang with my girls then spend all my time stressing out about some lame boy who I know I'm gonna dump before too long anyway.' That was more like it – some pro-girl, empowering message that they could stick in a pull quote.

'But what kind of guys do you like?' God, this journalist was persistent.

Candy stifled a yawn. 'Everyone thinks I go for these slouchy slacker types, but I'm so over boys who can't get their shit together,' she said. 'I like boys who are passionate about stuff that isn't the latest Wii game or mope-rock anthem, like art or photography or whatever. And he's gotta be able to make me laugh and he gets that I'm weird and that sometimes I can be a pain in the ass 'cause he's like that too. And he's got to be taller than me, not that that's difficult. Look, I'm going to have to go now, we're just getting to the airport.'

'But—'

'If you need anything else, call my publicist and we can set up another ten minutes,' Candy lied, knowing that Kris would do no such thing.

The plan was that Candy would sleep like a baby for the duration of the twelve-hour flight. But every time she closed her eyes, the image of her perfect boy taunted her with the knowledge that he only existed in her head. And even if he was real, standing in front of her with a soft smile, there was absolutely no way he'd be interested in a drama queen like Candy. He'd want some ethereal, dreamy girl who'd never cause scenes or dress up as a Sumo wrestler on live TV.

Candy gave a groan of frustration, much to the alarm of the businessman in the seat behind her, and thumped her pillow in the vain hope that that would be the key to unlocking the mysteries of sleep.

Candy eventually fell asleep while watching the new Kirsten Dunst movie and woke up as they were serving lunch. As she wrestled her suitcase off the baggage carousel, she felt as if there were rocks in her head. She also felt like she should go home and go to bed and sleep until the middle of next week.

It was such a tempting thought. The cleaning service would have been and her bed would be redolent of the scent of meadow flowers and she could snuggle down . . . A yawn threatened to split her face in two as Candy wheeled her suitcase towards the driver holding a sign with her name on it.

It was on the tip of her tongue to tell him to take her to Camden and to leadfoot it all the way, but it was Monday morning – well, Monday lunchtime – and she was meant to be interning. She'd even told Nico that she'd be in late when he said they weren't expecting her. 'Oh, I never get jet-lag,' she'd said grandly.

Well, she had jet-lag now, or acute sleep deprivation, and she wasn't in the mood to deal with Alfie and his rampant OCD, not without stabbing him in the eye with something sharp. But she *was* going to work, because she wasn't a lightweight or some empty-headed dilettante. Candy could just imagine Sophie's smug, triumphant smile when she was a no-show. 'Hackney,' she grunted at the driver. 'And can we stop and get some super caffeiney coffee on the way?'

Candy tried to do her make-up on the way to Hackney. Something pink and glowy so she didn't look so street urchin, but she failed miserably.

'You look like crap warmed over,' Ivy chirped when Candy staggered in. 'Are you going down with something?'

Out of the corner of her eye, Candy could see Alfie put a protective hand on his dress form as if Candy was sending out all sorts of toxic, airborne germs. She felt like marching over and coughing obnoxiously, but before she could take a step in his direction, Nico was bounding up the studio steps.

'Candy! You're back from Tokyo,' he cried enthusiastically. 'We need to have a handbag summit.'

Candy didn't have anything to do with Alfie for the next few days. Apart from being sent over to retrieve the Pantone book so she could start assembling a colour palette for Nico's second attempt at It bags. Anyway, Alfie had Sophie assisting him. She didn't seem to mind his psychotic tendencies, even when he made her wear white kid gloves to handle some lawn cotton. Candy sat on the other side of the room and stared in amazement as Sophie shot Alfie these doe-eyed glances, which he totally didn't notice because he was too busy gazing at a collection of swatches.

But if work was a source of all that was good, then home was the very essence of all things that were sucky. Irina had dropped in briefly on Wednesday night to leave a ton of dirty dishes in the sink, Hadley was still holed up with Reed and Laura was in St Barts. Which was fine. Except when Candy arrived home on Thursday night, looking forward to ordering some Chinese and watching TV until her eyes went blurry, she found three girls giggling and shrieking and trying on clothes. One of them was even trying to stuff her size seven feet into Candy's size three Miu Miu mules.

'I'm Jen,' one of them had said. 'We're on reading week from uni, Laura said it would be OK if we could crash here.'

It wasn't OK. Never had Candy wanted to throw such a mammoth hissy fit as she did right then. Well, that or burst into tears. 'Guys, I've been working all day,' she gritted. 'I need you to dial down the girlish shrieks and if you bust my Miu Mius, you pay for them.' Then she raised her eyebrow in a manner that usually made even Mimi back away slowly.

It worked on Laura's bridge and tunnel buddies. They probably thought Candy was a total despot, but at least they kept the high-pitched squeals of delight down to a less deafening level.

The Three Stooges were *still* there when Candy got home early on Friday afternoon because she had a big party, which needed mondo prep time. Jen and someone else whose name she couldn't remember started trying to regale her with tales of the thrilling time they'd had at the London Dungeon. They were *so* suburban.

'Where's the other one?' Candy demanded, but she already knew. She banged on the bathroom door. 'I need you out of there in five minutes and you'd better not have used up the hot water!'

She was moving out of this dump the very second she turned eighteen, Candy vowed as she continued to thump her fist against the door. 'Get out! Get out! Get out!' she chanted and she could keep it going for hours if she had to, but there was no need because the bolt was being slid back and the skinny one with the lazy eye was sidling out. They were all a bit scared of Candy after the incident last night when she'd yelled at them for accidentally wiping the Sky+ box of all the episodes of *Ugly Betty* she'd been saving up.

'All yours,' she squeaked.

'There's a courier coming round with some dresses that need to be signed for,' Candy barked as she blocked the bathroom entrance from anyone else who might try and sneak in. 'And Guido, my hair and make-up guy, is due, so let him in and don't stare like you've never seen anyone with tribal tattoos on their scalp before.'

But when Candy had finished a semi-intensive grooming regime and stomped into the lounge, the three of them were gathered around Guido, stroking his head. 'And it didn't hurt? Not at all?'

There were a pile of garment bags draped over the back of the sofa. Candy began to investigate the contents. Too long. Too long. Too low-cut. Too long *and* too low-cut. Eventually, she settled on an icy-silver cocktail dress that would require Candy's most supportive and binding pair of underpants if she wanted to maintain a sylphlike silhouette. She wriggled into it and watched the hem flutter delicately around her calves.

'It's meant to hit the knee,' Guido offered lazily. 'But I guess mid-calf is the new knee. Do you want pin curls?'

'I have some great rhinestone clips,' Candy said, putting her robe on over the dress. 'And maybe a little bit of glitter over my cheeks and browbone . . . What?'

Laura's three friends were gawping at her. 'So people send you clothes to wear when you go out and someone comes round to do your hair and make-up?' Jen asked enviously. 'Where you going then? Nandos?'

That must be an example of their earthy Northern humour. Then again, even when they'd been stony broke, Bette had always begged one of her gay entourage of stylists and make-up peeps to come round and get her ready for a night out. No wonder Candy's definition of normal was different to everyone else's. 'I'm going to the opening of a fashion exhibition at the V&A,' Candy bit out a little less scathingly than she'd originally planned, beckoning Guido with one finger. 'The light's best in the kitchen.'

Candy would have thought that the three of them could have come up with something slightly fun-related to do on a Friday night in London, but apparently not. All that they wanted to do was gather around the kitchen doorway and watch Guido work his magic. It was majorly annoying.

Not as majorly annoying as George ringing her a second later to completely blow her off. 'Sorry, Cands, I'm on my way to the airport. Got a callback in LA tomorrow morning.'

Candy swore she could actually feel something flake off one of her back molars as she ground them together. She really needed to see her dentist. George's no-show was a freaking catastrophe. He was her official 'walker', which was the technical term for a well-groomed gay friend who'd act as a date for a girl who, well, didn't date.

'Is Benji around?' she asked, because George's boyfriend was a good plan B.

''Fraid not – he's doing press in Belgium,' George said ruefully. 'Look, babes, I'm sorry to let you down at the last minute.'

There was a significant pause. Candy came in just a beat too late. 'Oh, I completely understand,' she insisted. 'Good luck with your callback. Like, break a leg and all that shit.'

'You don't need me to rock the red carpet,' George said

soothingly. 'And I'll bring you back something pretty from la-la land.'

Candy hung up and would have rolled her eyes if Guido hadn't been doing something lethal with a pair of eyelash curlers. She looked at him expectantly, but it would take too long to finish her hair and make-up, then stop off so he could get changed. And no way was she taking him to a Marina Facinelli retrospective when he was wearing a T-shirt with a drawing of two cowboys doing unspeakable things to each other on the front of it.

Just for a second Candy contemplated Laura's lame friends. Jeesh, she wasn't *that* desperate. George was right. She could totally rock the red carpet all by herself.

Chapter Nine

Three hours later, Candy was standing in the costume gallery of the Victoria & Albert museum and trying really hard not to scream.

Apart from the time she'd had an emergency appendectomy when she was ten, she'd never been in such acute pain. Several hairpins were skewering her scalp, her big chandelier earrings were pulling on her lobes and her toes were being pinched and crushed by her limo shoes into a shape they weren't meant to go. Also Candy's stomach was growling because she hadn't eaten anything since lunch. Not that she could actually eat, because her dress was so tight and her knickers so binding that all Candy could do was take little sips of air and hope she didn't faint.

'Candy, sweetie, love the dress,' a Nordic-blonde woman tweeted at her as she sailed by.

'Love your shoes,' Candy tweeted back, though she had no idea who the woman was.

That was always the deal at these kind of events. Very few people actually came over to talk to you, because they assumed you should be talking to someone else. Instead they gave Candy The Nod. The Nod said: 'Hey, I'm famous. You're famous too. By nodding we totally acknowledge that we're both in the famous people's club without actually having to make conversation, because we have nothing in common, apart from the fact we're both famous.'

At least if George had deigned to turn up, they could have bitched about some of the more whacked-out fashion choices on display. Candy stared at a buxom woman in a skin-tight mustard satin dress, which did nothing for her muddy complexion, and realized she was tilting backwards. She needed to stop that right away before she fell over. She yanked in her abdominal muscles for balance like Pei Yi, her yoga instructor, had taught her and started edging towards the nearest wall. If Candy could lean against something solid for a couple of minutes, it would take the pressure off the balls of her feet, which felt like they were being stabbed by millions and millions of tiny, red-hot needles.

She was almost at her destination when Candy felt a hand lightly touch her shoulder. Her heart sank but she pinned on a smile, which disappeared instantly when she saw who it was.

'Alfie! What the hell are you doing here?' It came out rather ferociously, but they weren't at work so she didn't have to respect him or his alleged genius status one little bit.

And she didn't regret her decision in the least, even though Alfie's tentative smile faltered and he took his hand away, which had been doing a good job of keeping her balanced. 'My tutor at St Martin's helped to curate the exhibition,' he explained stiffly. 'And I designed her dress for her.'

'It's not a little mustard number, is it?' Candy asked and

Alfie frowned. He was wearing a superbly-cut black suit, which accentuated his lanky frame, and his hair had been ruthlessly scraped back so apart from his dark skin and blue eyes, he looked very monochrome. *Plus ça change.*

'She's Scottish and mustard really doesn't work on a Caucasian complexion,' Alfie said, casting his eyes around the crowded room. 'Actually she's wearing green tartan.'

In that case, Candy had seen her: an aristocratic-looking woman with a silver grey crop wearing the most amazing Thirties-style dress in an unexpected but amazing tartan.

'Nice frock,' she said and then wished she'd reined it back in because she didn't want Alfie to think that she was another member of his fan club.

He obviously didn't because he was ducking his head and staring at the shiny toes of his black shoes. Probably spent hours polishing them just so. 'She was adamant about the tartan,' he muttered. 'I still think it would have been better in a grey georgette.'

Candy swayed suddenly, which made a nice change from the falling backwards, and Alfie's hand shot out to grab her elbow. They both squeaked in surprise.

'Sorry,' he mumbled, and that's when Candy noticed that he had a plate of canapés in his other hand. Canapés, which made her stomach gurglies come back for an encore. Alfie smiled when he saw where Candy's attention was riveted. 'Actually, I brought this over for you. You looked hungry.'

'I'm really not,' Candy denied flatly.

'Candy, I can hear your tummy growling,' Alfie insisted and the hand that was still on her elbow started leading her adroitly through the throng. Candy had no choice but to walk, her shoes weren't designed to have their heels dug in.

Alfie led her out of the gallery and into a smaller, quieter anteroom. 'There you go,' he said casually. 'You can stuff your face without worrying about people watching.'

Jeez, what kind of girl did he think she was? 'I do not and never have stuffed my face.'

'I saw you annihilate a jacket potato only a few hours ago,' Alfie pointed out because he was the king of the annoying detail.

'I can't eat, even though I'm freaking starving,' Candy gritted. 'I'm about to bust out of this dress as it is.'

Alfie ran a professional eye over Candy's butt. At least, she assumed it was a professional eye, because he didn't appear to be checking her out in the slightest. 'It fits beautifully,' he said. 'It's not too tight at all.'

'That's because I'm wearing the most ridiculous pair of gutbuster panties,' Candy said. It was worth the loss of dignity to see the horrified expression on Alfie's face. 'My feet are killing me, my hair is killing me, my earrings are killing me and I can barely breathe, let alone eat.' She gave an angry intake of breath as Alfie walked away without a word.

He was a jerk-off. A total douche bag. A fucktard. A son of a pox-ridden bitch.

'Hey, over here!' Candy's inner NC17-rated narrative was interrupted when Alfie waved at her from a narrow doorway she hadn't noticed. 'I think I have a solution to your, er, pain.'

Maybe she'd take it all back if he really did have a solution. Candy hobbled over and found herself in a deserted stairwell. Was Alfie planning to push her down the stairs to take her mind off all her other agonies?

Actually, no. He was shrugging out of his dinner jacket, which he handed to a bemused Candy so he could turn around and face the wall. 'You can use that to um, cover yourself up if you want to make some er, adjustments to your . . . dress,' he stammered.

Candy didn't need to be told twice. She hoiked up her dress so it was around her hips, rolled down the waistband of her knickers and then fashioned herself a skirt out of Alfie's tux so she could sit down on the stairs. 'You can turn round now, I'm decent.' Candy smiled as Alfie peered cautiously over his shoulder. 'Well, decent as I ever am.'

Alfie sat down next to her and passed over the plate. 'Aren't you going to take off your shoes?'

Candy investigated a miniature fishcake and dabbed it into a smear of wasabi sauce. 'I'll never get them on again if I do,' she confessed, before shoving the food in her mouth.

It should have been embarrassing to scarf down an entire plate of canapés while Alfie sat and watched as if he'd never seen a girl who enjoyed her food before. Candy wondered whether she should finish with a delicate belch just to tease another look of horror from Alfie, but decided against it. 'Thanks,' she said, licking her fingers, and he did look horrified then, like he was just remembering that she was in close proximity to his suit jacket. 'I was about to faint from hunger.'

'Why did you come out in such an uncomfortable outfit?' Alfie asked curiously.

'Because sometimes you have to suffer for beauty, especially when you're seven pounds too heavy for sample size,' Candy grinned.

Alfie ran another practised eye over the bits of Candy that weren't covered in black wool. 'But you're tiny,' he said, like Candy wasn't already aware that she was practically the same height she'd been in sixth grade.

'Oh come on, you're in the industry, you know how small sample size is,' Candy scoffed. 'It's not a real girl size.'

'Sometimes I forget that models are thinner than everyone else,' Alfie said, resting his elbows on his knees and leaning forward. His hair was starting to droop and he pushed it back, and Candy eased her foot almost out of her shoe and gingerly rotated her ankle. Both of them were becoming slightly unravelled. 'And also that when I make dresses, girls have to eat in them and um . . .'

'Hoist them up so they can have a pee?' Candy suggested sweetly. 'My mom, she used to be a model, said that there was only ever one designer who made his models go to the can in his dresses.'

That should have been Alfie's cue to start pumping her for gossip but he just nodded, like he was filing the information away for future use. 'Do you hate me a lot?' he suddenly asked. 'Because of how I am at work?'

'Kind of,' Candy admitted. 'Nico says it's because you're a genius and you can't help being a perfectionist blah blah blah, but spending fifteen minutes giving me a tutorial on how to wash my hands is just insane.'

Alfie thought about that for a moment. 'It does seem a little excessive when you put it like that, but I tend to get very preoccupied at work.'

'You can say that again.' Candy tilted her head to one side so she could get a good look at Alfie. He was really quite handsome. He probably needed to get laid so he'd be less uptight. 'Dude, you should get out more.'

Alfie spread his hands to encompass their dimly lit corner. 'I'm out,' he said rather unhappily, like he'd much rather be somewhere else, doing whatever he did when he wasn't at work. Though Candy still thought it involved protective gloves and a magnifying glass. 'And you don't have to be quite so belligerent all the time, you know.'

'I'm not belligerent, I'm from New York,' Candy drawled, and Alfie's eyes glinted just once.

'I'm trying to call a truce but you're not making it very easy,' he said sharply, at the same time that his hand reached up so he could gently and expertly adjust one of her hair pins. 'Sorry, it was crooked and it was annoying me.' His hand brushed Candy's cheek as he removed it quickly, and she'd been skin-starved for way too long because a jolt of . . . *something* hit her as hard as the wasabi sauce. Now she was jonesing for a bit of touch from one of George's people. How tragic!

Candy thought hard and she thought quickly. If George got the gig in LA, then she'd have a vacancy for a new gay best friend. They were the one accessory that never went out of fashion. So, maybe ceasing hostilities with Alfie might be a good thing. Not that she had him in mind as a GBF but he might have a friend who'd do.

Solemnly, she held out her little finger and hooked it around Alfie's. He didn't flinch away, but shook on it. 'Truce,' she said firmly. 'And you could try being nice to me at work too. I'm sure it wouldn't ruin your reputation as a control freak genius.'

Alfie looked doubtful. 'Well, I'll try,' he conceded.

Chapter Ten

Monday morning inevitably rolled around again. Candy wished it wouldn't roll round quite so frequently or early when her alarm clock woke her up at eight.

She'd actually had a pretty good weekend. After catching up on her beauty sleep on Friday night after the party, Saturday had restored Candy's good humour. She'd even taken Laura's friends to her favourite spa in Mayfair and paid for them to have mani/pedis and facials, and they'd taken her out to some gross pub in Camden to say thank you. The night had blurred into dancing on sticky floors, kissing random boys and eating chips in the all night café on Chalk Farm Road. Even better, on Sunday they'd all gone back north with promises to keep in touch on the fake number she'd given them. Candy had been able to spend the day trying out her latest pattern – on muslin first, instead of ruining a perfectly good piece of lawn cotton. Then, Irina had stumbled in just in time for a *Heroes* double bill and a large stuffed-crust pizza.

It wasn't a good weekend as far as New York weekends went, but it was pretty good. Candy still had a smile on her face as she arrived at Nico's studio and bounded up the stairs to the studio. She had her own little table now and her own pads and pencils. Marge, the ancient secretary, had even given Candy her very own day planner.

She glanced over to Alfie's pristine little corner but only Sophie was there, ready with the evil looks. Candy returned them with interest before she went on the first coffee run of the day.

When she got back, Alfie was sitting on his stool, shoulders hunched, while Sophie fussed around him. 'I'm sure he didn't mean it,' she twittered. 'I think it's beautiful.'

Alfie mumbled something indistinct and slumped a little more. Very interesting. Candy continued matching laminated sketches of bags with leather and fabric swatches. The second attempt at the It bags were being sent off today to the sample factory in Milan, and Nico promised Candy could name the finished bags, when she popped in to show him the final selection before they were picked up by courier.

'Anything else you need?' she asked hopefully, because she had some ideas for shoes too.

'Could you spend the day with Alfie? I think he's going out on a little field trip,' Nico said vaguely. 'Could probably use some company.'

Surely not Candy's company? Yes, they'd sort of buried the hatchet the other night, but if they had to work together again, Candy had a feeling she'd be burying the hatchet in Alfie's cranium. 'I guess,' she sighed. 'But if we go out and I end up pushing him under a bus, then don't get mad at me.'

Alfie was still sunk in a despondent slump when Candy got back to the studio. He barely looked up as she approached, just stared at the black dress on his form like it was about to assume a Yoda-like voice and start imparting wisdom.

'Nico said something about you and me on a field trip.' Candy's unenthusiastic tone was especially designed to let Alfie know how she felt about this, but he just grunted. Not that Alfie would do anything as uncouth as grunt, but it was as close as he would ever get.

'So . . .' Candy prompted. 'Shall I go and put my coat on?'

'What do you think of this dress?' Alfie enquired, summoning up the energy to frown. 'Be honest.'

'When am I not honest?' Candy walked over to the form and looked at the frock. Like everything Alfie worked on, it was exquisite; the heavy folds of fabric fell gracefully and it would look wonderful on whoever wore it. Each stitch was perfect, every seam as straight as a Roman road . . . 'It's kinda boring,' Candy admitted, then tried to hastily retract when she saw that Alfie looked as if he was about to commit hari-kiri with his scissors. 'No, don't get me wrong, it's a beautiful dress, it's just kind of a little bit on the dull side. My mom would love it. Well, actually most people's moms would like it; mine prefers something shorter, tighter and preferably with a leopard print.'

Candy decided to stop talking when Alfie began to massage his temples. 'That's what Nico said,' he whispered. 'Well, he was a little more tactful. He said that I was technically proficient but my design lacked *passion*.' He hissed the last word like it was really offensive. 'Then he told me to take the rest of the day off to get some inspiration that didn't involve looking at books or old photographs.' He cast a weary look at the Avedon print pinned to his mood board.

'So, where do you want to go? Where do you normally go?' Candy asked.

Alfie sank even lower on the stool. Soon he'd practically be on the floor. 'Usually, I go to the vintage magazine shop and buy old fashion magazines,' he sniffed. 'But apparently, I'm not allowed to do that any more. Any ideas?'

If Candy wanted inspiration, then she never went further than Bette's closet. But New York was several hours away and Alfie would probably cry if he saw the condition of some of Bette's vintage dresses, which had been worn on stage or had the buttons replaced with safety pins by Candy when she was going through her punk phase.

Candy also liked watching old movies to look at the pretty dresses, but wasn't that the same as looking at photographs? 'Why don't we just go out and start walking and see where we end up?'

'Couldn't do any harm,' Alfie agreed morosely, standing up and brushing off his lapels in case all that heavy moping had left specks on them.

The moment they got outside, Candy rooted in her bag for her red crochet beret and pulled it firmly on so it mostly covered her trademark black bob. Then she wound her Marc Jacobs stripy scarf so it obscured the bottom of her face and put her huge Jackie-O glasses on. Alfie looked at Candy as if she was deranged, but a civilian couldn't expect to understand what a major hassle it was getting stopped all the time.

'Left or right?' Candy asked Alfie.

He jerked his head to the right and they started walking.

Chapter Eleven

It wasn't quite as awkward as Candy thought it would be. They didn't talk, but it wasn't an uncomfortable not talking, more that Alfie was deep in thought and Candy was relishing the simple reality of just walking down a normal street with normal people, which was something she didn't get to do very often.

They stopped a couple of times. Once at a Jewish bakery so Candy could wolf down a smoked salmon and cream cheese bagel and again at a florist because Alfie wanted to buy some gerbera daisies because he liked the way the petals faded from cerise to the palest pink. Now, they'd been walking for hours and Candy didn't know where they were or how they were ever going to find their way back.

They were in the middle of a market, like the one on Fulton Street in New York where she used to go with Conceptua to buy exotic fruit and these really great sticky cakes. They passed a stall selling spices and Candy breathed in the pungent aroma appreciatively, admiring the sacks of saffron and dried chillies and the vibrant picture they made. 'Take a picture of this,' she urged Alfie, who looked at her in amazement.

'But this is just a market,' he pointed out.

'Pretty market,' Candy clarified. 'Look at the colours.'

She gestured at the spices. But then she was darting across the road towards a shop window and the tantalizing sight of a tangerine-coloured sari shot through with gold thread. 'Oooh! Take a picture of that too! I know that whole Bollywood thing was over five years ago but, like, if you lined that black dress with something in that orange colour and the skirt foofed out a bit more, that'd be cool.'

Alfie followed her, camera in hand, but grabbed hold of her wrist when she tried to go inside. 'Come on,' he urged. 'I've already taken a picture.'

'But they have tons of jewellery inside and we could buy some fabric and put it on your mood board.' Candy grinned. She was really getting into this. She expected Alfie to smile back, but he had that constipated look on his face again.

'It's getting late,' he protested. 'It will be dark soon.' Alfie still had his hand on her wrist. Now he tightened his fingers. Candy glanced down and idly noted how pale her skin looked against his before she gave an experimental tug that did no good.

'Dude, this caveman act is a whole new look for you, but we both know that if I want to go into that shop there ain't a goddamn thing you can do to stop me,' she told him sweetly. 'I'm a hair-puller from way back.'

Alfie's thumb was worrying against the soft part of her wrist where all the veins seemed to merge like a complicated contraflow system and her skin was at its most sensitive. It was momentarily distracting, but then Candy tore her gaze away from Alfie's intense blue stare.

Through the window she could see sequins and a shade of deep green that seemed to have been imported straight from a tropical rainforest and oooh, a tiara! There was no competition.

'I'm going in,' she said, and she meant it too. She was anticipating a fight, but Alfie suddenly dropped her hand like it was red-hot as a voice from behind Candy exclaimed sharply, 'Alfie, what are you doing here? You haven't been sacked, have you?'

Alfie groaned so softly that Candy could barely hear it. He briefly looked down at Candy and grimaced before raising his head. 'Hi Mum. Just on a bit of a work outing actually.'

Oh, this was too good to be true. Candy whirled around to stare at the owner of the voice, the woman who'd given Alfie life and somewhere along the way had managed to screw him up god-holy.

She wasn't expecting a diminutive woman in a shalwar kameez, being trailed by several children of differing ages and sizes but all of them laden down with supermarket carrier bags. And she wasn't expecting the broad grin on Alfie's face when he caught sight of them. 'Brats,' he said delightedly.

Candy was almost mown down as Alfie was besieged on all sides. One child managed to tread on her toes, another one knocked her into the shop window, and someone else caught the end of her scarf. She was only saved from choking by Alfie's mum, who was also intent on trying to snatch at small limbs, stop her shopping from going flying and castigating Alfie at the same time.

'You should have said you'd be in the area,' she snapped, as she retrieved a tin of coconut milk from the pavement. 'But that would mean you phoned occasionally. You don't even text, you ungrateful boy. Get off him, Harry!'

Alfie was being used as a climbing frame by a very small, very determined little boy until Alfie suddenly grabbed his feet so he could swing him upside down, while the kid squealed with joy. 'I've been busy, Mum,' he said. 'Anyway, I saw you last week.'

'Last week indeed,' Mrs Alfie muttered darkly. 'Perdy, if you don't stop pulling on your brother's jacket, there'll be no Gameboy when we get home. And who's your friend?'

They all turned to look at Candy, who was picking up a packet of dried apricots. Even Alfie seemed to have momentarily lost his memory because he was staring at Candy as if he didn't quite know who she was or how she got there.

It was left to Candy to make the introductions herself. 'I'm Candy. Alfie and me, we're, well . . .' Friends was stretching the truth a little too far. 'We work together.'

'You're the rude girl off the telly,' a voice piped up from the cheap seats, as Alfie's mum gave her a sweeping look. It reminded Candy of the frequent trips to the principal's office when she was back in high school; he'd managed to convey the exact same sense of disapproval too.

'We need to get going,' Alfie said, depositing a small child back on its feet. 'I'll call. Promise.'

Candy wasn't too sure who Alfie was most embarrassed

by, his mother or her. Though his mother was kinda intimidating.

'Nonsense,' she was saying crisply. 'You've got time for a cup of tea – and take a couple of bags from the little ones.' There was a pointed look and Candy realized that she was included in this directive.

Alfie was doing what he was told even as he tried to argue. 'Mum, I'll come round next Sunday, but we really should be getting back.'

His mother wasn't even listening but setting off at a fast pace, hands full of shopping and small children. Candy pulled a face. 'Are they all your brothers and sisters?' she asked with a smile. The two smallest boys were trying to pound the shit out of each other.

'Two of them are. Two of them belong to next door and the smallest one is my nephew.'

Candy had always dreamt of a huge, extended family spilling in and out of each other's houses. Sometimes she added in a couple of golden retrievers lolloping across a rolling lawn because her fantasy involved rolling lawns, white picket fences, apple pies and all sorts of other clichéd garbage that she'd never admit to anyone, even under extreme interrogation techniques. So she settled for a small smile. 'Must get noisy.'

'There's also my teenage sister, Pretty, and two other brothers,' Alfie sighed. He drew his shoulders back. 'Look, there is no way to get out of this, but don't show me up.'

'As if!' Candy gasped indignantly, although she'd already been making plans to ask Mrs Alfie to show her his baby photos and whether her son did his own ironing.

'No personal questions, nothing work-related. Don't swear, mind your manners and don't ask for coffee,' Alfie grimly recited. 'We're having one cup of tea, ten minutes of polite, inconsequential chit chat and then we're out of there. Right?'

He really was the complete opposite of fun. 'But, Alfie . . .'

'*Right?*'

'Like, I have any choice,' Candy grumbled as they turned into a street of terraced houses. She looked around with interest. Candy had always thought that the East End was a barren wasteland of curry houses, drug dens and boarded-up shops but each house was more immaculate than the last, until they came to number eighty-nine that had a manicured patch of lawn the size of a postage stamp. The brass knocker on the door positively gleamed, she could have eaten her dinner off the garden path, and only the Arsenal poster in one of the windows was any indication that a normal family and not a bunch of clean freaks lived here.

It was no surprise that Mrs Alfie was already opening the gate. Candy couldn't wait to follow her, but was slightly impeded by Alfie's death grip on her jacket sleeve. 'I'm warning you,' he growled in her ear, menacingly enough that the little hairs on her neck all stood up and waved.

'I'll be on my best behaviour,' Candy said wide-eyed, and Alfie had the nerve to bump her off the path with a well-placed nudge like he didn't believe a word of it.

Chapter Twelve

There was a flurry of taking off coats and putting away shopping, which seemed to involve so much commotion that Candy had no choice but to hang back. There were so many people charging up and down the narrow hall, in and out of the kitchen and through another door that Candy felt like a spare part.

She counted heads as four children ran upstairs, then Mrs Alfie was coming out of the kitchen towards her and Candy had to steel herself not to hang her head and stare at her feet.

'I'm Meera,' she said, touching Candy's shoulder lightly. 'What must you think of us? Come into the lounge.'

She opened the door and ushered Candy into a room that was obviously for best. It was also a room where dust or clutter or empty Diet Coke cans and piles of magazines were not tolerated. And on the mantelpiece were photos: baby photos, school photos, party photos. Candy couldn't wait to get a closer look.

'You have a very nice home,' she said politely, which was odd because David and Bette had never bothered to instil any good manners in her.

Alfie's mum gave her a tight smile. She wasn't completely down with the Candy Careless love but Candy could respect that. 'Would you like a cup of tea?' she asked.

Candy really wouldn't. She was a certified coffee drinker, but Alfie had been really particular on the subject of tea drinking. 'Yes please. Milk and three sugars, please. Thank you.' If it was any less sweet then she wouldn't be able to choke it down and why was she shoving in random pleases and thank yous? She was starting to think in British!

'I'll just be a minute.' Meera floated out of the door, oddly graceful even in her slippers, and Candy raced over to the photos to see if there was one of Alfie naked in the tub. There wasn't, but it seemed as if every minor event in the Alfie household was worthy of a picture. Candy's baby pictures were sparse and mostly involved some black-and-white shots taken by a famous rock photographer of her staggering around backstage at CBGBs in a fairy outfit when she was three. She could hear Alfie and his mum talking in the kitchen, though she couldn't hear what they were saying.

Then the front door opened and a pretty girl of about fifteen burst into the room, long dark hair flying in every direction as she unzipped a pink hoodie and bellowed, 'What's for tea? I'm starving!'

Candy was really beginning to wish that she'd backed Alfie up when he'd said that they had to be going. The girl threw her hoodie on the sofa and was about to toe off her trainers, then caught sight of Candy. Her face was easy to read; confusion, recognition, shock, more confusion. 'Oh. My. God,' she said sharply and bolted from the room.

Candy fled for the safety of the sofa and sat there, back straight, hands folded on her lap. Even the freaking queen wouldn't have been able to find fault with her, though it was possible that Alfie's mum had higher standards.

She looked up as the girl stormed back in with her phone in her hand, snapped a picture of Candy's startled face and ran out again. Candy was still blinking as Alfie walked in carrying a tray, followed by his mum, who wouldn't let him put it down on the coffee table until she'd made sure there was a mat on it.

Alfie sat next to Candy on the sofa as Meera poured tea and proffered digestive biscuits, which were arranged in fan formation on a doilyed plate. 'So, you're American?' she announced. 'I have a cousin in Boston.'

'Cool,' Candy said, though actually Boston was just a tenth-rate substitute for New York. She blew on her tea and hoped to God that she didn't spill it over anything.

'Pretty says you're very famous – why are you working with Alfie? Is it for the TV? Are you going to be on the telly, Alf?'

'Well, I am on TV on this, like, genre-defining . . . on this reality show with my parents,' Candy tried to explain. 'They're in this band, y'know, like the whole rock 'n' roll thing meets mid-life crisis, but I'm trying to move away from that and I want to get started in the fashion business so Nico, Alfie's boss, is letting me get a taste of the industry.' Candy frowned, but Meera gave her a regal nod of approval.

'Very sensible,' she said. 'Showbusiness seems very flighty. Look at that Britney Spears.'

Alfie choked on some biscuit crumbs. His shoulders

seemed to be shaking in a mirthful sort of way.

'You have a very large family. They must keep you busy . . .' ventured Candy.

That was Meera's starter for ten. After that, there was no shutting her up. Alfie was the oldest and obviously not just the apple but the pear and orange of his mother's eye. Then there was Av, who'd just qualified to be an accountant, Sanjay, who worked with Mr Alfie, Pretty, the only girl, and Perdy and Harry, the two youngest. Six children! And apart from Alfie, they all lived at home.

'I wish you'd move back,' Meera said. 'It's not the same without you here.'

'There's no room,' Alfie said stoutly, but he flushed and jiggled his long legs so one of his knees banged against Candy and she almost spilt her tea, which was just as gross as she thought it would be.

'And how old are you, Candy?'

'Seventeen,' Candy said, wondering where this was going.

'That's very young to be away from home,' Meera said and Candy knew *exactly* where this was going. At least Meera was seeing her as an ally now rather than an object of suspicion. 'You must miss your mother and father.'

'Fuck, no!' Candy yelped before she could stop herself. Alfie didn't seem too pissed – his shoulders were shaking again – but Meera had her pinned with a look that could melt steel.

'We don't use language like that in this house,' she said icily, and it was *so* time to go.

'I'm very sorry,' Candy mumbled, placing her cup carefully back on the tray as a prelude to getting up and getting the hell out of Dodge, but Alfie patted her arm gently.

'Stop hauling her over the coals, Mum,' he said softly. 'Candy hasn't sworn at all in the last hour, which has to be a personal best.'

Way to make her come across like some foul-mouthed little harpie, but Meera smiled and finally she seemed to relax. 'You'll stay for dinner, the two of you?'

There weren't two of them. There was Candy and there was Alfie. Two entirely separate entities both saying the exact same thing.

'I'd love to but I need to get back . . .'

'Mum, I already said I'd come round on Sunday . . .'

'But your father will be playing football on Sunday and I know he'd love to meet Candy.'

There was some weird tension at the mention of Mr Alfie. Why was Alfie doing his utmost to avoid him – maybe it was the whole gay thing? But even Candy had been brought up better than to come right out and ask about it, especially as Pretty was back and she'd brought reinforcements: three other girls in hoodies who crowded around the living-room doorway so they could stare at Candy and not say a word. It was like being in the monkey cage at the zoo or on MTV's *TRL*. Same diff.

Candy nonchalantly sipped her tea and tried to act like there weren't three chavs studying her like they had to take a test on Candy Careless the next morning.

'What's for tea, Mum?' Pretty whined again. 'Do we have to wait for Dad?'

'Don't say "tea", it's common. We're having sausage casserole and Alfie's friend is staying for *dinner* too. Isn't that nice?'

Alfie's friend was going to do no such thing, but Pretty was already tossing her hair back so her gold hoop earrings jangled ferociously. 'You can't give her sausage casserole,' she spat, her friends sniggering in the background. 'She's *famous*.'

They had the sausage casserole because Meera was having no truck with either Candy or Alfie vacating the premises before dinner or that anyone could be too famous to eat what she put in front of them.

Mr Alfie, or Eddie as he told Candy to call him, came home just as she was helping Pretty lay the table in a dining room that didn't seem like it was going to fit everyone in it.

He was as tall as his wife was tiny and dressed in a pristine pinstripe suit complete with waistcoat. Even Alfie didn't wear a waistcoat, unlike his other brother, Sanjay, who followed his father into the room.

Were they investment bankers or did the men in Alfie's family really dig bespoke suiting?

Eddie was almost as pale as Candy, with wispy blond hair, so she didn't get why he was down on Alfie for being gay when they were down with the whole mixed-race thing. 'So, how come some of you have English names and some of you don't?' Candy asked as Meera dished up the casserole, which she'd been pretty dubious about, but which smelt delicious.

There was a long explanation about honouring different grandparents and a Bollywood actor that Meera had had a crush on when she was a slip of a girl, and any worries that Candy had about offending someone, or the conversation lagging, melted away.

Probably because she was sitting next to Pretty, who was over her initial attitude and kept firing names at her. 'Have you met Justin Timberlake? Is he fit in real life? Is Lindsay Lohan as big a cow as she seems? Do you have their phone numbers? Can you, like, call them whenever you want? That model Laura that you live with, would you say she's fatter or thinner than me?'

Eventually Eddie told her to shut up, even though you could tell that he cut Pretty a ginormous amount of slack because she was the only girl.

'Are you Alfie's girlfriend?' Harry demanded shrilly as soon as his sister went mute.

There was a palpable tension in the air, which was just ridiculous. Because they had to know that Alfie didn't go for girls. And if he did, they wouldn't be small, mouthy girls, but someone who had the exact same measurements as Alfie's dress form and probably an intense love of German Expressionist cinema, or something equally pretentious.

Candy looked at Alfie, who was steadfastly gazing at his plate, and she started to get suspicious. Like, this whole aimless wandering so they ended up right round the corner from the family home had actually been an elaborate ruse! An elaborate ruse so Candy could meet Alfie's parents and they'd think he was completely straight. In which case, Sophie would have made a much better candidate. Parents loved girls like Sophie.

'No, I'm not,' Candy insisted vehemently. 'Alfie just tries to boss me about at work in a non-boyfriendly manner.'

'I don't boss you about,' Alfie said crossly. 'I mentor you. It's entirely different.'

'You say mentor, I say tinpot dictator,' Candy drawled, and maybe she shouldn't be quite so bratty but sometimes she just couldn't help it. Anyway, Meera and Edward were exchanging fond smiles, so maybe the fact that Alfie had brought a girl home, any kind of girl, meant they were prepared to overlook Candy's shortcomings.

'How is work, Alfie?' Eddie asked casually, and again that strange atmosphere was back, everyone stiffening. Even little Perdy put down his fork and cowered slightly as if World War Three was about to break out.

The painful little knot appeared between Alfie's eyebrows. 'It's fine,' he said tersely.

'Fine,' Eddie repeated with just a *soupçon* of scorn. 'Fine, he says. Milan was fine. Then Milan wasn't fine. And now this is fine.'

'Don't start . . .' Alfie almost growled.

'The problem with you, son, is that you have ideas above your station. You don't belong in that world and it's high time you realized it. It's not a proper profession.'

Candy's head was whipping back and forth like she was witnessing a ping pong match. What the fuck was going on and why was it going on in front of a guest?

Alfie's face flushed and he gripped his knife a little tighter. 'It's what I want to do and I'm doing it. End of discussion.'

Actually it wasn't. 'Five generations of Tanners have worked at Pryce & Giles,' intoned Eddie. 'Every eldest son in the family. You couldn't have wounded me more if you'd become a Spurs fan.'

Unbelievably, a grin ghosted across Alfie's face. 'Well, I quite fancy their chances in the Premiership this season.'

There was a collective gasp of horror and then Alfie started to laugh and all the other Tanners began to laugh and Candy decided that they were insane. Not insane in the way that her family was but insane in this seething, buttoned up, unintelligible British way.

'What was *that*?' she hissed at Pretty, who was giggling away like the rest of them.

'We're all mad Arsenal supporters in this house. Dad says we'd be dead to him if we ever followed another team,' she supplied.

Candy shook her head. 'No, the stuff before the soccer.'

'It's not soccer, it's football!' Pretty screeched, and now it was Candy's turn to have Eddie's wrathful gaze on her.

'Sorry,' she cooed, suddenly finding her plate very interesting. 'Lovely casserole, Meera.'

She never did get to the bottom of it. As soon as pudding was finished and Candy was still scraping the last crumbs of apple pie from her bowl, Alfie was standing up. 'Right, we really have to go now.'

Meera looked dismayed, though Candy didn't kid herself. She just wanted Alfie to stay a little longer. 'You won't have a cup of tea?'

'You stay,' Candy urged Alfie. 'I'm going to phone my car service.'

'You have a car service?' Pretty breathed, and starting tapping furiously away at her mobile phone.

Alfie looked around wildly as if he was trapped. 'Well, I'm going to Stoke Newington, it's on the way. Can you give me a lift?'

Candy had no clue whether it was on the way or not but she nodded. And fifteen minutes later, there was the sound of a car horn and she was being loaded up with tinfoil packages of leftovers after Candy had let slip that the only cooking she could do involved pressing buttons on the microwave.

'It was lovely to meet you,' she said as Meera and Eddie saw them to the door. 'I'm sorry about swearing and the soccer thing.'

Meera had unbent so much by now that she laughed and gave Candy a little hug, and Eddie ruffled her fringe, though if anyone else had tried a move like that Candy would have shut them down. She really would. But somehow, this time, she didn't mind. Eddie and Meera were like proper parents. And although there were tons of them and they asked deeply personal questions that weren't their business, Alfie had a proper family.

'That was awesome,' she sighed happily, when they were nestled in the back of the car. 'Your family pretty much rock, you do know that, right?'

Alfie's brows snapped together. 'Awesome isn't the word I would use.'

'You all eat dinner together and you talk about your day and shit,' Candy reminded him. 'And your mom's a great cook. Her apple pie was way better than anything my room-mate's mom bakes.' She felt a slight guilty twinge at betraying Mrs Laura and her miraculous chocolate cake. Previously, she'd been Candy's first choice as an adoptive parent, should Bette and David ever die in a freak accident. 'And Bette can barely order Chinese,' Candy noted sourly.

'Bette?' Alfie echoed. 'Is she one of your flatmates?'

Candy looked at him incredulously. 'Bette's my mom! Have you never watched *At Home With The Careless*?'

Alfie squirmed just a little bit so one of his long legs banged into Candy. ' 'Fraid not. But I did Google you.'

Candy wasn't sure how she felt about that. She was eminently Googleable though. 'Oh, yeah?' she said challengingly.

'Yes, and I have to ask, is Careless really your surname? I mean, seriously?'

She gave a little gurgle because of all the things Alfie could ask that wasn't one that she'd been expecting. 'Well, my dad was originally a Krakowski but he legally changed his surname to Careless when he was eighteen because it was more punk rock.'

It was the one thing she'd never forgive David for. Being

cursed with Careless for a surname was a hard cross to bear, especially when Candy spilt or dropped something at school, or got an answer wrong. Or did anything that was even one degree away from perfect. Candy Couldn't Care Less — and that was just the teachers.

'Candy Krakowski,' Alfie said, like he was trying it out loud. 'Well, it's better than Alfie Tanner, which sounds like I should be running a pie and mash shop.'

'What the hell are you talking about?' Candy demanded. 'And what was that whole thing at dinner with the "fine"'s, when it was so not fine, and you not going into the business . . .'

Alfie already had his hand on the door handle. 'Oh, we're in Stokey already,' he said with obvious relief. 'Anywhere along here is great.' And the car hadn't even purred to a halt before he was getting out. 'I'll see you tomorrow when you won't breathe a word to anyone about anything you saw or heard tonight,' he added silkily, shutting the door before Candy could protest.

Chapter Thirteen

Alfie wasn't at work the next day. Not that Candy minded one way or another. Especially as she spent most of the day leafing through Alfie's reference books, much to Sophie's consternation.

'Alfie doesn't like people touching his stuff,' she pointed out when she saw Candy with Alfie's treasured copy of *The Golden Age Of Couture*.

'I'm not people,' Candy said airily. 'Alfie's my mentor. I'm his, like, mentee.'

'You shouldn't be eating at the same time.'

Candy was halfway through a bag of lemon sherbets, which were her tenth favourite thing about living in Britain. And anyway, they were medicinal lemon sherbets because the air conditioning was making her throat dry. 'I thought we had this whole *quid pro quo* thing going on where we were going to stay out of each other's way. So stay the hell out of my way.'

'If Alfie wants to know why there are grease stains on his books, I'm telling,' was Sophie's parting shot.

Candy stuck her tongue out behind the other girl's back and rubbed the bridge of her nose. Talking to Sophie always gave her a pain in the head, which was weird 'cause actually Sophie was way more of a pain in the ass.

Turned out that Alfie had flown out to fit a private client

in Germany and wasn't expected back for a couple of days, so Candy didn't feel the least bit guilty for taking home the books she hadn't had a chance to look at. It wasn't like he'd ever find out, especially as Sophie had been banished to the post room to do a mail-out for the rest of the afternoon.

Candy was even careful to make sure she didn't spill chocolate milk over any of the pages when she was reading them in bed later that night. She wasn't usually big on warm milk, even when it had half a packet of chocolate Nesquik in it, but her throat was still sore. Still it was nothing a good night's sleep wouldn't put right.

Alas, a good night's sleep was not going to happen. Two hours after she'd turned out the light, Candy woke up because she was shivering so hard that her teeth were rattling. Pulling back the covers and padding across the room to make sure the central heating hadn't broken was a Herculean task that left her panting and ragged as she flopped back into bed. The radiator was toasty hot, but Candy felt as if she'd been submerged in ice and someone had rubbed sandpaper across her throat.

Candy dozed fitfully, because now she was feverish hot and sweating what felt like gallons into her sheets. Again, kicking off the covers made her feel like she was running a marathon, and the pounding head and earache accessorized beautifully with her aching throat.

Candy didn't know how long she lay there, trying to sleep in between the convulsive shudders when she suddenly got too cold or the tropical sweats because she was too hot.

So she lay there until it was eight and someone *had* to be in the Fierce office. Someone who could call a doctor and diagnose chronic bronchial pneumonia. But how was she meant to get to the door and open it for the doctor when just pressing three on her speed dial left her wrung out and exhausted?

It took ages for the doctor to arrive. Almost as long as it took Candy to stagger down the two flights of stairs to let in a woman who didn't look old enough to practise medicine.

'You do seem peaky,' she said, as Candy practically crawled back up the stairs. The examination was brief and mostly consisted of peering down Candy's throat, shoving a thermometer in her mouth and running cold fingers over Candy's elbows and knees because her joints ached.

'Flu,' she diagnosed. 'It's a virus so I can't give you any antibiotics. Just take some anti-inflammatories for the joint pain and lots of fluids so you don't get dehydrated.'

'Flu?' Candy croaked. 'But I'm dying!'

'Yes, it does feel like that,' agreed the doctor cheerfully, because she really needed to work on her bedside manner. 'Is there someone you can call?'

There *was* someone she could call. But Conceptua proved very resistant to the idea that she come to London and nurse Candy back to health. And though she could understand English perfectly when she was watching Jerry Springer, she unleashed a torrent of Portuguese at Candy.

'But I need you,' Candy whimpered. Even hacking up a lung, and not because she was playing the sympathy card

121

either, wouldn't get Conceptua to leave Manhattan.

Tears didn't work either. Candy was sobbing down the phone when Irina and Javier walked in with their suitcases. Candy had never been more pleased to see anyone in her whole life. 'I have flu,' she whined, holding out the phone to Javier. 'Tell Conceptua that if I die it will be her fault because she won't come here and make me chicken soup. In Portuguese, *per favore?*'

Javier took the phone warily, like it was covered in flu germs. Actually it probably was, but he was soon jabbering away to Conceptua. 'Your mom's at a yoga retreat and she's not contactable,' he told Candy, which meant that she was probably having some more cosmetic surgery. 'Conceptua is really sorry that you're ill but she says to tell you that it's Jorge's first Communion on Sunday. She can't miss that, Candy!'

It was a goddamn Catholic conspiracy. Though actually, Irina, who never ever went to church though she had plenty to confess, was managing to look sympathetic, while rummaging in her duty-free bag. 'I could make you the hot chocolate with vodka and the chilli powder. Soon have you back on your feet,' she said threateningly, like there was going to be a major problem if Candy refused to be cured.

Javier put the phone down and took a step away from Candy. 'Sorry, I've got a shoot for *Dazed and Confused* tomorrow, don't want to catch anything,' he said with one of those beguiling smiles, which would have made Irina kill Candy if she'd responded to it any way, shape or form. 'Conceptua says she's going to light a candle for you and she's given me the chicken soup recipe.' He held up a copy of *ELLE*, which he'd been scribbling on.

Javier and Irina shared a helpless look. 'We not cook the chicken soup,' Irina decided. 'Unless you want the food poisoning too, but Jav'll go to KFC and get you a bargain bucket instead.'

Candy snuggled up on the sofa with her eyes closed and wished Javier and Irina would stop talking about food because it made her want to hurl. All of a sudden she was hit by a wave of homesickness. Until she remembered that Bette was a pretty terrible nursemaid. When Candy had got the chickenpox back in Junior High Bette had swathed her own face in a scarf, while she spoon-fed Candy iced tea, in case she caught it herself. Talking of which, where was Irina with the hot chocolate?

Heading for the door, that's where, after barking down her phone very loudly. 'Actually we have to go now,' she said without preamble. 'I have the flu shot but was almost a year ago and I just booked the cover of *Skirt*. We check into a hotel.'

Candy could feel her face collapse in on itself. 'Oh,' she said. She was far too sick to even pretend that it was OK. 'Oh.'

'We'll phone to check up on you,' Javier said soothingly. 'And we'll try to find someone with an up-to-date flu shot to come round.'

Irina pulled a face. 'But she might die before then,' she protested. 'She lead the very unhealthy lifestyle. Really, is no surprise she's ill.'

'Jesus, Irina, she's just got flu, nobody's going to die.'

'She might,' Irina insisted, pointing at Candy. 'Look, now she's too weak to bitch at me.'

Candy tried to glare but gave up and shivered instead. 'I'll be fine,' she sniffed.

Irina rolled her eyes. 'I'm calling Reed.'

'Not Hadley,' Candy spluttered, because she might be ill but she'd still pitch a hissy fit if that brother-stealing bimbo turned up.

But Hadley wasn't coming round for the simple reason that she was with Reed, who was in LA. There'd been a time when Reed hadn't even left Camden without her knowing about it. But that was in the days of BS – Before Sadley.

Candy's eyes started leaking in tandem with her nose as Irina got medieval on Reed's absconded ass. 'In Russia, we take care of family,' she said furiously, conveniently forgetting she'd gone nearly a year without speaking to her mother. Though she had bought her a house so that kind of made up for it. 'I not care if you are meeting the distributors. Is that more important than your sister?'

Irina was really good at laying on the guilt. Candy flapped her hands feebly to let Irina know that she was overdoing it, but Irina turned her back. 'Maybe it's flu. Could be meningitis.'

Candy sincerely hoped that it wasn't. 'Give me the phone.' It was hard to pull off menacing when it sounded like you smoked sixty a day, but Irina did as she was told, after telling Reed that he was 'an uncaring bastard'.

'I'm all right,' Candy said, listening to the faint hiss of static coming off the transatlantic line. 'Really.'

'Oh, Cands, you sound *dreadful*,' Reed purred, and it was like the four months of Candy being vile to him was instantly forgiven and forgotten. 'Poor baby. Where's Bette?'

It took a superhuman effort not to cry again. 'Either a spiritual retreat or having the fat sucked out of her ass again.'

'You've seen a doctor? What did they say? Why did no one at Fierce make you get a flu jab?' Reed was asking all the right questions that an over-protective, elder half brother should ask and Candy felt like crawling down the phone line so she could be wrapped in his arms when she finally reached LA.

'I feel pretty crappy but I totally don't have meningitis,' Candy choked out. All this talking was making her throat super dry. 'You're gonna be home soon, right?'

'As soon as I can. I'll raincheck some meetings.' Reed's voice was muffled and Candy could hear someone talking in the background. 'Hadley says hi. Hang on . . . What? She says that you should take some echinacea tablets and try some wheatgrass shots.'

And maybe Candy really was on the verge of death because she couldn't think of a single savage retort but just coughed, 'Er, yeah, thanks.'

The next day or two drifted past in this horrible haze of shivering fits and feverish interludes.

But actually Candy didn't mind being on her own, once she'd made an executive decision to stay on the sofa, rather than going back to bed. It was nearer to the bathroom and the kitchen and she couldn't hear the *beep beep* of the pelican crossing.

Time played funny tricks as she dozed on and off. She'd have these vivid dreams about the most mundane shit, like going to the kitchen for a glass of water, but wake up five minutes later to find that her throat was still parched and she hadn't actually moved.

It was hard to sleep, mostly because the phone didn't stop ringing – usually it was either Reed or Irina checking to see that she hadn't died in the ten minutes since they last called her. One of Fierce's celebrity bookers had called to ask if Candy would be well enough to do a TV show in Manchester the next day. She got really snippy when Candy said she wouldn't.

'I've seen Christina Aguilera perform with laryngitis,' the woman informed Candy snottily. 'I'm phoning Mimi.'

That was when Candy turned her phone off, only to be woken barely a minute later by the doorbell ringing. Correction. Someone leaning on the doorbell with no intention of getting off it any time soon.

Candy shuffled over to the window and craned her neck downwards to see if there were any lurking photographers. Whoever it was was travelling alone.

Getting to the front door took ages. And being upright was totally overrated. Candy paused to catch her breath, which made her break out in an unpleasant, all-over cold sweat again, and opened the door to find a furious Alfie standing there.

Chapter Fourteen

For a second, Candy thought she was having another of her not-really-asleep, not-really-awake dreams until Alfie started to speak. And there was no way her unconscious would ever be able to conjure up that exact same note of peevishness.

'Well, thank you for disappearing without telling anyone. I suppose fashion was a bit too much like hard work. But how dare you take my books with you?' Alfie paused for some much-needed oxygen, while Candy edged away from the door because it wasn't just her whacked-out inner thermostat, it really was freezing. Cold enough that she could see Alfie's breath coming out of his mouth in these frantic little puffs as he continued to get his rant on.

'Have you any idea how valuable that *Nova* book is? No! Because you never think of anyone but yourself. Well, I'm not leaving until I get the books, and the least you can do is apologize to Nico and actually tell him that you've quit instead of just not turning up,' Alfie finished with his best glare.

Candy opened her mouth to refute all of Alfie's heinous claims, but nothing really came out except a few wheezy exhalations, which were a prelude to a coughing fit. After she'd finished choking and heaving, Candy straightened up and blinked at Alfie. 'I'm ill,' she said, because it was the simple truth and her throat really couldn't take a longer explanation or any harsh glottal swearing.

Alfie stopped narrowing his eyes and give Candy a quick once over. It seemed to take in everything from her greasy, sweat-soaked hair to her crumpled cupcake PJs that had a few orange juice stains down them and her frozen feet clad in stripy socks. 'You look *hideous*,' he exclaimed.

They were not words designed to make any girl's heart go pitter patter. But Candy felt too wretched to care very much. Especially when she eyed the huge expanse of stairs, which seemed comparable to scaling Everest. 'Come up,' she said. 'I'll get your books.' She wanted to point out that actually she hadn't taken them, she'd *borrowed* them, but it would take too much effort to explain.

As it was, Candy got halfway up the stairs and then felt the need to sit down with her head between her knees, while Alfie stared down at her, with a pissy expression on his face no doubt.

'Head rush,' Candy said tersely, and he made this weird clucking noise at the back of his throat, which had to be impatience.

'Harry and Perdy have been off school all week. You might have caught something off them,' Alfie said apologetically. Apparently, the weird clucking noise was guilt. 'Have you been sick at all?'

'No, I'm too busy being totally delirious and having gross sweats,' Candy grumbled, trying to hoist herself aloft again. Alfie's arm shot out to steady her and, despite the huge disparity in their heights, which resulted in a lot of jostling and Alfie banging his elbow on the banister, he helped Candy the rest of the way.

Once they were back in the flat, Candy collapsed face down on the couch. She couldn't bear to see the look on Alfie's face as he surveyed the wreck she'd made of the place. She'd cancelled the cleaning service and the lounge was a mess of empty orange juice cartons, balled up tissues and a congealed plate of toast that she'd decided not to eat two days ago.

'Who's looking after you?' Alfie asked. 'Surely you're not on your own?'

It took ages to get the whole garbled story out about Bette's mysterious disappearance, Reed's LA trip and Irina's almost out-of-date flu jab, especially as Candy had to pause to sneeze and cough at regular intervals.

'The books are on my nightstand,' she finished, blowing her nose on the last tissue in the box. She'd have to start using the contents of her sock drawer next. 'I'd avoid looking from left to right when you're in there.'

For someone who'd been incandescent with rage about the plight of his *Nova* book, Alfie now seemed supremely unconcerned. 'Never mind that,' he said breezily, taking off his black wool coat and looking around frantically before he hung it on the hook on the back of the front door. 'There must be something I can do to help?'

Oh, where to start? First, Candy wanted Alfie to surgically remove the bit of her body that made the mucus, then she wanted him to book her into the penthouse suite of the Sanderson and hire a twenty-four-hour nurse, but she settled for, 'A glass of water and I'm due some more Sudafed. There might be some in the kitchen.'

'When did you last eat?' Alfie wanted to know, taking off his suit jacket and rolling up his shirt sleeves. He probably hadn't kicked it this freestyle since Arsenal had won some soccer cup or other.

'Eating makes my throat hurt,' Candy mumbled into the cushion, and Alfie was making that strange clucking sound again.

'No tablets until you've eaten,' Alfie decided, like someone had made him the boss of Candy, and yeah, she might be ill but she'd have remembered that conversation. But Alfie had disappeared down the hall and when he returned a few minutes later, he had a bowl of hot water scented with Laura's lavender bubble bath, some wash stuff and a pair of clean PJs.

'I'm going to get you some supplies while you, er, freshen up,' Alfie said, clearing a pile of magazines out of the way so he could put the bowl down on the coffee table. 'Are those your door keys on the hall table?'

'Yes, but—'

'You have nothing edible in your fridge. I'm amazed you don't have rickets or scurvy. I'll be as quick as I can.' Alfie was already out of the door, scooping up her keys as he went.

By the time he got back, carrier bags bulging promisingly, Candy was as clean as she could be from her makeshift bath. She was pleased to be in fresh pyjamas though the head rush as she tottered to put the grungy old ones in her laundry bag had nearly finished her off.

'Sit,' Alfie said when Candy cannoned off the kitchen door as he put things, leafy green things that she wasn't going to be eating, in the fridge. 'Go back to the sofa.'

It seemed that Alfie's superpower was to walk into rooms carrying bowls of hot liquid; this time it was tomato soup. Alfie sat next to the huddled lump that used to be Candy Careless and started tearing a roll into bite-sized pieces, which he dumped in the soup.

'There, doesn't that smell nice?' he cooed, as if Candy was a finicky toddler.

'Can't smell anything,' Candy groused, struggling to sit up and take the spoon, in case Alfie had any bright ideas about feeding her.

But actually, after half a bowl of soup and a couple of tablets, Candy did feel better. Or at least something resembling human. And able to concentrate on other things, like how gross she looked.

'Don't tell anyone I had greasy hair,' Candy whispered hoarsely, as Alfie started putting the worst of the debris into a rubbish sack. 'Or that I had baked goods on my pyjamas.'

'It's OK. I'll take your secrets to the grave,' Alfie said solemnly, but his eyes twinkled and getting unbuttoned really suited him. He hadn't fussed with his shirt cuffs or tie once in all the time he'd been there. 'I bought you some get well soon presents while I was out.' Yup, Candy definitely preferred this incarnation of Alfie.

Alfie's other superpower was the buying of items for the

sick and infirm. Candy put that down to the gay gene. There was dry shampoo, a cute little tub of menthol Vaseline for her chapped lips, and the posh tissues with the added balm. He'd even bought her a copy of *Grazia* and some sugar-free throat lozenges, as well as Belgian chocolate ice cream, which would slide down her sore throat with the greatest of ease.

'Alfie . . . I don't know what to say.' Candy could feel her eyes tearing up. Being ill really brought the sap to the surface.

'Then don't say anything,' Alfie said, leaning over Candy to deposit the empty tissue box in his bag. 'You should be resting your voice.'

Which sounded like a great idea. But all of a sudden she wasn't feeling so good again. Not like the other times when she hadn't felt so good. This took feeling-not-so-good to a place where it really wasn't meant to go.

'Are you sure you're all right?' Alfie asked, leaning in even closer. 'You've gone grey.'

And Candy didn't answer because she was too busy hurling regurgitated tomato soup all over Alfie's snowy shirt front.

Chapter Fifteen

Candy didn't remember anything much after that – just a series of fleeting impressions: cool hands stroking her hot head and someone crooning words at her in a language that she didn't understand. Being carefully laid down on fresh sheets and someone patting her shoulder as she bit back a sob because even that soft touch hurt.

Mostly there was sleep. And waking up took long minutes of trying to force her eyes open. Not because they hurt, but because they'd been shut for so long that it was hard to get out of the habit.

And really Candy wished that she hadn't bothered because the first thing she saw when she did open her eyes was Alfie sitting on her bed and looking down at her with a troubled expression.

Shit! Shit! Oh, *shit*! It was all coming back to her now in glorious technicolour. Alfie opened his mouth to say something, probably to shout at her for puking all over him, but Candy got there first even though she couldn't remember the correct way to express your apologies when you'd thrown up on someone.

'I'm really, really sorry,' Candy blurted out, noticing the black shirt Alfie was now wearing and the way he was slightly edging away from her as if he was expecting another hurlathon. 'I'll totally pay for the dry cleaning.'

'You sound like you're feeling better,' Alfie said, giving Candy another keen look, while she itched to hide under her quilt. To think that he'd seen her all crappy and sweaty and pukey and gross. And it didn't make it any better that Alfie was gay. It made it worse, because Candy knew gay boys and they were very exacting when it came to issues of personal hygiene. 'I was looking for an excuse to get rid of that shirt anyway. The collar points never seemed to be even. It was very annoying.'

'I feel beyond humiliated. What I did, like, *on you*, was ungodly.' Candy covered her flaming face with her hands.

Alfie was busying himself with plumping up her pillows and straightening the duvet, which was freaky and unnerving. 'Actually I was far more worried about what you did afterwards,' Alfie said, and he could stop sounding so amused any time soon.

'What did I do afterwards?' she asked, though she really didn't want to know the answer.

'You practically fainted, then you went all floppy and delirious. I nearly called an ambulance, but I called my mum instead. She has a quicker response time.' He lowered his voice as he stood up. 'She phoned your agency, got put through to a number in Hawaii and had words with your mother. Then she rushed over so she could administer to your needs.'

'I bet it didn't lead anywhere good when she talked to Bette.' Candy shuddered and finally decided to get out of bed before she got sore from staying in a recumbent position for too long. 'Your mum and, well, you too, you've been awesome. And you hardly know me and I bet you think I'm a grade A pain in the butt.'

Candy tottered a bit as she followed Alfie to the kitchen and watched as he made himself a cup of tea. He glanced at her and smiled, one of those smiles of his that Candy didn't see too often and that didn't really match his over-starched exterior. 'Well, you were a grade A pain in the butt with a really virulent flu bug, and my mother loves nothing more than fussing over people. Really, you were doing her a favour.'

'It was so nice of her,' Candy muttered. Where she came from, there wasn't a whole lot of nice, unless there was something in it for the person bestowing favours. A horrible thought occurred to her. 'No one took any pictures of me while I was doing my dying swan thing?'

She totally deserved Alfie's sneer. 'You have a really worrying tendency to think the worst of people.'

'Yeah, kinda comes with the territory, you know?' Candy said softly and a little sadly.

There was a small, uncomfortable silence, which was broken by Alfie rustling a carrier bag ostentatiously in her face. 'Now that you're on the mend, I have contraband, even though my mother has very strong ideas about what constitutes a suitable diet for convalescents, which involves a lot of stewed fruit.'

It felt as if Candy hadn't eaten chocolate for weeks as Alfie held up a chunky KitKat. She looked up and caught a horrifying glimpse of her reflection in the hall mirror – she'd lost so much weight that she was starting to look alarmingly Olsen Twinish. 'I should probably eat that just to make sure that my sense of taste has come back.'

'There's plenty more where that came from,' Alfie said with another smile like he'd had a total personality transplant while she'd been ill. 'If I don't have to mop your fevered brow, we might as well watch a DVD.'

They watched *Funny Face*, which was the perfect film to watch when you were getting over nearly dying. There was Audrey Hepburn being all gamine and totally rocking the Capri pants and Fred Astaire being all charming and soft-shoe-shuffling. And Candy was starting to have a whole new appreciation for Alfie, who was definitely shaping up as a perfect gay best friend. He didn't even get huffy when she wanted to re-watch the *Think Pink* dance routine, and he supplied a running commentary about Audrey's fashion choices all the way through the last act.

The final credits were rolling and Candy was feeling like she might vomit again if she ate another bar of chocolate. It was still early and Alfie was already making noises about watching *Breakfast at Tiffany's* so they could rate Audrey's outfits out of ten, when the phone rang. The phone had been ringing all afternoon and Candy was sick of having the same conversation a gazillion times. Yes, she was feeling better. Yes, it was just flu and not meningitis. Yes, she'd probably have to have her schedule for the rest of the week postponed. And hell no, she wasn't going to do a phone interview with a Brazilian newspaper at eleven p.m. tonight.

But it wasn't anyone phoning to find out when Candy was going to get back on the celebrity treadmill again. It was Meera. 'Candy, dear, I just thought I'd phone before you have an early night. I told Alfie to get you some camomile tea so make sure you have a mug now and remember to rub some expectorant on your chest but don't forget to wash your hands. And I left some lavender oil on your nightstand so put a couple of drops on your pillow and it will clear your sinuses and help you to sleep better. Alfie will make you a couple of hot water bottles and the emergency doctor's number is on the board in the kitchen.' She paused once for a quick intake of breath. 'My sister Asha will be around at nine tomorrow morning but please don't swear, dear, because she's not as easy-going as I am. Goodnight!'

She was gone before Candy could respond or even ask her why the hell she was so bloody nice?

Alfie grinned knowingly. He'd thrown caution to the wind and toed off his shoes so he could put his socked feet up on the coffee table. 'I suppose that was my mum, not letting you get a word in edgeways? Hey . . . *hey* . . . Candy, why are you crying?'

Candy didn't even realize she was until she put her hands to her face and they came away wet. Why the fuck was she crying? Because *People* magazine said she was the eleventh most famous person in the world but Candy had been all alone and forced to rely on the kindness of strangers. Because Alfie and Meera had been great, and their nursing skills were second to none, but at times like this, when you were still below par and feeling vulnerable, you needed a hug.

Then the unthinkable happened. It wasn't just unthinkable. It was unimaginable. Alfie was shuffling forward and nervously wrapping one long arm around Candy so he could pat her on the back, like he was trying to burp her. 'There, there,' he said gingerly. 'No need to cry.'

It was the worst hug that Candy had ever had. Not that she was an expert or anything. Alfie's fingers nervously prodded at her shoulder as if she was covered in a light coating of something radioactive, while he held the rest of his body stiff and still.

It just made Candy cry harder because she wanted something more. She *deserved* something more. And Alfie . . . well, he was there, so that meant he was the only person able to give it to her, which is why she flung her arms around him and buried her face in the bony bit where his neck met his shoulder so she could ruin another of his shirts by making it soggy with her tears.

Alfie was marginally better at the hair stroking (the *greasy* hair stroking) than he was at the hugging, which wasn't saying much. 'Please stop crying,' he begged, his voice almost frantic. 'I hate it when people cry.'

Candy wrenched herself away from him. 'Why can't you just behave like a normal person for once?' she demanded. 'Instead of like a complete freak?'

Alfie tried to smooth down his shirt, realized it was

damp and pulled a face before he could stop himself. 'I could say the same about you. If I'm the kettle then you're the pot.'

'What?' Candy didn't even have to fake that top note of scorn.

'It's like the kettle calling the pot black? Oh, never mind,' Alfie drawled, sitting back so he could fold his arms and look prissy. Really, he should have worn little half-moon specs just to complete the picture. 'You're so overly dramatic all the time. It's very trying.'

'I am not at all dramatic. Hello! I'm, like, practically drama-free – and don't snort at me. Have you any idea how majorly annoying that is?'

'Maybe it's even more, like, majorly annoying than you talking like a character from a TV show all the time,' Alfie said in a stupid, crappy American accent that didn't sound anything like Candy's.

'I *am* a character from a TV show!' she yelled, which wasn't ideal for a throat that was recuperating and not the best thing to say when you knew your life had become an entertainment format but you hoped that no one else had wised up to that. 'That is, I'm sorry I contaminated you with an unseemly display of genuine emotion. Why don't you just go home and colour code your socks or whatever it is you do for fun? It sure isn't hanging out with me.'

Candy didn't know how the fight had started. Though she was pretty sure that she was in the right and Alfie was elbow-deep in the wrong. Alfie showed no signs of budging, though he looked extremely offended. 'All my

139

socks happen to be black,' he said with enough quiet dignity that Candy didn't laugh in his face. 'And I can see that this return to temper-tantruming form means that you're better and I probably should go.'

And when he put it like that, Candy realized that she didn't want Alfie to go. Not just because he was the only person between her and a few hours of loneliness, but because they'd been having fun and he'd bought her chocolate and sic-ced his mom on her when she'd been ill, and they still hadn't watched *Breakfast at Tiffany's*.

She wasn't telling Alfie any of that and he was already getting to his feet, but she was saved from trying to spit out, 'Fine,' in her most truculent voice by a ring at the door.

'Do you want me to see who that is?' Alfie asked reasonably, like they hadn't spent the last five minutes hurling insults at each other.

Now it was Candy's turn to do the quiet dignity thing. 'I can manage,' she said, hurrying for the door on legs that still weren't quite steady.

'Put a cardigan on at least,' Alfie called after her, like he could give a good goddamn, as she hurried down the stairs.

It was probably more flowers, Candy decided as she wrestled with the bolt. Though why they were being delivered so late at night, she didn't know.

'Candy, my little baby girl,' Bette cried, as Candy opened the door. She was gathered up in a big Chanel-No-5-scented hug. 'Baby, you look dreadful!'

Chapter Sixteen

You had to be careful what you wished for. Candy had wished for hugs and Bette had only been in the flat five minutes and wouldn't stop touching, petting and stroking her, as if Candy had turned into a lap dog since the last time they'd seen each other.

Which was humiliating enough, without an audience. Alfie looked as helpless as Candy felt. He kept edging towards the door and twisting his fingers nervously as Bette vacillated between a flirty playfulness, which was beyond inappropriate, and injured pride. 'Your mother was very rude to me on the phone,' she confided in a stage whisper. 'No one cares more about Candy than me, but I was at a retreat in the Napa Valley and we had to turn off our cell phones.'

It seemed as if the spiritual retreat wasn't actually an elaborate cover-up for more surgery as Bette wasn't displaying any visible signs of bruising or swelling. Although she seemed positively radiant so maybe all that yogic chanting had worked. Candy thought that Alfie had said her mother was holed up in Maui, not Napa, but she was distracted by Alfie actually trying to tell Bette off. 'Well, Candy was very ill. She was almost comatose for two days,' he said, swallowing hard. 'Someone should have been here.'

'Well, someone was and I'm so grateful to you and your family for looking after her,' Bette said sweetly. 'Does your mother like spas?'

Alfie looked even more helpless. 'Um, why?'

'I want to gift her a spa day,' Bette said, as if that should be obvious. 'I bet she'd love a hot stone massage.'

'She'd hate it,' Candy butted in. 'I'll sort out a thank you present. Now let Alfie go home.'

Bette opened her eyes wide and gave Candy a conspiratorial smile. 'Of course,' she said. 'I'll leave you two alone to . . . *say goodbye.*'

God, she saw smut and scandal everywhere. 'Jesus! We just work together,' Candy barked, before turning to Alfie who was looking longingly at the door. 'Go! I'll see you at work or something.'

Alfie didn't need to be told twice. He was out of the door in a blur of black wool, muttering a hurried, 'Bye,' over his shoulder.

Candy turned to glare at Bette, who was making herself comfortable on the couch. She beamed at her daughter, completely oblivious to Candy's furious face. 'Baby, come and tell Bette all about the beautiful boy. Then we'll wash your hair before it crawls to the bathroom all by itself.'

Due to her unceremonious departure from the spiritual retreat or what*ever*, Bette had a couple of days free in her schedule. Time which could be put to good use shopping, seeing her London friends, even performing acts of charity for the poor and needy. Instead, she decided to dog Candy's footsteps, until Candy was tempted to fake a relapse so she could take to her bed and pretend that she was still contagious.

David wasn't flying in until the end of the week and Bette hated being on her own almost as much as Candy did. 'It'll be great to have some girl time,' she kept saying, like if she said it often enough then Candy would climb on board too.

So, they had a fricking spa day because that was all they could ever think of to do with each other. Besides, the steam room totally cleaned out Candy's sinuses. They shopped for vintage clothes together at Candy's favourite retro boutiques. They went to the theatre. They went to dinner. And on Friday, when Candy couldn't think of anything left to do or talk about that didn't involve clothes, she agreed to let Bette come to Nico's with her.

'It's work, Mom,' she said for the tenth time as they shared a cab to Hackney. 'It's *my* work and *my* workmates and it's really important that you don't do anything to embarrass me.'

Bette paused from applying yet another coat of lipstick. 'Sweetie, I think I know how to behave in a design studio,' she said without rancour. 'And will your beautiful boy be there?'

'OK, let's get this straight right now. He's not beautiful. He's not mine. He prefers to be addressed as Alfie, and he's borderline OCD so I'd steer well clear of him if I were you.'

143

'Oh, baby, he's very beautiful,' Bette said, blotting her lips. 'That bone structure, those eyes.

'Excuse me! I think I know when someone that I see on a daily basis is beautiful or not,' Candy insisted haughtily. She wasn't even going to bring up the gay thing because that was Alfie's business and she didn't want Bette all over it like white on rice.

Bette patted Candy's arm. 'Whatever you say, baby. But you really should get a second opinion.' She peered out of the window as the car pulled in to the kerb. 'Is this it? Hmmm, it's very gritty. I love it!'

Having the flu must have addled Candy's brain otherwise she'd never have agreed to let Bette come to work with her. Because Bette didn't know the meaning of 'incognito'. Within ten minutes, she had an eager audience as she regaled them with tales from the modelling frontline. Even Sophie was hanging on her every word.

'Mom! Come on,' Candy yelped, tugging on one of Bette's wrists and moving in the direction of the stairs that led up to the workroom. 'People have work to do.'

'Of course,' Bette agreed. 'I even dressed down so I wouldn't show you up.' Dressing down for Bette meant wearing a new season Diane von Furstenberg frock that hadn't even hit the shops yet, teamed with a scuffed leather jacket and a pair of Fendi boots. 'I can't wait to see where my little working girl spends her days.'

'Way to make me sound like a hooker,' Candy grumbled, as she pushed open the door to the workroom.

Ivy and Lola rushed over instantly and, after a really

perfunctory enquiry about Candy's health, gushed over Bette. Not just about her star turns on *At Home With The Careless* but 'I used to have that shoot you did for French *Vogue* on my wall when I was a student,' Lola enthused. 'Where you're in the black leather on the white horse.'

Bette gave a mock shudder. 'That horse was practically feral. And each time we got the shot set up, it would crap everywhere. Mind you, that was nothing compared to the time I was naked on an elephant in Tangiers . . .'

'Oh, was that the shoot you did with David Bailey?' one of the accessory designers asked, and Bette was off.

Bette didn't pause for breath once in five minutes, she was too busy dropping names and playing up for an audience. Eventually Candy's withering stare penetrated Bette's synapses. 'Really, you mustn't ask me any more questions,' she said firmly, like anyone had been able to get a word in. 'I'm here to be a proud mama, so me and my Candy Cane are going to sit over there and you're not going to hear another peep out of me.'

'Can I have that in writing?' Candy muttered under her breath as she led the way to her workstation.

'Oh, look at your little mood board,' Bette cried. 'And your little pincushion.' The pincushion *was* actually noteworthy. It was a voodoo doll that Reed had bought her as a gag gift, which Candy had put to good use. 'Why don't you have a sewing machine?'

'Because I'm only an intern and most of the machines are in the sewing room. Look, just sit down and don't touch any of my stuff,' Candy warned. The moment she'd been dreading was fast approaching. She steeled herself to start walking over to Alfie, who was making lightning quick alterations to something on his dress form.

He looked up as Candy approached and, even with his mouth full of pins, Candy was sure that he was smirking at her. 'Hey,' she said uncertainly, which was odd because she never usually did uncertain out loud.

'Hey,' he mumbled.

'About the other night . . .' Urgh! That was so not what Candy had meant to say. She tried again. 'I was a heinous bitch and I'm sorry.' Apologies were best when they were simple and didn't go into too much detail. Candy set a large, flat box down on Alfie's workstation. 'I got you a little thank you present.' She'd already sent flowers and a Fortnum and Mason's hamper to Meera.

Alfie felt moved enough to take the pins out of his mouth and stare at the Paul Smith box in consternation. 'You really didn't have to.'

'Yeah, I really did,' Candy said softly. Alfie carefully worked the tape loose and opened the lid. 'See, I've already ruined two of your shirts so the least I could do was replace them, but I wasn't sure about the collar size – why do men's shirts go by collar size? – but they said you could exchange them . . .' She tailed off as Alfie shook out one white shirt and one black shirt, because she was babbling like a dumb, babbling babble-head.

'They're fine. Good. Thank you very much,' Alfie said, like he was reading the words off a prompt. Then he came to a smaller gift-wrapped box. 'No, this is too much.'

'The shirts were replacements,' Candy pointed out. 'This is a thank you for not leaving me to choke on my own vomit.'

Alfie winced, but his long fingers were carefully prising the package open to uncover a pair of lapis lazuli cufflinks. Candy had been side-tracked by a pair in the shape of dice until she'd seen these and realized that they were almost the exact same shade of blue as Alfie's eyes; the same eyes that were staring at her, unblinkingly. 'I don't know what to say . . . these are . . .'

'I still have the receipt,' Candy said quickly, because it was hard buying presents for guys. Her dad could be fobbed off with a new effects pedal and Reed liked Criterion Collection DVD boxed sets and Prada toiletries. Anything else was outside of her remit.

'They're perfect,' Alfie said, like he really meant it, holding them up to the light. 'I think my impeccable taste might be rubbing off on you.'

Whoa! Was that a joke? Candy gave a start. Alfie didn't do jokes. Apart from the time she'd been at the Tanner family dinner and he'd cracked a funny about the soccer. 'Have you ever thought that my taste is way more evolved than yours?' Candy asked icily.

Alfie solemnly shook his head. 'No, I can't say that I have.' And that was definitely a joke for real and his lips were twitching. Alfie had hidden depths but why had he suddenly decided to reveal them to Candy? And why was she ridiculously pleased that he liked the cufflinks? And why was she going bright red as Alfie leaned in really close?

'I think you should know that your mother's rifling through your desk drawers,' Alfie whispered in her ear, his cheek brushing against hers. Candy felt the need to cling on to the edge of the table – only because she still wasn't a hundred per cent better.

Anyway, there were more pressing things to worry about.

Candy whirled around in time to see Bette having a good snoop in her drawers and even daring to pop a chunk of Dairy Milk in her mouth. She had no respect for Candy's privacy or her chocolate stash.

Alfie was temporarily forgotten as Candy rushed over and closed the drawer so quickly that Bette's fingers nearly got caught in the crossfire. 'Back off, Bette!' Candy bellowed loudly, so that people were turning to stare like they were getting their own *At Home With The Careless Unplugged*.

Bette was supremely unconcerned. She waggled her fingers at Alfie, who raised a stiff hand in salute, and then had the nerve to start getting out of her chair.

'Don't even think about it,' Candy growled. 'Alfie has lots of work to do.'

'Like admiring the lovely presents you've just given him,' Bette murmured, because she just couldn't help herself. But she obviously realized she was talking herself towards matricide because she visibly pulled herself together, shaking out her jacket and folding her arms. 'So what do you do all day, baby?'

One of the few good qualities that Bette possessed was

her unfailing enthusiasm. Normally, it made Candy seethe, but today as she showed Bette her sketches and the bodice she'd been working on that had sent Alfie into a fit, it was cool that Bette *ooh*ed in all the right places.

And when it came to fashion, Bette and Candy rarely came to blows. 'That hemline is off by about three inches,' Bette noted, as she looked through Candy's sketchbook. 'It needs to be shorter.' Then she sorted through Candy's swatches and pulled out a pink Swiss dot cotton that Candy hadn't been sure about. 'This would look wonderful for the pin-tucked blouse but I'd contrast it with something edgy like a pencil skirt in a really nubby tweed.'

Of course, it couldn't last. But it lasted until Nico suddenly descended on them, wrapping his arms around Candy so he could plant a kiss on the top of her head. 'You feeling better, ducks?' he enquired, but before Candy could even reply, he was going into paroxysms of delight.

'Bette Careless in my squalid little studio,' he exclaimed and lifted up the hand Bette was holding out so he could make a big show of kissing it. 'Candy, you should have told me we had a VIP on the premises.'

'I loved your last collection,' Bette trilled, not fazed in the slightest. 'I picked up the grosgrain skirt in Barney's – they'd sold out of everything else.'

Nico was already hustling her out of the chair. 'I'm sure we can find you a few gorgeous things from the new collection,' he said, practically rubbing his hands in glee. 'Oh, Candy, we've got the bag samples back. Why don't you make us all a coffee and we can show your ma what you've been working on? It's funny, you two really don't look alike at all.'

Candy seethed all the way through the coffee-making process. She waited impatiently for the coffee to brew so she could push down the cafetière with great force. She knew that she didn't look like Bette; Bette was a former supermodel, tall and leggy, with a glossy look that all the years of hard-living and smoky clubs couldn't destroy. Candy took after the females of the Krakowski clan; none of whom ever managed to clear five foot. And they all ran to fat in later life. Candy settled for cute. Cute was OK for now, but there was nothing less cute than a girl who didn't realize that she'd passed the cute sell-by date. And then she'd better have something real to fall back on.

Like handbags. Nico hadn't even waited for Candy to make with the hot beverages. As she nudged his door open with her foot, he was already extolling the virtues of Candy's favourite tote with the polka-dot lining and the red top-stitching. 'I promised Candy I'd name a bag after her,' he was telling Bette.

Candy deposited the tray on the table just in time to catch the wistful look on Bette's face. 'I've always wanted a handbag named after me,' she sighed plaintively.

'Marc Jacobs named a shoe after you,' Candy pointed out, but Bette pulled a face. Or tried to. Her facial muscles really hadn't been the same since a dodgy batch of Botox.

'But bags have more prestige,' Bette countered. 'Everyone knows that.' She opened her eyes very wide and fixed them on Nico, who started to squirm. Really, she was absolutely shameless. 'I think it's adorable that Candy's having a bag named after her when she's *only* seventeen.'

It didn't happen very often, but it happened enough, that Candy wondered if Bette considered her a rival rather than the best friend she claimed Candy was. She couldn't compete with Bette in the looks department and no way would she ever find a guy who was as totes besotted as her dad. But Candy was always going to be thirty years younger than Bette, no matter how many surgical procedures and gross stuff Bette had injected into her face.

Candy could understand where Bette was coming from. Fashion was a fickle bitch and Bette had done really well to last as long as she had, *then* get to have a successful comeback. But no way, nohow, was she going to muscle in on the little patch that Candy had been cultivating. So Candy scooped the bags away from Bette's avaricious gaze and put them back in their bubble wrap. 'When I'm a famous fashion designer, I'll name a whole range of bags after you,' she said, which was pretty damn nice of her in the circumstances.

'Yeah, but that might never happen,' Bette pouted, then realized what she'd said as Candy clenched her fists and Nico's mouth dropped open. 'I didn't mean it like that, baby. I know that you'll be awesome at whatever you decide to do. So, Nico, can I have that first look at the new collection now?'

It looked like the mother/daughter bonding portion of Bette's stay was now officially over.

151

Chapter Seventeen

Bette was back at her hotel and all was right in Candy's world. Being ill had pretty much sucked, but the post-illness thing was really working out for her.

She'd arrived home from work to find Laura anxiously waiting for her with a hoard of get well goodies from her latest trip to Paris: pyjamas from Fifi Chachnil, scented candles from Diptyque and a box of chocolates from Ladurée that was almost as big as Candy. Laura buying chocolates, that she'd have to watch someone else eat, was an entirely selfless act that wasn't to be taken lightly.

'I only phoned because Jen thought she'd left her phone charger under the sofa and some strange boy answered,' Laura told Candy when they were curled up on Candy's big bed, sharing a conciliatory can of Diet Coke because real friends didn't mind if you backwashed. 'And he said you were too ill to come to the phone and I could hear you wheezing and spluttering in the background.'

'Actually I was practically comatose at that point,' Candy revealed casually, unable to resist piling on the guilt a little. 'I nearly had to go to hospital.'

That merited another hug from Laura. She gave pretty much the best hugs of anyone Candy knew; they were soft yet completely unyielding at the same time. Like, Laura had you shoved up against her amazing boobs and she wasn't going to let you go until she was good and ready.

'I thought I'd hang here for a bit if that's OK,' Laura said warily because this unspoken truce of theirs was a fragile, fragile thing.

'Well, you're still paying rent,' Candy agreed. 'And it's cool to have some company.'

Laura pulled a face. 'It's nice to have my own pad, but the place is full of builders and dust and Cath can't move in until they've finished her room.'

'What about Danny's place?' Laura and Danny had been surgically attached to each other for the last six months so it was a fair question.

'He's right in the middle of the season and he says he can't concentrate on his game when he's with me because I'm too distracting.' It was obvious that Laura didn't know whether to be offended or flattered, so she settled for a faintly smug look.

There was a moment of silence until Laura nudged Candy's elbow.

'So . . . ?' she prompted.

'So, what?' Candy hedged. 'I've been ill, it makes me muggy-headed.' She might as well milk that excuse while she could.

'Who was the boy who answered the phone that time? I thought you'd sworn off boykind.' Laura was the only person Candy had told about her lucky escape from kiss and tell hell and the whole snog-the-boys-and-make-them-cry-but-never-go-beyond-first-base philosophy.

'I have. God, I haven't even locked lips with anyone

for two weeks,' Candy said with feeling because she'd been having a total kiss famine since her night out with Laura's friends.

'Right, so there just happened to be a stray boy on hand while you were ill to answer the phone and mop your brow?' Laura asked sceptically.

'It was no one, just Alfie,' Candy said. 'He works at Nico's with me and there was a whole thing with his mum when I was ill. They're a really cool family. She cooks as well as your mum.'

'No one cooks as well as my mum,' Laura snapped, but it was the good kind of snapping with no bite to it and Laura had been successfully put off the scent. Not that there was anything suspicious about Candy's relationship with Alfie because there wasn't a relationship. Just those unbelievable tingles when he'd got up close and personal to whisper in her ear, which Candy had kept replaying over and over again. But that was because he'd been there when she was all snotty and phlegmy and needy. Like, when kidnap victims fall in love with their captors because they are so reliant on them. It was like the monster flu equivalent of Stockholm Syndrome.

'You've totally tuned out again,' Laura laughed, giving Candy a sly dig in the ribs. 'Or are you thinking about this mysterious Alfie?'

Candy was just contemplating whether she should 'fess up when the doorbell rang. Right on cue. Candy's heart lurched for a second in this strange mixture of fear and excitement that it might be Alfie, but Laura was getting up to answer the door and, a couple of minutes later, she was leading a familiar figure into the flat.

'Dad!' Candy cried, and if Laura's hugs were good then being swept up in David's arms so her feet left the ground was awesome.

'I'm so sorry that I couldn't be with you when you were ill, baby girl,' he muttered in her ear and then he placed her back on the ground so he could get a good look at her. 'You're too pale,' he decided, stroking her hair back from her face.

'Dad, I'm always pale,' Candy laughed, clutching hold of his hand so she could drag him to the couch. 'This is my friend, Laura.'

Laura shook hands with the tall, wiry man who was the same age as her own dad but had black nail varnish and blue hair. 'Pleased to meet you,' she squeaked, eyes widening as Candy let herself be pulled down on David's lap so she could press her head against his chest like she used to when she was little. One of the benefits of being practically a midget was that she'd never got too big to curl up on David when she was feeling down. It was her happy place. And she didn't even care that Laura might think she was a wuss for being such a daddy's girl.

Besides, Laura's dad was really ordinary. He was handy at performing small acts of DIY when he visited, like mending the bathroom taps, which had a tendency to leak, but he wasn't cool. David was cool, and Candy could see that Laura was impressed at the way David talked to her. Not like Laura was a teenager or a really beautiful girl, but like she was an interesting person whose opinions mattered.

Even when Laura was tweeting on about Danny and how worried his coach was about his tight hamstrings.

'We've started doing yoga together,' she confessed with a sly giggle. 'Don't tell anyone though. He thinks that if anyone sees him do a sun salute his rep will be in ruins.'

'I miss yoga,' Candy sighed. Since Laura had more or less moved out, it hardly seemed worth booking Pei Yi, her yoga teacher, for a solo lesson. 'I probably got sick because my chi was all unbalanced and shit.'

David chuckled and thankfully saved them his usual rant about bogus Eastern mysticism. 'So you're all hooked up, Laura?' He tugged Candy's nose. 'What about you?'

'What *about* me?' Candy asked innocently.

'Have you been breaking any hearts lately? Do I need to kick some scrawny boy's ass for not treating you right?'

Candy snorted at the image that conjured up. 'You'll be the first to know,' she said, except he wouldn't, because there was nothing to know.

'There's just Alfie,' Laura piped up. 'Alfie who does the Florence Nightingale thing when Candy gets sick.'

'Who's Alfie?' David asked in this over-protective, he's-not-worthy-of-you way that sent little chills up and down Candy's spine.

She was getting really bored of explaining who Alfie was. So she just went for the flashcards version. 'We work together. I got sick when he was here on a work thing. His family took care of me. End of.'

David wrinkled his brow in consternation. 'I know something about an Alfie,' he said. His short term memory had been completely fried by all the drugs. 'Alfie! Would this be the Alfie whose mother phoned up and shouted at Bette and threatened to report her to Social Services?'

Candy grimaced. 'Maybe,' she hedged.

'Same Alfie who Bette swears on her Hermes Birkin is just perfect for you,' David smirked and Candy knew he was just yanking her chain, and she shouldn't play but . . .

'For fuck's sake, she doesn't know what she's talking about,' she exploded predictably. 'He's not my type! And I'm *so* not his type! Why is that so hard for her to grasp?'

Laura perked up. 'But Danny wasn't my type and now look at us,' she cried, ignoring the fact that the only way Danny could have been more her type was if he'd come in a box with *Laura's Perfect Boyfriend* stamped on it. 'Why isn't he your type? I bet he is really!'

'He's not,' Candy said hotly. 'We're too different. Alfie's very . . . he's like . . .' Candy ran through her inner dictionary and tried to pick an adjective that adequately described Alfie. There didn't seem to be one. 'He's odd,' she settled for in the end.

'Odd. What do you mean by odd? Like, scary serial killer, bodies stashed under the floorboard odd?' David asked, looking at Candy's rapidly reddening face curiously.

'He's a little eccentric, quirky, whatever, but he can't help it and he's good people and he's looked out for me and I don't want to talk about it any more.' Candy struggled out of David's lap and shook her hair over her burning face. Way to completely not play things cool.

'Well, Bette thinks we should meet him. Seemed very taken with him.'

Candy's head whipped back and forth trying to silence the room with a laser-beam eye effect. 'Subject. Change it!' she barked.

Chapter Eighteen

Candy knew it was time to face facts. She seemed to be experiencing a major Alfie crush. It was so damn typical of her to get a crush on someone like Alfie, she decided as she sat at her desk flicking through Nico's spring/summer lookbook. She couldn't get moony over a guy who might actually in some small way fancy her too. No. That would be way too simple for Candy. She had to start jonesing for the most unobtainable boy she'd ever met.

The same boy who was giving her a look of abject horror and holding out a phone. Candy came to with a start. Had she been drooling?

'It's for you,' he stage-whispered. 'It's your mother.'

Well, that explained the look of horror. 'Why the hell is she ringing you?'

Alfie looked as if he was about to pass out. 'Please, just take it. And, for the love of God, try to get me out of it.'

Candy frowned. But Alfie was already hurrying away. 'Hey Bette, what's up? And why are you calling Alfie, you frightened the b'Jaysus out of him.'

'Oh, don't be silly, baby.' Bette's laugh tinkled down the phone, but it sounded a little forced. 'I just phoned to invite him to dinner tonight, and you, of course. Did you forget that it was Thanksgiving?'

'Thanks for asking. FYI, we've never celebrated Thanksgiving once in my seventeen years, and anyway Alfie has a thing, he can't do tonight and you're going back to the States tomorrow, aren't you? Aw, shame.' Candy's voice was so saccharine sweet it should have sent her mother into a sugar coma.

'But he already said that he'd love to come,' Bette wailed and Candy rolled her eyes in frustration. How was she meant to extricate Alfie from a hideous evening if he'd already agreed to it? 'And it's my last night and I want to spend it with my baby girl and the man who saved her from an untimely death.' Then again, when Bette turned the melodrama up to eleven, it was pretty damn hard to say no.

'You must have misunderstood. They always say that hearing is the first thing to go,' Candy drawled. Saying no to Bette was pretty damn hard but it wasn't impossible.

'Baby, you *have* to come and you *have* to bring Alfie. Your father wants to meet him, and I promise we won't ask him any embarrassing questions, and it's the last night that we can all be together, and please, Candy. Please. Please. Please. Ple—'

'My God, are you ten?'

'Please. Please. Please. Please.'

Candy recognized it as the last resort of a desperate woman. When Bette couldn't go for reason, she went for repetition instead. 'OK, we'll come. But stick to religion and politics and don't you dare make any personal remarks. I'm warning you!' Candy finished on a growl.

162

The tinkling laugh was back in all its irritating glory. 'I'll be on my best behaviour, baby,' Bette trilled. 'I've booked a table at the Ivy for eight. Love you!'

Candy put the phone down and approached an unsuspecting Alfie, who was happily slicing through a length of white silk and was unaware that the apocalypse had not been averted.

'I'm going to make you do nothing but intricate beading work for the rest of the week,' Alfie told Candy as they got out of the cab on St Martin's Lane. The traffic was backed up and it was easier to walk the last five minutes. 'And if you get through that, you can hand-stitch hems.'

He'd been like that for hours – ever since Candy had told him that his presence was still required. Any other boy would have just blown her off, but Alfie had been brought up too well for that. Candy had given it a lot of thought during the afternoon and apparently that was one of the reasons why she liked him. Who would ever have thought that it was nice boys that got Candy Careless all hot and bothered?

Except, actually she was freaking freezing. The chill November air seeped through Candy's coat as she wrapped her scarf tighter around her. Alfie took her elbow as they crossed the street and then walked on the road side of the pavement. Really, he was like something out of a nineteen-fifties etiquette guide. 'It will be fine,' Candy assured him, though she was also trying to convince herself. 'My dad's OK and Bette can be quelled with a harsh look. I'll make sure I give her a really good glare. Plus, I don't actually think we're going to have to eat turkey. Thanksgiving, schmanksgiving.'

There was a little throng of photographers waiting outside the Ivy as usual. Candy tugged free of her scarf as there was absolutely no point in trying to be incognito about this. In fact, Bette's publicist had probably tipped them off.

'It's Candy!'

The little throng quickly became a snapping horde, flashbulbs popping in Candy's face as they got closer.

'Good God,' she heard Alfie breathe, and Candy angled her head to see him staring at the approaching paparazzi like a small woodland creature trapped in car headlights and about to become roadkill.

Candy tugged on his sleeve. 'Look, cross over the road, circle round and I'll meet you in the lobby,' she said quickly. But it was too late – they were surrounded on all sides.

Alfie was bug-eyed, which wasn't going to make for a good photograph. There was only one possible course of action. Despite the Arctic temperatures, Candy slipped her coat off, grabbed Alfie's nerveless hand so she could pull him close, and posed.

'This way, Candy. Give us a nice big smile. Can we see a bit of cleavage, love?'

'Dude! You kiss your momma with that mouth,' Candy smirked, holding her own mouth so it looked as if she was smiling, rather than actually smiling. It made no sense, but she looked prettier that way. She put her hands on her hips and rested her weight on one foot and let them take their stupid photos so next week the girls at Go Fug Yourself could rip her green dress/pink tights combo to shreds. But, whatever. Candy had learnt really quickly that if she played nice with the photographers, they rarely turned vicious. Besides, they'd get far more money for their pictures if she started scowling and giving them the finger.

'Who's the fella, then?' someone shouted as Candy and Alfie, who was stiff as a board next to her, slowly made their way to the restaurant's door. 'How serious is it?'

Candy fluttered her eyelashes and played up her bratty charm for all it was worth. 'He's just my stylist,' she murmured, which was tabloid code for 'he's gay and there really is no dirt to be dug here'. 'Now, come on boys, I'm seriously starving and if I don't get fed soon, things are going to get ugly.'

There was a good-natured chuckle and finally the crowd parted and the doorman already had the door open for them. Candy gratefully stepped into the cosy warmth of the lobby and sniffed appreciatively at the faint aroma of what she hoped was her dinner.

'David and Bette will probably be at least an hour late so let's get a drink,' she said to Alfie as she off-loaded her winter woollies at the coat check. 'Hey, are you going to get over the shellshock any time soon?'

Alfie slowly shook his head. 'That time we went on the field trip and you put your dark glasses on so you wouldn't be recognized, I thought you were being pretentious.' His lips twisted. 'Just how famous are you?'

Why couldn't Alfie watch television and read trashy gossip mags like everyone else? 'Very famous,' Candy said, because there really didn't seem to be much point in false modesty. '*People* magazine put me at number eleven on their most famous celebrities poll.'

'But you go to the sandwich shop and you buy pints of milk and you have holes in your tights,' Alfie argued. 'Celebrities don't do that sort of thing.'

Candy steered him towards the bar. 'How many celebrities have you actually met on a day-to-day basis?'

'Fair point,' Alfie conceded, holding out a chair for Candy to sit in as a waiter hurried over.

'A bottle of champagne,' Candy said quickly as Alfie's eyebrows shot up. 'It's my treat for dragging you into this.'

Alfie settled into his chair with the look of a man who was just about to take a long walk to the nearest death chamber. 'I really have to learn how to start saying no,' he commented dolefully.

'Oh, you'll be fine,' Candy said brightly, but actually it was getting really boring to keep repeating that. 'Look at it this way, you've saved my skin a couple of times, now I get to return the favour.'

Thankfully, Alfie didn't point out that Candy had been the one to shove him into a situation where his skin needed saving. He just crossed his legs and folded his arms and made it clear that he wanted to get this over and done with as quickly as possible.

It was a relief when the champagne arrived. Candy

watched eagerly as the waiter coaxed out the cork with a practised ease; the small *pop* almost drowned out in the general hum of the room. Alfie eyed the golden bubbling liquid in his glass with suspicion.

'I'd get it down ASAP,' she advised, raising her own glass. 'We can't drink alcohol in front of my dad, he's in recovery.'

'Recovery from what?' Alfie asked, taking a small sip like he thought Candy had slipped the waiter some money to put arsenic in his glass.

There was no easy way to say it. 'You name an addiction and he's in recovery from it. Well, except for sex.'

Alfie flinched just like Candy knew he would, but then he took a proper gulp and grinned. 'To think that you accuse me of being a freak.'

'I never have!' Candy gasped, though actually she totally had. 'Or, like, if I did I was only joking.'

Alfie scoffed and somehow the tension snapped and they were both leaning back in their bucket chairs and having an actual conversation with the jokes and the laughing, which Alfie didn't do nearly enough because it gave his thin, clever face an almost boyish look. Bette was right; Alfie was beautiful, albeit in a tightly laced sort of way. And Candy vowed there and then that she had to get this crush under control because normally she never agreed with Bette. Crushing on Alfie was bad for her mental health.

Then another waiter was at Candy's side and murmuring discreetly in her ear that Bette and David had arrived and were waiting in one of the private dining rooms.

'Why are we dining in a private room?' Alfie asked, as they were led up to the first floor.

'No idea. Maybe it was the only way they could get a last-minute reservation,' Candy replied as she stepped through a door and nearly tripped over a cable. A cable that was attached to a camera, one of three cameras in the room, all trained on the table where David and Bette were sitting.

'I don't fucking believe this!' Candy spat. 'You never said this was going to be filmed.'

David shrugged, which was shorthand for 'take this up with your mother'. Bette shot them a bright smile. 'I really thought I'd mentioned it. I'm sure I said something about a Thanksgiving special, didn't I?'

'No, you really didn't,' Candy snapped. 'There was a whole load of bullshit about wanting us all to get together on your last night but you forgot to mention that it was going to be recorded for posterity.'

'Well, it's a bit boring filming just me and your mom,' David said, uncoiling himself from the chair so he could hold out his hand to Alfie. 'I'm David Careless. Sorry to spring this on you. Thought Bette had mentioned it.' He shot his wife one exasperated look, which Candy knew was all the punishment Bette would get, but Alfie was shaking her dad's hand and gingerly sitting down.

'Hey Candy,' Bethany, the assistant director, chirped as she pinned a mic to Candy's dress. 'We need to get your friend to sign a release form.'

Alfie's head shot up from silent contemplation of his

place setting. 'I'm not signing anything!' he yelped. 'Is this going to be on TV? Candy, no . . . I just can't.'

He was already getting up to leave and Bethany was giving Candy a look that promised certain death. 'The ratings are down,' she muttered.

When the ratings went down, the ad rates went down, which meant that the network might not renew the show, and if they weren't on TV, then those lucrative product endorsements and nightclub openings would dry up. Candy wasn't proud, she liked making money and starting her own fashion label one day was going to take more than change.

So she grabbed hold of Alfie's wrist. 'Hey, it really won't be that bad,' she said soothingly, tugging him back on to his chair. 'I'll swear a bit and play the brat card, Dad will do a puppet show with the cutlery and Bette will go into her *Whatever Happened to Baby Jane* shtick —' Candy felt a moment of triumph as Bette gave a tiny outraged huff '— no one's really going to be paying much attention to you.'

It was the sad truth. The three of them had their assigned roles and Alfie was just there for window dressing. 'I'm really not comfortable with this,' Alfie insisted, tugging at his shirt collar like he was being garrotted.

'I promise you that they won't air anything you're not happy with, right, Bethany?' Now it was time for Candy to pull out her own look of certain death, and hers was much better.

Bethany didn't look too happy about it, but she grunted 'Yes' and put the release forms in front of Alfie. 'You just

169

need to sign there and there,' she said, producing a pen.

Candy knew everyone was holding their breath, until Alfie gave a deep sigh and signed his name carefully. 'I'm going to pour a million different coloured sequins on the floor and make you sort them out one by one,' he grumbled, but if he was making a joke about it, then he couldn't be *that* mad.

Candy realized that she still had Alfie's wrist in a vice-like grip, so she patted the back of his hand and let go. 'Be really nice to Alfie or I'm going to pitch the biggest hissy fit you've ever had nightmares about,' she warned her parents.

David grinned proudly like she'd just brought home a report card full of As. 'That's my girl. Now, Alfie, let's get you something to eat while they're still screwing about with the lights, because this is going to take hours.'

Alfie didn't know what to expect because he'd never seen a genre-defining, reality-based dramedy before. From the way he was twitching three hours in, as they re-shot a scene where David went off into a *bleep*-tastic rant about organic food and what a total rip-off it was, he'd expected it to be strictly fly-on-the-wall, Candy shot him a sympathetic smile as the make-up girl took away the shine on his forehead.

'Won't be long,' she lied grimly, as their plates were replaced with half-full ones because the food was wilting under the hot lights. 'You've been great. Why don't you try some pumpkin pie?'

Actually, Alfie had been the opposite of great. He'd smiled politely, chimed in with a few monosyllabic replies to questions when he really had to, and folded his napkin into a swan. Or maybe it was a flamingo? 'I'm not very good in social situations,' he explained in a whisper. 'I dress other people so *they'll* be good in social situations.'

It was the most he'd said all night. He'd hadn't even chimed in when Candy and Bette had rowed about the corsages in the *Sex and the City* movie. 'Y'know, I am really sorry about this,' Candy said again. 'If I'd known she was going to pull this kind of crap, I'd never have let you come.'

Alfie smiled bravely. 'It's OK,' he insisted.

'When we're re-shooting, it feels really staged, but most of the time you forget that the cameras are even there,' Candy confided. 'One time I even sat on the can with the door open—'

'Please don't finish that sentence,' Alfie begged, but he was smiling for the first time since they'd sat down, and her Stockholm Syndrome sponsored crush was back for an encore because Candy felt her heart give one honest-to-goodness thud in appreciation.

'You two are so adorable together,' Bette husked across the table, and Candy realized that David had finished ranting to camera and that all attention was fixed on them.

'We're not together,' Candy stated firmly. 'Alfie's my mentor. I already told you that.'

'You've been whispering together all evening,' Bette pointed out, turning her most mega-wattage smile on Alfie, who did look kinda dazzled. 'I'm so glad that Candy's found a nice young man. You should have seen the losers that she used to hang around with in New York.'

Candy bristled instantly. 'Like I ever brought them home to meet you,' she sneered.

'What was that little punk's name?' David suddenly snarled. 'That jerk-off who thought he could treat you like crap and get away with it. Jack? Jake? I wanted to kill that sone of a bitch.'

'His name was Jacob and we're not meant to be talking about this,' Candy growled. 'He's history.' And she'd probably have forgotten about him ages ago if David and Bette didn't keep bringing up the topic of her one failed relationship at every opportunity.

'He broke your heart,' Bette wailed, but Candy could tell from the glint in her eye that she was enjoying herself immensely. 'You crossed an ocean to get away from him.'

'To get away from you, you mean,' Candy shouted, aware that there were expressions of glee from the crew because no matter how much the show was staged, they loved it more when an impromptu fight broke out.

Alfie cleared his throat. 'I don't think you should speak to your mother like that,' he offered. 'She's just looking out for you.'

Candy smiled thinly. 'Alfie, you've met my mom twice before, which is not enough times to actually have an accurate opinion about her. She's a shark with lipstick.'

Bette put a hand to her forehead. 'Baby, I can't wait for you to grow out of your terrible teens,' she sighed wearily. 'I get that you have to push me away to try and forge your own identity, but it's really hurtful.'

Candy snorted until she saw Alfie pull a sympathetic face. He couldn't actually be buying Bette's crap, could he? 'Keep your surgically-altered nose out of my lovelife!'

'Not my business,' Bette said, holding her hands out in front of her. 'Just as long as you two are practising safe sex, baby. Remember, no glove, no love.'

Candy could feel her face burning with the heat of a thousand fiery suns. Next to her, Alfie was about to upgrade the twitching to a full-on spasm. 'We are not having sex,' she yelled. 'He's gay! C'mon, it's obvious that he's gay and that he's not my boyfriend, so shut the fuck up!'

That was TV gold right there. Candy wondered why she could never self-censor. Or just, like, keep her mouth shut. Alfie was getting to his feet and calmly folding his napkin back into a square. 'Thank you for a lovely evening,' he said stiffly to Bette and David, who were both giving him what-the-hell? looks. 'I really have to be going now.'

Then he unclipped his mic and, before Candy could even process what was happening, he neatly stepped over the cables and walked out.

There was a moment's silence before David spoke. 'Can't believe you just outed him, baby girl. Maybe you should go after him and apologize?'

Candy slowly shook her head and grimaced. 'Shit. I really don't think he was ready to come out of the closet and on television and all.' She looked helplessly at the spot where Alfie had been sitting.

173

'Do you think you could get him to come back, Candy?' Bethany ventured. 'And maybe this time he could throw his napkin down on the floor before he storms out? Or maybe we could get some bread rolls and he could chuck them at the wall?'

Candy rounded on her furiously. 'He's not coming back! I've just totally humiliated him on camera and it's all your fault!' Then she turned and pointed an accusatory finger at Bette, who was retouching her lipstick. 'Actually it's *your* fault.'

'I don't know what all the fuss is about,' Bette said, because her vapidness could be truly overwhelming sometimes.

'Jesus, where were you two minutes ago?' David asked her, but Bette just rolled her eyes.

'He's not gay,' she said simply.

'He so is!' Candy spluttered. 'I swear he measures the exact amount of shirt cuff that he allows to poke out from his jacket sleeve.'

'He dresses well, doesn't mean he's into boys,' Bette countered, nudging a stray smear of lipstick with her pinkie finger. 'Though it is a little unusual.'

'But he doesn't like girls in that way,' Candy bit out. And he especially didn't like her in that way.

Bette smiled like Candy was trying to be funny. 'Baby, I hate to pull rank on you,' she said, which was an absolute lie. 'But my gaydar is faultless. It's bulletproof. And that boy is one hundred per cent straight, which is wonderful because you two are so good together. I know you like to work that edgy thing, honey, but deep down you really hanker for something a bit more *staid*. Really, he's perfect for you.'

Candy gaped at her for a second because Bette hadn't just hit the nail on the head, she'd completely bludgeoned it. Pity she had to be so snide while she was doing it. 'Oh, screw this. I'm out of here,' she snarled, picking up the basket of bread rolls that had suddenly appeared in front of her and hurling them at the wall, before she stormed out in a huff that wasn't even a little bit faked.

Chapter Nineteen

It was a relief when Bette finally left the country. It was an even bigger relief that Candy had celebrity commitments, which prevented her from having to face Alfie's wrath.

David and Candy flew to Sweden to take part in a high-falutin conference on the future of television. And while she was there, Candy signed up to be a spokesmodel for a new youth-orientated line of mobile phones.

It was odd that the more famous and rich that you got, the easier it was to find people willing to pay you stupid amounts of money for a couple of days' work. Candy still couldn't get used to the feeling she had when she walked into a store and knew that she could buy pretty much anything she wanted without having to check the price tag first. Unless the store sold, like, space ships or priceless works of art or something.

Candy didn't even know how much money she had. It wasn't like she checked her bank statements. She had financial advisors and accountants and off-shore holdings so that her money made more money, which made even more money. She'd asked Mimi once if she was a millionaire and Mimi had just laughed like it was the funniest thing ever. 'Oh Candy,' she'd said. 'How far would a million get you? If you were only a millionaire then I wouldn't have been doing my job properly.' Which Candy took as a yes.

And apart from the whole avoiding-Alfie thing, because Candy kept getting these flashbacks of the way his lip curled and his eyes flashed dangerously after she'd outed him, it was cool to have quality time with David and not have Bette there to distract him.

Going out with a forty-five-year-old man who didn't drink, take drugs or smoke should have been a drag, but it never was. All Candy's doom and gloom about returning to London melted away because she saw the city through David's eyes. He might pride himself on being a cynical bastard, but there was nothing jaded about her dad.

He'd talk to anyone: cab drivers, the bus boy at the restaurant they went to for lunch, a posh old woman buying chocolates in Selfridges. And even walking down the street with him opened Candy's eyes to new things.

'Look up,' he'd say. And Candy would look up and see something she'd never seen before. A gargoyle clinging to the turret of a Victorian house, a splash of brilliant red in a window box, even a man walking about his living room absolutely butt-naked while he vacuumed.

All too soon it was David's last night in London. Candy was his plus one to some magazine's music awards. It was the main reason why David had flown over in the first place; he was due to give a Lifetime Achievement Award to some whiny-ass singer who was ten years younger than him, had sold about a gazillion times more records but cited David Careless as a major influence in every single interview he ever did. It might also have been why David was in such a foul mood.

'Look, you'll shove the award at him, snarl at the photographers, then we scram,' Candy said soothingly as they sat in their limo, except she wasn't very good at it and David was as close to furious as he ever got. 'I'll take you to my favourite Chinese restaurant; they have an Elvis impersonator.'

David slid further down in his seat and stared sullenly out of the window. 'I'm just a caricature,' he said suddenly 'Like a performing seal dressed in black leather.'

'You *so* are not,' Candy protested, though he kind of was to the general public. But, then again, so was she. 'Remember – Chinese Elvis impersonator after we've fulfilled your contractual obligation. What's not to love about a guy who can sing "His Latest Flame" in Cantonese?'

But nothing could cheer David up when he got like this. And as soon as their car finally pulled up outside the theatre where the awards were being held, he got out, grabbed Candy's hand and dragged her along the red carpet. There were flashbulbs exploding on all sides and cries of 'Candy, give us a smile!' but David scowled and was intent on getting them inside as quickly as possible.

The moment they found their table, he pushed Candy into a chair and vaguely patted her shoulder. 'Back in a minute,' he grunted, leaving before Candy could protest.

He was gone for *ages*. Long enough to miss dinner, which was a dried-up piece of chicken because they always

179

served chicken at these kinds of events. And long enough for the awards to start and a whole crowd of musical non-entities to troop up on stage to get their gongs. Even worse, Candy was forced to make polite conversation with a dude from *Hollyoaks* and a singer who'd she slagged off in a magazine the week before. Across the room, she could see Laura and her lame footballer posing for the photographers. Danny kept whispering in Laura's ear, then she'd throw her head back and laugh. It was impossible to catch her attention, even by waving frantically. Candy couldn't tell if Laura was playing up to the cameras or was still so sappy and in love that everything Danny said made her pee her pants with laughter. God, she missed the old, single Laura who'd hadn't been such a goddam wuss.

Out of the corner of her eye, Candy could see a girl with an earpiece and a clipboard scurrying towards her for the fifth time in half an hour. 'Where is your father?' she gritted as she reached Candy's side. 'He's due on stage in ten minutes.'

Candy was not her father's keeper. Though she decided not to point that out. 'He's probably just catching up with some old friends,' she improvised gamely. If David hadn't been clean for the last two years she'd have been seriously freaking out right about now. 'I'll text him,' she offered. 'Make sure he knows that you're looking for him.'

The woman hurried off and Candy sent David yet another text message, not that she expected it to do any good. He'd probably made a run for it and was back at his hotel. So why hadn't he called her?

Candy was just wondering if she should call Mimi, not that she could do much, when the awards host stepped up to the mic. 'It's now time to honour someone whose contribution to the music industry can't go unrewarded. He's a colossus of creativity, a champion of other talent, both young and old, and he always gets his round in. To present our Lifetime Achievement Award, I'd like to welcome to the stage, David Careless, who's been a formative influence on this man's music . . .'

Candy shut her eyes as the room went quiet and a spotlight picked out the empty seat next to her where David Careless wasn't waiting to trot obediently to the stage like a well-trained dog.

'Is there a David Careless in the house?' the host asked in a feeble attempt to mask the blind panic with a little light humour.

There was nothing for it. Candy would have to go up instead. And make some fake, insincere speech about the talentless douche, even though he'd never had an original idea in his life. Candy started to scrape her chair back when an unsteady figure suddenly stumbled on stage.

Candy sat down with a thump and forced herself not to cover her eyes with her hands. Not when there were photographers poised to pounce. Her father unsteadily weaved his way from the wings so he could approach the host, who was looking at him with undisguised alarm.

'David,' he said jovially. 'Aren't you meant to be carrying a Lifetime Achievement Award about your person?'

David Careless peered over the top of his dark glasses. 'No,' he said baldly. 'I'm not giving an award to some jumped-up little fucker who owes me back royalties for ripping off just about every song I ever wrote.'

There was a collective gasp from the room – and Candy . . . Candy was seriously conflicted. Because part of her wanted to punch the air in jubilation that her dad still had more attitude and fire than any of the stiffs sat here smug in their own mediocrity. And the other part of her wanted to crawl under the table and hide because David was bobbing around on stage like a prize fighter after ten bloody rounds and he was slurring his words and it all meant that he'd fallen off the wagon with a spectacular thud.

Before she even realized what she was doing, Candy was on her feet and threading her way towards the stage where David Careless was pointing a belligerent finger at the nearest camera and still getting his rant on. 'You're all a bunch of greedy sycophants,' he hissed venomously. 'I put twenty years of blood and guts into those songs, but you only wanted to know me once I'd agreed to become a comedy turn on primetime TV. Where were you when I still had my integrity?'

It was awful. Candy could see her father's face contorted with rage in the monitor as she yanked up the tight skirt of her dress so she could run up the steps that led to the stage. There was a faint smattering of applause as Candy appeared, though she couldn't imagine why, as she seized David's hand, which he was still swinging wildly about. He immediately clutched her fingers tight enough that there'd be bruises tomorrow and blinked at Candy as if he didn't know who she was.

Then reality hit and he slumped into her arms, his whisky-sour breath hitting her in the face. 'Oh, baby girl,' he muttered – and how could he be so drunk and still manage to get wired for sound? – 'How did we get so lost?'

There was no other choice but to yank David to the podium, shake hands with the host and spit out some garbled apology about jet-lag and one of their pets dying before Candy read the speech scrolling down the autocue that lauded the furiously angry Lifetime Achiever, who finally strode on stage to get his award.

'You used to be my hero,' he said witheringly, snatching out of Candy's hands the stupid glass plaque that had just been placed there by one of the stage crew. 'Now you're just a tired old has-been.'

For one awful second, which was even more awful than all the other seconds that had gone before, Candy thought David was going to take a swing at the glowering singer/songwriter who, up close, was covered in a really orangey foundation. Thankfully, he thought better of it.

'Better to be a has-been than a never-was,' David said almost thoughtfully. 'And your wife's been shagging your guitarist for years.'

The award shattered on impact with the floor when the singer dropped it so he could lunge for David's neck, but Candy was already pulling him down the stairs.

'For fuck's sake, Dad!' she screamed, because he was dragging his Cuban heels. 'Come on!'

Candy didn't care that everyone was staring or that she was whacking at photographers with her clutch bag as they fought their way out of the auditorium. She didn't care about anything until they were finally out on the street and running over rain-soaked pavements to come to a halt outside a taxi rank.

It was only once they were safely in a black cab and Candy's heart rate had slowed to a less fatal beats per minute that she realized that David was chuckling with unbridled glee.

'What the hell's so funny?' she growled, because he was *this* close to being strangled for the second time in the space of ten minutes.

He didn't answer at first – too busy wiping tears of laughter away – but then he sniffed triumphantly. 'That was the best fun I've had in ages,' he declared.

Chapter Twenty

There were already photographers circling the entrance to David's hotel so Candy told their driver to take them back to her flat. It wasn't ideal, but hopefully she could have David inside and halfway to sober before the press realized where they were.

It took three pots of coffee and two rounds of ham sandwiches to sober David up enough that Candy could tell the gazillions of people calling that: 'He's all right. No, seriously, he's OK. I think he reacted badly to these cold and flu tablets that I've had in my bag for, like, ever.'

Only Mimi was unconvinced when she called to say that a clip of David was already up on YouTube. 'Is he using again?' she asked baldly.

'No, nothing like that, I told you already,' Candy hissed, striving for aghast and not sure if she was hitting it.

'And I don't believe you. Please tell me that he was only drunk. That's manageable. But if he's using again, the show's lawyers will start making noises about breach of contract and that's bad news for everyone concerned. I'm sending Derek round to get him to a hotel before the press track you down.'

'But he's not on drugs,' Candy said quickly, maybe too quickly, but when she glanced at David, his long, skinny frame sprawled over every available inch of sofa, he shook his head. 'He's not, Mimi. And he hasn't been drinking either and I don't see why you're so twisted about it. I bet we make all the front pages tomorrow and that means you can find a few more conglomerates who have products that need endorsing,' she finished bitterly and then she hung up on her godmother before she said something that she *really* regretted.

Candy caught sight of her reflection in the mirror. Her usually poker-straight hair was sticking out in all directions and during all the excitement her red lipstick had smeared its way across her chin. She looked like crap and the black satin dress she'd been so proud of tonight, at how grown-up it made her look, was ripped at the hem.

'You don't have to lie for me,' David said softly. He'd been pretty quiet up till then. 'I had a drink, that's all. In fact, I had about five drinks and all of them were large ones.'

'You're not meant to be drinking at all,' Candy protested and it was weird that she never got really angry with her dad. No matter how much crap he pulled – and he'd pulled plenty in his time. Instead her voice got soft and throbby, even though she swore she wasn't going to cry. 'Y'know, if you're not happy we could just not do *At Home With The Careless*. We've already made a ton of cash so let's just bail out. You could start making music again, get back into the studio . . .'

David shook his head decisively, like a dog that had just had a bath. 'We can stick it out for a bit longer. Bette loves the fame. Let her have her moment in the sun, Candy.'

They always stuck up for each other. Hid behind

each other. And Candy was always the odd one out. The third wheel.

'But there are three people in this family. Four if you count Conceptua and—'

'No!' David's voice was sharp, which it never normally was with Candy. 'Let it go.'

And she did cry then. But silently crying like that made it slightly better. David just rolled over because he could only deal when it was other people who made Candy cry.

Candy felt like the loneliest girl in the world until she was miraculously saved by Reed suddenly coming through the door, followed by a foot-dragging Hadley. 'Hey, how are you?' he asked, his voice soft and his hands full of cases. 'Are you feeling better now? And what the hell happened at that awards show?'

God, the monster flu seemed like years ago and really wasn't Candy's most pressing concern right now. 'Yeah, just about,' she hiccupped, deciding to completely ignore Hadley's presence. She could only cope with so much. David was motionless and Candy wondered if he'd passed out or maybe died from alcohol poisoning.

'We got back from LA as quickly as we could,' Reed said, perching on the arm of the chair. 'More to rescue you from Bette's ever-loving care than anything else. Spiritual retreat? Whatever. And then we heard about David's latest adventure.' He leant over and gave David a hard poke on the shoulder. 'Are you using again?'

That got David's attention. He rolled over so he could glare reproachfully at Reed. 'No,' he grunted. 'Do you want to check my arms for needle marks?'

Reed looked as if he was seriously considering it. 'Well, once a junkie, always a junkie. Didn't you write a song called that once?'

'Reed, that's way harsh,' Hadley admonished, still not entirely sure whether she was allowed in the living room. She gave Candy a tentative little wave and smile. 'Did you get my message about the echinacea and the wheatgrass when you were ill?' she asked uncertainly.

Candy decided that, just this once, she could afford to be magnanimous. Besides, anything that stopped the almighty row that seemed to be brewing between Reed and David had to be a good thing. 'Yeah, thanks, but I couldn't really keep anything down.'

'You've lost loads of weight,' Hadley said from the doorway. 'Being ill is better than colonic irrigation for detoxing.'

Once again, Candy wondered what on earth Reed could possibly find so captivating about Hadley, especially if she wasn't putting out.

'And you have mascara smudges on your face,' Hadley continued, which was a good point. Candy's face felt really sticky, like her make-up was sliding down towards her feet. She'd probably feel a bit more battle-ready if her pores weren't so clogged. And she was all set to head to the bathroom with a warning to Hadley to come and get her if things turned ugly, but it was too late.

'You don't come in here and start throwing your weight around,' David said to Reed, his voice still slightly slurred.

'I'm not taking drugs and it's none of your business.'

'Well you've sunk a skinful at least and you were with Candy, so that makes it my business,' Reed growled, and it had been so long since he played the big-brother card that Candy would have had a major case of the warm fuzzies if it wasn't David he was glowering at. 'So much for your well-publicized sobriety.'

'Candy's a big girl. She can handle herself,' David pointed out with pride, like he'd raised Candy to be all self-sufficient and stuff. When actually she'd learnt to be self-sufficient because her mother was a narcissist and her father was a drug addict. 'My girl's got stones.'

'She's seventeen,' Reed gritted. 'And believe me, she doesn't do such a great job of handling herself.'

'Excuse me,' Candy interrupted furiously. 'I'm standing right here so . . .' She tailed off because actually she didn't know what to say. She was too angry to think. Angry with David for letting her down *again* and angry with Reed because the last few months had shown his love wasn't exactly unconditional. And that last crack of his had just about proved it. 'This isn't helping the situation.'

At least both David and Reed lost their fight faces, which was something. Hadley was still hovering in the doorway but now she smiled brightly. 'I'll put the kettle on,' she decided. 'Who wants some nice Chai tea?'

Reed smiled vaguely. 'That sounds great, baby.'

'Do you want some more black coffee?' Candy asked David, who shrugged. He seemed pretty sober now, but Candy didn't want to ask for a status report in front of

Reed and she certainly didn't want David to snap at her in that icy-cold voice he'd used before. God, why couldn't she have a family like Alfie's who managed to dial down the drama to a bare minimum? But the mere thought of Alfie and how furious he was with her was somewhere that Candy didn't want to go. It felt as if there wasn't a single person on the planet who was actually Team Candy right now.

It was a relief when Derek from Fierce turned up to whisk David away so there could be some respite from all the sitting round not talking and sipping Hadley's foul-tasting Chai concoction. David complained bitterly but let himself be led out into the night without more than a cursory wave at Candy, even though he was flying back to the States the next morning. She'd forgotten what drunk David could be like and, what a surprise, she really hadn't missed him.

'I'm going to get this crap off my face,' Candy muttered as soon as the door had shut behind David, and she hoped that Reed and Hadley would take the hint and leave. She didn't know why Reed had bothered to come round, especially with Sadley in tow. Apart from the perfunctory enquiry about her health, Reed hadn't seemed particularly bothered about Candy.

As she smeared cleanser over her face, Candy contemplated what a needy little critter she'd become since she moved to London. Not that it did her any good. She held that thought as the sounds of a commotion from outside the bathroom door interrupted her pity party. It was . . . Laura and Irina going at it just like old times.

'I don't even know why you're here,' Irina shouted. 'You have your own flat, go live there.'

'Oh, shut up,' Laura rapped back. 'You're only annoyed because you thought that you'd have the place to yourself so you and Javier could have really noisy sex.'

Candy opened the bathroom door in time to witness the truly smug look on Irina's face. 'A healthy sex life is nothing to be ashamed of unless you have British uptightness and a fat ass.'

Laura was saved from having to think of a comeback – because really there wasn't one – by the sight of Candy emerging from the bathroom. It was hard to have a soothing deep cleanse when Anglo-Russian relations had broken down outside.

'Are you all right, Cands?' Laura asked with a fairly credible amount of sincerity. 'Danny and I were at the awards do.'

Candy remembered that she was actually still kinda pissed at Laura for ignoring her before, but at least she sounded like she cared.

'Is your father doing the heroin again?' Irina asked baldly. She, on the other hand, didn't sound like she gave a flying crap. 'No wonder you turn out the way you have.'

'Are you both staying here tonight?' It was too much. The one time that Candy wanted to be by herself to cry and eat loads of ice cream and possibly wear her pyjamas with the cupcakes on them, and they had a full house. Over Irina's shoulder, she could see Javier and Danny (who got on far better than either of their girlfriends would have liked) watching English football on the telly and Reed and Hadley having a smooch that made Candy want to dry-heave. No wonder her top lip was curling up like it was going to permanently stay that way.

'Is not your flat, Candy,' Irina barked. 'I still pay rent. Is not my fault that I'm such a successful model that I never here.'

'Don't worry, we're leaving,' Laura snapped, her temper already nicely riled by Irina. 'Forgive me for wanting to check that you were OK.'

'I'm surprised you managed to tear yourself away from Danny's mouth long enough to notice,' Candy muttered, as she marched into the living room. It dawned on her that, once again, she was the odd one out. Three couples and one single girl who didn't belong with anyone. Jeez, when would this night stop sucking?

Hadley obviously thought the exact same thing. 'Guys, guys, let's not fight,' she cooed, sliding off Reed's lap even though there was a perfectly good armchair right next to her. 'This should be a happy occasion.'

'I don't see why,' Candy grumbled, but then she did. Or rather she saw the obscenely large diamond on Hadley's finger. It was hard not to, when Hadley was waving her hand around like she was trying to swat a fly.

Reed shot Hadley a warning look. 'Baby, we said we'd wait . . .'

It was too late because Hadley was opening her mouth and breaking Candy's heart. 'Reed and I are going to be married. Isn't that the best news ever?'

Chapter Twenty-One

Five minutes later, Candy was still shouting. 'Do you know when's a good time to announce your engagement? Any other night than the night my father gets absolutely shitfaced for the first time in three years! That would be a good time!'

'But it's good news,' Hadley repeated for the tenth time. 'Good news makes bad times better.'

'Good news for who?' Candy took a deep breath to try and centre herself, but it didn't work. 'Not for me, that's for sure.'

'But this isn't about you,' Reed reminded Candy coldly. He'd been quiet, though silently disapproving as Candy had ranted and cried. 'It's about Hadley and me. You could try being happy for us.'

'Why?' Candy demanded, brushing an impatient hand across her leaking eyes. 'It's not going to last. I bet you break up before you even make it down the aisle. You haven't even had sex!'

And it was the God's honest truth. They weren't compatible. They had nothing in common and Reed lost tons of cool points just by being in the same room as Hadley, let alone intending to join with her in a state of holy matrimony. Any fool could see it. Apart from the fools who were standing right in front of her.

Like Laura, who'd been content to only coo over Hadley's ring up till now. 'That's a really bitchy thing to say, Candy,' she gasped, hand on her heart for emphasis. 'Hadley's always been nice to you.'

'Which goes to show just how dumb she is,' Candy snapped, because as far as she was concerned, equal opportunities niceness was the mark of a truly suspect person. How could you ever respect or trust anyone who always had a kind word or a smile? Niceness was just Hadley's gameplan.

But no one agreed with her. Not if the filthy looks aimed in Candy's direction were anything to go by. Javier and Danny were wisely sticking to the sidelines, but Irina marched over so she could get right up in Candy's face. 'Hadley has the heart of gold,' she insisted vehemently. 'You just jealous because you have the twisted love for your brother, which is illegal.'

'What the fuck are you talking about?' Candy shouted, because God, that was just wrong on so many levels. And judging by the horrified look on Reed's face, he thought so too. 'I barely knew I had a brother up until two years ago and then Hadley worms her way in and he might just as well not exist again. Reed was the one person who was on my side and now I'm back on my own and it freaking sucks!'

'It's not about being on anyone's side,' Reed shouted back. 'Christ, Candy, you're so judgemental! If you're feeling lonely then it's because there isn't a person around who's willing to put up with your bad moods and temper tantrums. Look around you! There are no TV cameras so it's time to stop acting like a pint-size diva!'

There were so many horrible, hurtful accusations in that speech that Candy didn't know where to start. So she burst into tears again. 'Get out!' she screamed, flailing her hand and attaching it to Laura's wrist because she was the nearest. Then she started to tug her to the door. 'Get out! Get out! GET OUT!'

'You are being absolutely ridiculous,' Laura said furiously, tugging her hand free. 'I really don't think I want to be your friend any more.' She flicked her head in Danny's direction, who was staring at the floor. 'C'mon, Danny, let's go back to yours.'

'All of you – get out! If I'm such a vile psycho bitch queen then you can all screw off and let me get on with it!'

'Always with the drama,' Irina sneered. Then she had the audacity to put her arm round Hadley, who was white-faced and trembling. About the only point in Hadley's favour was that she hardly ever cried. 'I think you and Reed look funny together, but I hope you'll be happy.'

'I'm OK,' Hadley said quietly. 'Reed, we should go. The negative energy in here is giving me the beginnings of a tension headache.'

Candy made a scoffing sound because, well, come on – every time Hadley opened her mouth the most ridiculous things came out of it, but she was obviously in a minority of one. Laura and Danny were already out of the door,

Irina following with a terse, 'You're a very silly girl,' aimed at Candy.

Only Javier had a lopsided smile for her and a gentle touch on her shoulder as he went, which left just Reed and Hadley.

'Go on then,' Candy snarled. 'Don't let the door hit you on the way out.'

'It's a pity that we didn't know each other before,' Reed said grimly as he helped Hadley into her coat, though she had two working arms and could have done it all by herself. 'That way I might have had some influence and stopped David and Bette absolutely ruining you.'

'I am not ruined!' Candy growled. 'It's not like they spoilt me or anything. Quite the opposite. And you know—'

Reed held up his hand. 'Don't even think about playing the shitty childhood card,' he warned, his face pinched with anger. 'That's not an excuse. Bette walked out when I was five, Hadley's parents were monsters. So you had a tough childhood? For God's sake get over it and grow up!'

He flung the last words at her as he practically hauled Hadley towards the door. And if they were dishing up home truths then Candy had one for him. 'The only reason you're with *her* is because she's exactly like Bette,' she informed Reed, her voice dripping with contempt. 'Like, Freudian, much?'

'You little bitch . . .'

Hadley was already there in the narrowing space between Reed and Candy. 'Don't,' she said, though it wasn't clear which one of them she was talking to. 'Don't.

You say a whole bunch of mean stuff because you're mad at each other and then you can't come back from it. Now, please, Reed, I want to go home.'

And when Hadley Harlow became the voice of reason, things had got really, really bad.

Chapter Twenty-Two

Heading back to work on Monday was possibly the scariest thing that Candy had ever done. It was even more scary than the time she'd had to tell Irina that she'd accidentally put her Versace dress in the washing machine when she was dyeing some old antique nightdresses black. If the row with Reed and, well, *everybody*, had one silver lining, it was that it had taken Candy's mind off Alfie. The weekend had involved a lot of crying and being angry and vibrating with the unfairness of it all. But now her mind was firmly back on Alfie, and not in the delicious way it should when you had a crush on someone. There was nothing like alienating the object of your affections by outing him to kill a crush stone dead.

But the actual reality of going back to work wasn't so bad. People were treating her with kid gloves and sympathetic looks because of all the garbage in the papers about David. Surely they wouldn't have done that if Alfie had told them about the disastrous dinner and Candy blurting out his sexual preferences for everyone to hear?

But maybe Alfie wasn't out at work. It was all very confusing, Candy thought as she lurked in the kitchen. Even Sophie had given her a lukewarm smile and asked if she was OK, and Marge had wrapped Candy in a lavender-scented hug. 'You were very dignified on the telly, my girl,' she said gruffly. 'That dad of yours, he wants rehabbing, he does.'

There was no putting it off any longer. Candy slowly took the stairs up to the studio and crept to her desk without looking at Alfie. She was kicking it low-key today, all in black without any colourful tights or corsages to draw unnecessary attention to herself, but her butt hadn't even touched the seat before she was aware of a wintry presence behind her.

'Now that you've finally decided to grace us with your company, I've got lots of jobs for you,' Alfie announced coldly before Candy could even turn round. 'I've made a list.'

Boy, had he made a list. It ran to several pages of typed A4. Candy stared at it dolefully, then spent the rest of the morning reorganizing ribbons. Not just by colour. Because where was the fun in that? No, she had to organize them by material and shade and thickness. And when that was done and Candy's fingers were about to walk out in protest, she had to start filing patterns.

By Tuesday lunchtime Candy wasn't even halfway down the list, much to Alfie's icy disapproval as he surveyed the order she'd brought to the fabric room. 'I would have thought you'd know the difference between ivory and cream by now,' he sniffed before he went to lunch.

Candy had to resort to sticking her tongue out at Alfie's departing back, which wasn't remotely satisfying. But George was back from LA and waiting for her in reception so he could take her to lunch.

'We're pretty limited for options,' she told him as they walked out into the biting November wind. 'But the pub on the corner does a good roast or there's an Italian place that doesn't actively suck.'

George decided on Italian 'because it's almost impossible to screw up a Caesar salad and I'm giving up carbs until the New Year.' He looked around at the boarded-up shops and the local winos camped out in a nearby bus shelter, and gave a theatrical shudder. 'It's like downtown Tehran or something.'

'Like, you'd know,' Candy scoffed, tucking her arm in his and marching him towards the Italian. George kept up a constant commentary of gossip: who was wearing what, who was doing what, who was doing what to whom, and Candy realized how much she'd missed him.

'I'm so glad you're back,' she said feelingly, once they were seated. 'Things have been kinda draggy.'

'You and Hadders still haven't kissed and made up?' George asked, pushing away the breadsticks like they were infected with the Ebola virus.

'We kinda did for five minutes until she announced her engagement to my brother. Can you even believe it?'

George pulled a face, because at least he was Team Candy all the way. 'I wouldn't bother getting them a wedding gift,' he muttered darkly. 'I give it six months before he removes her vocal chords under cover of darkness.'

Candy giggled as she got a mental image of Reed clamping Hadley's mouth open, and then abruptly stopped as she saw Alfie seated on the other side of the room, deep in conversation with some tall, thin, impossibly elegant girl who was big with the hand gestures.

'What just happened?' George wanted to know. 'You went from happy to glowery in five seconds.'

It took ten minutes and a glass of red wine to bring George up to speed on the Alfie situation. Then it took another five minutes for him to read her the riot act. 'It's not big or clever to out people without their permission,' he said crossly for the tenth time. 'It's actually, like really rude.' Hadley had outed George and his boybander boyfriend, Benji, in the pages of a national newspaper.

'It didn't do you any harm,' Candy muttered, her face flushing because it wasn't like she'd done it on purpose. It had been in the face of extreme provocation. 'You were wasted on that crappy sitcom and now you're doing pilots in LA.'

'And signing development deals with major TV networks,' George announced smugly, pausing to preen, before he rapped Candy over the knuckles with his discarded breadsticks. 'That doesn't make it all right, little missy.'

Alfie and *his* . . . the girl were deep in conversation. She kept reaching over to touch his hand and he was laughing and hanging on to her every word in a way he never did with Candy. 'I wish we'd gone somewhere else for lunch,' Candy snapped, as the waiter brought their food over. 'It's bad enough that he makes my work hours abject fucking misery without cutting into my lunchtime too.'

George had his back to the room, but he was starting to

twist in his chair. 'I want to see! Where's he sitting?'

Alfie hadn't noticed them because he only had eyes for the girl, but George couldn't do anything discreetly. 'Stop looking!' Candy hissed. 'He'll see us.'

'Is he the good-looking Indian guy in the corner?' George demanded, making no effort to lower his voice.

'He's Anglo-Indian,' Candy corrected. 'I think. Or Pakistani or Bangladeshi or . . . Stop staring, George, for Christ's sake.'

It was too late. Almost as if he was aware that two pairs of eyes were scrutinizing him, Alfie suddenly looked around, caught sight of Candy and said something to his companion, who looked over too. She was even more distressingly beautiful face-on than she was in profile. Candy stared at the sun-dried tomatoes on her pizza in mortification as George gave a little wave. Candy kicked him hard under the table, glad that she was wearing her boots with the really pointy toes.

George turned back to her with a pained gasp. 'What did you do that for, you vicious little harpie?'

'I'm never telling you anything ever again,' Candy promised, eyes still fixed on her plate. 'You're so embarrassing.'

'I know,' George agreed happily, investigating his salad suspiciously for stray, carb-laden croutons. 'But I don't get it. How can that be Alfie?'

'Because it is. I work with him, I've puked on him, I think I recognize him by now,' Candy said smartly.

'Yeah, but you said Alfie was gay – and that guy is

not gay,' George stated firmly. 'I'm disappointed in you, Candy. I'm going to have to revoke your fag hag membership status.'

It was like déjà *ewww* all over again, with people denying what was so very obvious. 'I knew you were gay within a second,' Candy reminded him. 'Even though you were pretending to date Hadley.'

George held up his hand in protest. 'Look, I can recognize my chosen people because that skill is, like, engraved in my DNA – and that boy is not one of us. Pity though. God, he's pretty. I didn't get a good look at his eyes. I bet they're all intense and see-right-through-you.'

They kinda were, but that wasn't the point. What was Candy missing here? Why did everyone who wasn't her think that Alfie was straight when she knew that he wasn't? He couldn't be. It was such a distressing thought – that Alfie was out of bounds not because he fancied boys but because he wouldn't fancy her even if there'd been a nuclear holocaust and the whole future of the planet depended on them doing the nasty.

'Oh, shut up, George,' Candy snapped again. She had to totally skip dessert even though there was tiramisu on the menu because her teeth were aching painfully from being ground so much in the last ten minutes.

Instead she hurled down three espressos because the cups were really tiny, and watched from beneath her lashes as Alfie and the girl paid the bill. Then he helped her into her bright red princess coat and they walked out together. And when Candy told George to get his fat head out of the way, she saw Alfie give the girl a kiss on the cheek, then a hug goodbye. Which didn't prove anything anyway.

Candy was jittery to the max when she got back to work. It had to be the coffee. It couldn't be anything else, like waiting in dread for Alfie to demand to know why Candy had had the audacity to eat lunch in the same restaurant as him.

When Alfie finally started walking towards her with a grim expression on his face, Candy felt relieved. She'd just rather get it over and done with so she could get back to yet another boring and mundane task that Alfie considered appropriate punishment for daring to speak of his sexual preferences.

Without saying a word, Alfie handed her a black dress with a skirt made out of metres and metres of fabric. It was so voluminous that if someone had needed to put up a marquee in a hurry they could have used it and still had some material left over.

'The hem needs hand-stitching,' he announced, with the faintest note of smug satisfaction. 'And I need it all done this afternoon.'

For one second, Candy was tempted to tell Alfie where he could stick his issues and his hand-stitching. But she decided against it. She was made of stronger stuff than that. Besides, her big mouth was the reason why she was in this horrible holding pattern in the first place. So she settled for a 'Fine,' and if it came out sounding sullen and surly, then so be it. She could understand why Alfie was *still* so mad at her, even if she didn't necessarily agree with it.

And it was then that the three cups of espresso turned out to be the worst idea that Candy had had in a long time. Hand-stitching with black thread on slippery black satin was bad enough. But when your hands were acting independently of your brain and your fingers seemed to have turned into fat sausages, it was well-nigh impossible.

Candy aimed the spotlight above her workstation at the dress and squinted furiously as she tried to place neat, even stitches along the hem, which seemed to be increasing in length, the more she worked. Every now and again, for a nice change of pace, she'd get up to press the section she'd just worked on, which was almost heartbreaking because it was always a paltry amount of hem, no matter how long Candy had been beavering away.

She hadn't even completed a quarter of the hem when people started packing up to go home. Candy glanced over at Alfie expectantly. At this rate, hemming the dress would take until the end of next week, so surely going home so she could pluck out and soak her aching eyeballs wouldn't do any harm. But Alfie shook his head decisively, so Candy bent over the dress once again with all sorts of creative curses rattling through her head.

An hour later and only she and Alfie were left. Candy had a crick in her neck, a stabbing pain between her eyes and a blistering stream of invective working its way to her vocal chords, when Alfie suddenly materialized behind her.

'You know, it's hard enough to sew black on black without you blocking my light,' she muttered venomously.

It was even harder when Alfie leaned over and placed his hand on the next section of hem. Candy thought about plunging the needle in the webby bit between his fingers, but didn't. She was really making great strides with the self-restraint, not that Alfie was likely to appreciate it.

He carefully gathered up the dress so he could scrutinize her handiwork, while Candy listened to the blood rushing in her head. She was definitely over her Stockholm Syndrome and not a moment too soon either.

'These are a disgrace,' Alfie said flatly. 'Your stitches are a mess. Unpick them and start again.'

Candy shut her eyes and thought about counting to ten. 'Fine,' she spat again. 'I'll do it tomorrow.'

Alfie flared his nostrils, and his face shouldn't have looked so pretty from upside down, but it did. 'No,' he said, like he was hanging on to his temper by the most fragile of threads. 'You'll do it now. I did say that this was a rush job. Of course, if you've decided that the world of fashion and putting in an *honest* day's work isn't everything you thought it would be, you're welcome to leave.'

Now it was Candy's turn to flare her nostrils so hard that it felt like she might have sprained something. 'I'm not going anywhere,' she warned Alfie, so he'd know that he was stuck with her and her inferior hemming skills.

'Just unpick the bloody dress,' he said, already walking away.

And Candy was going to suck it up. She even went as far as rooting through her sewing basket for the unpicker. But that was as far as Candy's good intentions went, because then she was getting to her feet and marching after Alfie.

'So, do you want to talk this out, then?' she demanded, as he tried to sit down and found his way blocked by Candy, with her hands on her hips.

'Talk what out?' he countered, edging ever so slightly away. 'Go back to your table and leave me alone.'

Candy wasn't going to be put off that easily. 'You obviously have your panties in a bunch because I told my parents you were gay . . .'

'Your parents and a camera crew filming every thrilling second, don't forget,' Alfie reminded her. He smiled thinly. 'And that has nothing to do with my reaction to your substandard, shoddy work.'

'Bullshit,' Candy hissed. 'Why else have you been giving me these crappy, boring jobs to do if it wasn't to punish me?'

'Because they needed doing,' Alfie insisted, but it lacked conviction and his gaze kept dropping to his sewing box, though Candy couldn't tell whether he was worried that she was going to attack him with sharp implements or if he was planning to get medieval with the pinking shears himself. 'I have absolutely nothing to say to you that isn't about work.'

He was so infuriating. He had to have taken lessons because no one, not even Hadley, was that infuriating without professional help. 'Look, I'm sorry, OK?' Candy burst out. 'I shouldn't have said it in front of everyone.'

'You shouldn't have said it at all,' Alfie said savagely. 'And you should have apologized days ago.'

He had a point. Candy hung her head. 'You were really angry when you walked out of the Ivy and I didn't want to make things worse,' she admitted in a small voice.

Alfie actually snorted. 'You're the queen of confrontation. You thrive on winding people up and then stepping back to see the results.' For someone who claimed he didn't have anything to say to her that wasn't work-related, Alfie sure seemed to be whipping himself up into a frenzy. 'Is it fun, Candy, to casually destroy someone's reputation just because you're feeling bored?'

'That's not what I was doing!' Candy didn't even have to fake the note of horror. 'I was trying to get my mom off your back. I was practically doing you a favour.'

'You're playing the altruism card?' Alfie opened his eyes super-wide, which was a needlessly dramatic gesture, as far as Candy was concerned. 'That's ironic because within five seconds of meeting you, I realized that your colossal self-obsession was the biggest thing about you.'

Candy felt the throb of imminent tears. She'd reconciled herself to the fact that Alfie wasn't dying to jump her, but his utter contempt was an exciting, new development. 'I get that you're mad at me,' she choked. 'But it's not my fault you can't own your sexuality and you're freaking out in this repressed, British way because I dared to mention it. So you're gay. Like, big whoop! You're working in the fashion industry and—'

'I'm not gay!' Alfie shouted, shocking Candy into silence for probably the first time in her tender, young life. She stood there and watched him clench his fists and breathe

209

deeply like he was trying to rein in his temper. 'I'm not gay,' he repeated quietly. 'I don't have a problem with people being gay, other than the fact that I'm not.'

'You are,' Candy reiterated. 'And I'm cool with it. What I'm not cool with is you being so embarrassed about it. I was there at your folks' house when your dad was being all weird about you working in fashion and he obviously knows that you're gay and you should just be open about it. Then you wouldn't have to get all pissy about stuff like this.' Candy finished with a top note of self-righteousness, which made Alfie's jaw tighten. And when Alfie's jaw tightened, Candy's stomach dipped like she was on a rollercoaster.

'Not that it's any of your business,' Alfie bit out. 'But my dad is annoyed that I'm the first eldest son in the Tanner family for four generations not to work in the same tailor's shop in Savile Row. He doesn't think there's any career prospects in "sewing sequins on frocks".'

'Yeah, whatever,' Candy sniped, and Bette and George's insistence that Alfie was straight as a die (and what was a die anyway?) was starting to seem a little more convincing. But if Alfie wasn't gay and did like the ladies, she was one lady who he didn't like. Not one little bit. 'Are you sure you're not gay? Maybe bisexual?' she added hopefully.

Alfie drew in an exasperated breath. 'You seem unhealthily fixated on my sex life,' he said softly, and Candy's stomach-dipping upgraded to a full-on churning motion. 'I wonder why that is?'

'Well, I'm glad that we got all that cleared up,' Candy

squeaked, because Alfie was looming over her now in a way that seemed to eat up every spare inch of space between them and suck all the air from the room as an added bonus. 'I'm going back to the hemming from hell now.'

Candy managed three steps, before Alfie's hand curled around her wrist and tugged her back. She wasn't sure why, until his other hand cupped her chin so he could tilt her face. 'You know, I don't think we've cleared anything up,' he mused, a half-smile on his face that Candy couldn't decipher. Well, actually she wasn't capable of doing anything much but revelling in the feel of Alfie's hands on her, and she'd worry about everything else at some later date. 'I think you still have doubts about my orientation.'

'I don't,' Candy started to assure him, but Alfie was obviously sick to death of the sound of her voice because he shut her up in a really simple and effective manner.

He kissed her.

It was a tentative kiss, so tentative that the part of Candy's brain that was still capable of rational thought started to get back on the gay train, but then Alfie realized that Candy wasn't tearing her mouth away and screaming about inappropriate touching in the workplace, so he kissed her properly.

Alfie kissed with the same intense precision as he did everything, whether it was sketching out a pattern or basting seams or making coffee. All his attention was focussed on Candy, so when she started to sway, like she was some goddamn Victorian virgin swooning from her first kiss, his hand glided to the small of her back to keep her steady.

His mouth moved so unhurriedly, like he was memorizing the feel and smell and taste of her, his thumb rubbing the hollow behind her ear so Candy opened her mouth on a sigh and the kiss became more urgent. Candy stopped being this motionless, swooning kissee and realized that this wasn't some fevered relapse back into flu land but actual reality. Alfie was kissing her. And she could kiss him back.

It meant that Candy could reach up and tug at the one unruly lock of hair on Alfie's head and tug it, like she'd been dying to do for days. It also meant that she could pull her mouth away and, if she stood on the tippiest of her tippy toes, use it to kiss along the high planes of Alfie's cheekbones.

Then Alfie was kissing her again, but she was so small and he was so tall and the craning and the bending was getting so uncomfortable that it was completely distracting away from the kind of kisses that Candy would remember when she was a wizened old lady. So it made perfect sense when Alfie suddenly lifted her up and sat her on the edge of his table. But that didn't really work because he still had to lean down to kiss her again.

It worked out so much better when Candy scooted back with a tight grip on Alfie's lapels so they were both horizontal. Horizontal as in making out on a table, which should have been very bad, but actually was very practical with the difference in their heights. The kissing led to touching and Alfie didn't seem to mind that Candy was still clutching great handfuls of his jacket, wrinkling it between her frantic fingers as he did something with his mouth and her neck that made her go a little crazy.

It all seemed to be heading towards something inevitable that should have been scary and wrong, but Candy didn't care. Not when Alfie kept kissing her like he'd die if he didn't. Then, over the panting sound of their breathing, a box of pins scattered noisily to the floor, followed by the dead thud of a bolt of tweed, and the kissing stopped as abruptly as it had started.

Candy's eyes had been screwed tightly shut, but she opened them as the heavy weight of Alfie was suddenly removed and he made this noise in the back of his throat. Not a happy noise. She sat up and pulled down her dress, which had got rucked up and slightly unbuttoned, so she could peer down at Alfie, who was squatting on the floor. His jacket was half on, his tie hanging forlornly in a loose knot and his hair was sticking in all directions. Not that he seemed to care. He was methodically checking the tweed, brushing away invisible smuts of dirt, like it was an injured child.

Once Alfie had established the fabric wasn't any the worse for its harsh treatment, he started picking up the pins one by one. Could this really be the same boy who'd been rolling around with Candy on the table?

'Alfie?' Candy asked hesitantly, which was a new look for her. Normally she'd have shouted at him by now.

Alfie stood up, put the box of pins back on the table and then tutted as he saw the creases in his trousers. 'You should probably go,' he muttered, resolutely not meeting her eyes.

'It's late. You can redo the hem tomorrow.'

Unbelievable. Fucking unbelievable. It wasn't until Alfie raised his head and then hurriedly looked away again, that Candy realized she'd said it out loud.

'What was that just back there?' she asked, because she really needed to know. 'And why are you being like this?'

'I don't know what you mean,' Alfie said stoutly, like he hadn't had his tongue in her mouth ten minutes ago. 'Come on, I need to lock up.'

As far as Candy could recall, even Jacob, who was the biggest rat bastard she'd ever had the misfortune to meet, had taken five days before he started giving her the silent treatment. Five days was industry standard, not five minutes.

And all of a sudden, the whole kissing thing was making the kind of sense that Candy wished it didn't. 'Either you really are gay and you were trying to put me off the scent or you were body-swapped for a brief period of time or . . . or . . . I totally sucked at the kissing.'

'None of the above,' Alfie said testily, jangling his keys. 'Will you please go?'

Then it dawned on Candy, and really she should have known. 'If you think you're going to go to the papers with some big kiss and tell on your five times a night sexcapades with Candy Careless, my lawyers will sue you so hard and for so long that even your grandchildren's grandchildren will wish they'd never been born,' Candy bit out.

Alfie looked like he'd been hit over the head with an anvil – all he needed were some cartoon stars to complete the picture. 'What the . . . ?' he began and then as if someone had flicked a switch, he went from confused to cold in the blink of an eye. 'Sometimes I think that you might actually be a decent human being and then you open your mouth and I'm forced to rethink that theory,' Alfie said, and it was such a great exit line that he had no choice but to throw the keys at Candy's feet and walk out.

Chapter Twenty-Three

Usually Candy's MO was to kiss the boys and then skedaddle. But this was different. Alfie was different. And he'd walked out on her. Which made the whole complicated situation even more complicated. David wasn't the kind of dad given to imparting fatherly nuggets of wisdom, but he'd once told Candy that she should never shit on her own doorstep — and now she knew exactly what he meant.

One thing was for sure, Candy thought, as she sat cross-legged on the couch later that night, she was *never* going back to Nico's. There was no point in having all these good intentions about learning a trade and getting her hands dirty, when she'd made out on a work table with her mentor, who'd had a bad case of the regrets two minutes later. And Candy would do everything in her power to make sure she never had to see Alfie again.

When she phoned Mimi a few hours later, her godmother was wonderfully helpful. 'I'm so glad you've come to your senses,' she said crisply. 'I've had to put all sorts of offers on hold while I waited for you to get this out of your system.'

Candy bit back all sorts of impassioned denials. 'Can you phone Nico and say that I won't be back?' she asked. Though she didn't really need to ask. Mimi took twenty per cent commission and in return she cleaned up Candy's messes. 'And can you be nice about it?'

'Darling, I'm always nice.' Mimi had had years to perfect her aggrieved tone. 'Now are you ready to get back to work, right?'

Damn straight she was. 'Yup, ready and able and hoping that it involves travelling to another continent,' Candy agreed.

'That accessory company is still sniffing around,' Mimi offered casually. 'I'm sure I could get them to let you have some kind of creative input on the products, but the only thing is that they're based in China and—'

'I'll go,' Candy said eagerly. 'Can you get me on a plane today, and tell them I want one hundred per cent creative control and in return I'll make sure that I'm regularly photographed with their crappy goods?'

'I don't know what's going on with you, darling, but I like it,' Mimi murmured. 'Start packing and I'll call you back in an hour.'

Even though she wasn't expecting to, Candy fell a little bit in love with Shanghai. It helped that it reminded her of New York; the impossibly tall buildings hogging the skyline, millions of people rushing like there wasn't a second to spare and giving it attitude. And then it was like nowhere on earth she'd ever been.

There were restaurants right up in the heavens shaped like flying saucers, walls of shimmering neon, and shops selling mind-boggling, high-tech gadgetry. But it was also a city steeped in exotica, from the old-fashioned junks floating in the harbour to the temples she visited on the first day when she had a little time to explore. Plus, Candy got to eat pork buns for breakfast, and oysters and crispy chicken any time she felt like it, which was an awful lot.

But the best thing about Shanghai was that it wasn't London and there was absolutely no chance of running into Alfie. Even better than that, there were no lanky Anglo-Indian boys in well-cut suits half glimpsed out of the corner of Candy's eye, who'd make her start hyperventilating. When Candy and Jacob had imploded, she'd realized that the Village was overrun by tousle-haired hipsters in scruffy jeans and each one had given her a jolt straight to the heart. No wonder it didn't work so well any more.

Candy would have been happy to wander the streets of Shanghai for months, but there was work to do. She was anticipating the accessory-designing portion of the trip to involve much arguing and flouncing. When she turned up at the HQ of Le Sac and was led into a big conference room with views of the harbour, Candy was surprised to see two Western women in their twenties who looked as if they'd just stepped off the dance floor of some sceney little club in Hoxton or Williamsburg. They were eyeing her with just as much suspicion.

'We're the design team of Le Sac's youth division,' one of them said half-heartedly. 'We're going to be working together.'

Candy wasn't sure if they'd got the memo about her

one hundred per cent creative control but, whatever. She wasn't here to make friends. She was here to make bags that were going to have her name on them and that meant 'No leopard print, no skulls and crossbones, and absolutely no pink or glitter,' she said firmly. 'That's absolutely non-negotiable.'

Both girls let out a huge sigh of relief. 'Thank God for that,' one of them said. 'I'm May. Do you want to brainstorm some ideas then?'

By the end of the week, Candy, May and Elise had sketched out a whole range of accessories that looked expensive and covetable, even though the priciest was a $75 suitcase. Everything else was pretty much affordable if you lived off allowances and babysitting money. There were purses, pocketbooks, clutch bags, totes, book bags, make-up bags, pencil cases, cell phone cases, iPod covers and the famous suitcase, in a choice of the same dark denim as Candy's favourite pair of jeans or a brushed khaki twill like Elise's combat pants with red top-stitching and a cotton lining that had tiny shooting stars printed all over it and a very discreet CC logo embroidered in the corner.

Once May and Elise were certain that the workplace was going to be a leopard-print-free zone and they'd got over the whole being-in-the-presence-of-the-eleventh-most-famous-person-in-the-world, they started treating Candy like a regular person. And that meant hanging out. Turned out there was a huge ex-pat hipster community who worked in Shanghai's burgeoning fashion and computer games industries.

So there were many nights in clubs, drinking imported beer and blinking from the glow of the disco lights. And there was a boy; the kind of boy Candy usually went for – messy of hair, smirky of mouth, bad of reputation. His name was Jared and he designed Easter eggs for computer games, and she kissed him in some dark corner of some dark club. But it was a bust because it didn't get rid of the Alfie taste in her mouth, so Candy made Jared go and get her another beer, then she slipped out of the club while he was waiting at the bar and took a taxi back to her hotel.

Working flat-out every day was much more effective at making Candy's blues a little less blue. When they showed their sketches to the CEO of the youth division, some yuppie idiot called Charles who was wearing chinos and Converses to show that he was down with the kids, he practically started drooling. 'We could reverse them as well, and have the lining on the outside and the khaki or the denim on the inside. Could you come up with another print idea as well as the stars. Maybe leopard print?'

'Leopard print is so over,' Candy sighed. 'What about ripping off Andy Warhol's flower paintings?'

'Love it,' he enthused. 'We could get these in production so they're ready for Back to School 2010. Or Back to Cool as I like to say. I don't suppose you'd like to turn your talents towards something a little more grown up, Candy? We're having a little trouble conceptualizing our high end collection for Spring/Summer.'

Candy stayed another three days and left with the title

of Creative Director to add to her résumé. It was proof that she wasn't just another celebrity famous for being famous. And when her fifteen minutes were up, she had enough talent to make it on her own instead of relying on her fading star to open the right doors for her.

It was enough to finally put a smile on her face as Candy hauled her suitcase inside. The thought that she'd be eighteen in a couple of months and could shuck off parental consent and move to an apartment with a lift, broadened the smile so it felt a little more genuine.

The flat was empty, a stale, hollow sort of empty as if it had been that way for ages. Hadley had obviously been in residence because she'd left a note and a pile of coins on the kitchen worktop. 'Very sorry. Had to use your soy milk and Mr C–C peed on one of your patterns – has bladder infection. Let me know if I haven't covered the cost.' Candy's groove was definitely not back in full working order because she couldn't muster up a hissy fit. Instead she sneered at Hadley's penmanship and the little smiley faces dotted over the 'i's. Then she vowed to get even with that vile little mutt if it was the last thing she did.

Even tackling the huge pile of post that had mounted up while she was in China seemed like too much hard work. As she munched her way through a bowl of coconut noodles, Candy idly flicked through it. Junk mail got put in the recycling bin. Bills were stacked in a pile to be forwarded to Fierce. There was a postcard from Courtney, her erstwhile babysitter now primetime TV star, from some press junket in Australia, a twenty-per-cent-off voucher from her spa if she tried their new Ayurvedic head massage, and there was a parcel.

Candy picked it up and gave it a good shake. It was soft and squidgy and rustled intriguingly. Whoever had sent it had done a thorough job of wrapping it too, Candy realized when she tried to open it. The brown paper was covered in copious quantities of sticky tape so it was hard to dig her nail in and start ripping.

Once she was past the outer layer, there were sheets and sheets of soft tissue paper, and nestling at the centre was a black dress. A beautifully cut, beautifully constructed black dress lined in a tangerine silk shot through with gold thread that was instantly recognizable.

Candy stood up and shook out the dress so she could see that it would fit her like a glove, hugging her breasts and waist then flaring out into a swirly skirt that would swish about her legs. A folded piece of card fluttered down to the floor and, even before Candy scooped it up, she knew who it was from. There was only one person who could have made a dress like that, though why he'd made it for her, Candy didn't know.

Dear Candy

I didn't want to have to write something pathetic and cliché-ridden along the lines of 'about the other night . . .' But I do want to apologize for what happened after. So please accept this dress as a peace offering and if what happened is the reason why you haven't come back to work, I'd like

*to assure you that there are absolutely no hard feelings
on my part.*
Best wishes
Alfie

Candy stared hard at the neatly penned lines, searching for clues in the stiffly worded message. An explanation would have been nice. Even an enthusiastic indication that Alfie had missed her. But he'd made her a dress instead. Just once Candy wished that something in her life was simple and straightforward. She'd been trying so hard not to keep obsessing about the enigma that was Alfie, but now he'd made that impossible with his bullshit peace offering and his stupid note that said nothing but squeezed her heart just enough for it to start hurting all over again. Candy stuffed the dress and the note back in the tissue and the brown paper and shoved it in the overflowing black garbage bag that was waiting to go downstairs.

An hour later, Candy was frantically trying to rescue it and praying that the remains of the coconut noodles hadn't soaked through. There was no harm in trying it on.

It fitted perfectly, but more than that it felt as if the cool satin was Alfie's hands on her, stroking Candy as she stood in front of the bathroom mirror and posed with her hands on her hips. And now that she was calmer and had read the card again, she'd noticed from the date that Alfie had thoughtfully written at the top, that he'd sent it while she was in China. That was a fortnight ago, so he probably thought that she was an ungrateful bitch who didn't appreciate his frock and never wanted to hear from him again.

But it could all wait. Right now, all she wanted was her bed. She barely managed to brush her teeth before curling up under her comforter and closing her eyes.

Candy had only been asleep an hour when she was woken up by her phone. She started the long climb out of unconsciousness as the ringing finally penetrated. As she sat up, she was also aware that someone was ringing the doorbell. Scratch that. Someone was wedged against the doorbell. But the phone was nearer.

'Who is it and why the fuck are you calling me at two in the morning?'

There was a muffled noise on the other end of the line, somewhere between a sob and a choke. Candy rolled her eyes and was just about to hang up when Bette spoke. 'Baby? It's me. I don't know what to do. My God, I don't know what to do.' And then she stopped speaking because the sobs were getting in the way.

Candy was wide awake now, icy rivulets racing down her back, because actually phone calls in the middle of the night never led to anything good. 'What's up?' she said sharply. 'What's wrong?'

But Bette wasn't saying – she was too busy weeping. And it wasn't the kind of crying Bette did when she was in pain from another surgical procedure or she'd broken a heel on a favourite pair of shoes, or even like the times when they couldn't make the rent and the landlord would send his sinister cousins round to collect. It was much worse than that. A desperate wounded sound like Bette had gone to a place beyond words.

Candy could hear her own voice softening. 'Hey, Bette . . . Mom, come on, it can't be that bad. Just tell me what the problem is and I'll fix it. Whatever it is. Please, Mom.'

For a moment, Candy thought that Bette hadn't heard her, but she'd stopped crying so that had to be a good thing, right? Right?

'It's your dad,' Bette whispered hoarsely. 'It's David.'

Five words and Candy felt her whole world collapse. 'What about him?' she said, anxiety clawing at her. 'For fuck's sake, tell me!'

Bette gulped and the noise seemed as if it was magnified a thousand times. 'He's ODed. Jesus, baby, I didn't even know he was using again . . . it's all my fault. I should have known. Oh God, I just don't know what to do.'

Chapter Twenty-Four

It all made a horrible kind of sense. If David had started drinking again then drugs were the inevitable conclusion. 'He's OK though, isn't he? He's not, like . . .' Candy couldn't finish the sentence, but Bette was already rushing in to fill up what couldn't be said.

'No! No! I'm at the hospital now and he's going to be fine, but baby, they were filming. I thought he was just tired because he's been working so hard and I kept talking to him about hiring a contractor because we really need to get the bathroom fixed . . .' Candy let Bette ramble, only half listening as she tried to get her own thoughts in order.

'Hang on! Rewind? They caught the OD on tape? OK, Mom, you need to call Mimi and get her on damage control and you need to make sure they hand over the tapes before it ends up on the internet. Can you do that?'

'I don't know!' It was a desolate wail. 'The police are here and Nick from the TV network . . . he's been really kind but I just don't know what to do. Candy, baby, I need you! Can you come home?'

Candy was already out of bed and rummaging for clean clothes. 'Like, you even have to ask. Phone Mimi and make sure she gets me on the first flight out of London.'

It wasn't until she put the phone down that Candy realized there was still someone ringing the doorbell, but before she could do anything about that, her phone started beeping again. She snatched it up.

'Hi, Candy? This is Lorna Matthews from *The Daily Gazette*,' a voice oozed down the phone. 'So sorry to hear about your dad . . .'

'How the hell did you get my number?' Candy shouted.

'You must be devastated. There's a rumour that David ODed. Did you know he was back on drugs? Can I have a quote for this morning's edition?'

Candy hung up and within seconds, the phone was lighting up and ringing again so she switched it off. No way was she answering the door, but she rushed to the living room so she could peer out of the window and, sure enough, there was a mob scene of camera crews and photographers outside – and now the landline was ringing too.

Candy sank to the floor with her hands over her ears and started to cry. It seemed like the right thing to do. But only a couple of minutes later and she was all cried out. Blubbing wasn't going to solve anything, and she had work to do. She hauled herself to her feet and switched her phone back on so she could call Mimi because Bette wouldn't remember half the stuff that Candy had told her.

Halfway to Heathrow, Candy's driver decided that they'd both get killed *en route*, thanks to the hordes of paparazzi on motorbikes intent on cutting them up to force them to a halt so they could hold their cameras up to the tinted windows. Candy's vision was blurry, thanks to the countless flashes popping in front of her eyes.

Finally, they flagged down a police car, which called for back-up to keep the mob of paps at bay. Mimi phoned with a plan B, and then there was a police escort to City Airport, where the TV network had paid for a private plane to fly Candy to New York. At any other time, Candy would have thought the whole circus was ridiculous but just a little bit thrilling. But this wasn't any other time, it was right now, and all she could think about was getting to New York as quickly as possible. She barely gave the luxurious interior of the private jet a cursory look. And as soon as the pilot told her she could take off her seatbelt, she was back on the phone to Mimi for a progress report.

They flew into a private airfield in Queens so Candy could clear passport control with relative ease, but outside it was the same story. How was it that the press were always one step ahead, she thought as she climbed into the back of another car, not a limo because it was impossible to navigate the New York streets fast in a big, obnoxious town car.

Chapter Twenty-Five

A sobbing, heaving mess of Bette fell into Candy's arms as soon as the lift doors opened on the twelfth floor of the hospital.

Candy could feel her neck getting damp as Bette cried and wailed, and when Candy stroked her hair with one hand and patted her back soothingly with the other, she just cried and wailed harder.

'Thank God you're here, thank God you're here,' Bette chanted like it was some kind of magical mantra and now that Candy had arrived, things would miraculously get sorted out.

Very carefully and very gently, Candy prised her mother free. It had been a long time since she'd seen Bette this wrecked. Her shingled platinum hair was sticking up in tufts and, despite the lifts, her eyes were swollen and red from crying, faint remnants of her mascara now like dirty smudges down her cheeks.

'Is there somewhere we can go and freshen up?' Candy asked no one in particular, and they were led into an empty room. God knows what they'd done with the patients that usually occupied this floor.

Candy sat Bette on the edge of the bed and ran a paper towel under the tap so she could wash her mother's face. At some time during the procedure Candy started mouthing baby talk to Bette, which was beyond nauseating but it seemed to calm Bette down.

'There, there. It can all be fixed, you'll see,' she murmured. 'We've been to worse parties than this.'

They really had, and Bette had never gone to pieces before. She'd always remained her usual flaky self, like the latest crisis was something that was happening around her, rather than to her. Maybe Bette was starting to realize just how fleeting fame could be, and how family was really the only important thing.

Candy sat down next to Bette on the bed and let her mother rest her head on her shoulder while she stroked her hand, and eventually the sobs faded away to just the odd hiccup.

'So, did you talk to Mimi about making the network hand over the tapes?' Candy asked, still in the same soothing voice so Bette wouldn't freak out all over again. 'And what had he taken anyway?'

'Candy, please . . . not now,' Bette begged, clutching a hand to her forehead. 'I can't think straight. And you're asking me all these questions and it's just too much to deal with.'

Bette was definitely sounding more like her old self. Enough that Candy could start to open up a big can of bad-ass when the door opened and Candy's publicist, Kris, stuck his head around the door.

'Sorry to interrupt, but Candy, I've got make-up waiting and I sent someone over to Barney's to get you some outfit options. You need to be ready to read out a statement to the press in half an hour. I've got a draft for you to have a look at.'

Candy shut her eyes as the room started spinning around her. 'Look, Mom, you're obviously feeling better, can you do the press thing? I haven't slept in forty-eight hours – I just got back from China and—'

Bette crumpled before Candy could even finish pointing out how very dead on her feet she was. 'But you promised! You said you'd come and take care of everything and I just can't. I can't.'

It really was time for Bette to find a new song, Candy thought exasperatedly, but she pulled her shoulders back and gave Kris a tired smile. 'OK then, lead the way.'

Kitted out in a little black ensemble from Chloe, Candy was ready to face the press. There was a murmur of excitement when she walked into the conference room because if they were going to run a special segment on *E!News*, then her face was far more comely than some anonymous lawyer or hospital administrator.

'I'm not going to answer any questions,' Candy said crisply over the melee of shouts. 'I'm going to read a brief personal statement and then I need to get back to my family.'

'My father, David Careless, was admitted to this hospital yesterday evening after a bad reaction to some prescription drugs he was taking for a non-specific viral infection. He's in a stable condition and is continuing to respond well to treatment. My family would like to thank everyone for their good wishes and asks respectfully that we be left alone to get through this difficult time.'

Candy finished reading and looked up. Big mistake. At a conservative estimate, twenty microphones were shoved in her face.

'What did he take, Candy? We heard it was an OD.'

'Has David been depressed?'

'Where was Bette? Is there any truth in the rumours that she——?'

'That's enough,' Kris said sharply, bodily inserting himself between Candy and the baying hordes. 'No further questions.'

Candy was ushered out of the door and back into the elevator before the press could even process that she'd disappeared. She sagged against the wall and let out a breath. 'They really are a bunch of wankers,' she said to Kris feelingly.

'Hey, you're talking British,' Kris grinned. 'Do you want to go back in there and call them pillocks or bloody fools or something?'

'What I'd really like to do is see my dad,' Candy said and frowned. 'He is OK, right? I mean, everyone says that he is, but no one's even told me what room he's in. He's in a room, yeah? He's not, like in ICU or something?'

Panic was suddenly overtaking her, making it hard to breathe. It was a relief when the elevator doors opened and Candy could get out, because it felt like the walls were about to close in on her.

'He's fine. Really, really fine,' Kris assured her. 'Not saying that he's going to be taking up kickboxing any time soon, but he's on the mend.' He pointed down the corridor. 'He's in room 1217. I'm sure he'd love to see you.'

It felt like the longest walk of her life. Candy didn't have a clue what she was going to find on the other side of the door.

It certainly wasn't David sitting up in bed eating green Jello and watching the Knicks and the Lakers slug it out on pay-per-view.

For a second she wanted to laugh, because David was wearing a hospital gown and it really didn't go with the tattoos and the remnants of the black nail varnish he had on. And then Candy wanted to cry because he was her dad, which meant that he should be there to look out for her and take her for ice cream when she was feeling down and mend taps like Laura's dad. He shouldn't be in hospital recovering from an OD, and she shouldn't have to be the one to figure out what happened next.

David glanced up from the TV and saw Candy cowering by the door. His face split into an entirely spontaneous grin. 'Baby girl, what are you doing here?' he asked, like she'd just happened to be in the area and decided to surprise him.

There were so many things Candy could have said, wanted to say, but all that came out was a choked, 'How could you?'

Chapter Twenty-Six

David patted the bed. 'Come and give your dad a hug.' Candy stayed right where she was. 'I mean it. How could you put us all through this? I've had twenty-four hours of gut-wrenching terror and police escorts and fucking paparazzi and you're sitting there eating goddamn Jello like everything's right in your world.'

'Don't start on me, Candy,' David growled, and for someone that never used to have a cross word for her, like ever, he was beginning to make a habit of getting snippy with her. 'Just don't.'

'Oh, I think I'll start on you if I want to,' Candy growled back. 'God, to think I was worried when you got hammered in London. Were you using then? Did you go out with me when you were high? Did you?'

'Look, I have an addictive personality, you know that,' David said, like it was a reasonable excuse. 'Can't change who I am. There's a lot of things I can't change even if I want to.'

If Bette's hysteria was annoying, then David making with the cryptic ranked just as high. 'Mom's out of her mind with worry,' Candy informed him, because if she couldn't get through to him, then Bette usually could.

His reaction was a little sneer. 'Yeah, I just bet she is,' he drawled and something was really off, apart from the obvious, that Candy couldn't quite put her finger on.

'Did she get the stuff for you?' Candy asked, and it was all a horrible hangover to a life that Candy thought she'd left a long time ago.

Like, she couldn't remember the day that she discovered that her dad did drugs. More than that, that he was a drug addict, user, meth-head, whatever you wanted to call it. It had just been an everyday part of growing up, along with learning her multiplication tables and watching *Sesame Street*. She could still remember being three or four and Bette waking her up in the middle of the night, lifting her out of her little trundle bed and carrying her out into the freezing cold streets to flag down a cab.

'Daddy's sick,' she'd croon in Candy's ear, tucking her blankie tighter around her. 'And Mommy needs to go and get some money so we can buy him some medicine.'

Getting money meant going to this huge apartment on Central Park South to see a terrifying woman with a white streak in her black hair who always wore red. Bette would pull dresses out of her bag, shocking pink Schiaparelli, Fortuny velvets, a Patou gown; spoils that she'd found in flea markets during her modelling days that she was selling now for a handful of dollars to an avaricious witch, when they really belonged in a museum.

Then they'd get back in the cab and drive way downtown to where the numbers stopped, and this time the apartment building wasn't so luxurious. Bette would knock on a paint-scarred door and a metal grille would slide back so she could put the money through and then they'd wait long minutes for a little twist of paper to get pushed into Bette's hand.

Those were special occasions that really stood out, but the other stuff was more mundane, ordinary – a syringe nestling next to her Little Mermaid toothbrush in the holder in the bathroom. David passed out on the living-room floor as Candy stepped over him on her way to school. The strange, smoky, bittersweet smell that would linger in the air when David had friends over and Candy wouldn't be allowed in the living room. Bette would call Courtney and they'd go to the cinema, staying to see the movie three times over until it was time to go home.

It had been a strange way to grow up. And it hadn't been all bad because there were times when things were really good, usually when David wasn't high or coming down but somewhere in the middle, and he'd be mellow and happy to spend hours helping Candy paint animals on her bedroom walls. Or he'd scoop her up in his arms and Bette would put a record on and the three of them would dance and sing until Mrs Kim in the apartment downstairs would bang on her ceiling with a broomstick.

But then Candy had got older and there were no dresses left to sell and Bette would shut herself in the bedroom for hours and the sores on David's arm had all gone septic and things couldn't stay the same. Not when he'd got jumped by some thugs one night when he'd gone out to score and had ended up half-beaten to death.

He'd said it was a wake-up call and Bette had phoned

Mimi, who'd been maintaining radio silence because she refused to enable their lifestyle any more. David had been shipped off to rehab in Utah and Mimi had found Bette a job as a guest judge on some TV modelling show, and six months later, David had come back clean.

And now they were right back where they'd started. You stripped away all the money and the fancy clothes and the bigger apartment and nothing had changed. Except Candy was done with this.

'Did she get you the drugs?' she repeated harshly, and maybe this was the first time she'd ever spoken to him like this. 'Or did you manage that all by yourself?'

David shrugged. 'Bette was otherwise engaged,' he said bitterly. 'And I had nothing else to do but reflect on the cruel joke that my life had become. I needed a distraction.'

'Oh and I guess if you'd ended up choking on your own vomit and, like, dying, that would have really been a distraction,' Candy bit out. 'God, I hate you a little bit right now.'

For the first time, the sneer disappeared off David's face and he reached out a hand. 'Don't say that, baby girl,' he pleaded. 'I messed up. It's what I do. You could say I have a talent for it.'

Candy was already stepping out of the room. 'I cannot do this right now,' she muttered. 'I'll come back when I've calmed down and I'm not about to mouth off a load of stuff I'll really regret.'

There was a distinct lack of venues for Candy to calm

down in. She sat in an empty room for a bit, but various people kept peering in so in the end, she climbed up the emergency stairs until she found the door that led to the roof. It was freezing cold, the promise of snow in the air, and she only had a thin black dress on.

And actually she realized that calming down wasn't an option and being alone with her thoughts kinda sucked. Right now, Candy didn't know which parent she was most mad at, and if she tried to think about stuff that wasn't the almighty train wreck currently happening on the twelfth floor of the hospital, it involved Reed being engaged to Hadley and Alfie kissing her into the middle of next week and then acting like he wanted to be decontaminated immediately afterwards.

God, if they were handing out medals for the crappiest life, Candy would get the gold. All she needed on top of this was another bout of killer flu, she thought as she shivered and sneezed. It was time for round two of facing the music.

By a process of elimination, Candy quickly decided that Bette was still in the funky-smelling room where Candy had last seen her. Not for the first time, Candy wished that Reed were around. Bette always behaved better when Reed was around, like if she played the good mommy card, he'd totally forget that she'd abandoned him in his formative years.

'Hey Bette, I've seen Dad. He's being majorly weird,' Candy bitched as she burst through the door without knocking, which she really should have, because Bette was wrapped in a steamy clinch with some guy in a suit that made Candy's own shenanigans on certain tables look like a Sunday School outing.

Chapter Twenty-Seven

'How could you?' Candy heard herself say once again. And once again there was no reply, just a tiny squeak from Bette and a muffled curse from the man, who jack-knifed off the bed so he could grab Candy, haul her into the room and slam the door behind her.

'Baby, sweetie, honey, it's not what it looks like,' Bette said frantically as Candy wriggled in the suited jerk's firm grip.

'Oh my God, do your buttons up,' Candy hissed, finally wrenching free. 'You're disgusting!'

And it was exactly what it looked like, and all the oddities were becoming clear; David hitting the narcotics and his voice getting caustic when he talked about Bette. The way that Bette had mysteriously disappeared to either Napa or Maui when Candy had literally been on her death-bed and . . .

'Oh! Oh! Oh! I was wondering why Conceptua wasn't here, 'cause she adores Dad and it's because she found out and you sacked her!' Candy squawked.

'I did not!' Bette flung back. 'She got all religious and weird and she walked out.'

'Well, why did she get all religious and weird if "this isn't what it looks like"?' Candy air-quoted so furiously that she nearly poked her eye out. 'And who the hell is *this*?'

Bette visibly gulped. 'Candy, you know Nick de Laurentis, he's head of the network.'

Candy didn't know Nick de Laurentis, though they were going to be having words, but he was holding out a hand, which she pointedly ignored. 'We have met before,' he said smoothly, with a smile that Candy didn't like one little bit. 'At pre-season launches and the like, but you have to meet and greet so many people at those things that I won't be offended that you don't remember me.'

That was big of him, but even Candy knew that you didn't get lippy with the guy who signed each season's renewal notice, even if he was screwing your mom behind your dad's back. She settled for a terse 'What*ever*.'

Nick de Laurentis, who Candy hated more than anyone she'd ever hated in her life, which was really saying something, narrowed his eyes. 'Now, Candy,' he said in a patronizing voice. 'We all need to act like grown-ups about this.'

'Since when has she ever acted like a grown-up about anything,' Candy asked viciously, pleased when Bette flinched at her words. 'How long had it been going on?'

Bette wouldn't look at her, but Nick sat back down on the bed and crossed his legs. 'Over a year,' he said, as calm as could be. 'Obviously, we've had to be discreet, but your mother and I are in a serious relationship.'

'Well, isn't that just peachy for the pair of you?' Candy paced angrily, but there wasn't much room and she wanted to give the two adulterers a wide berth. 'No wonder you won't release the footage of my father ODing, you want to use it as blackmail in case he tells everyone what a lying, deceitful pair of fuckers you two are!'

'Darling, please . . .' Bette stretched a hand towards her and then thought better of it, which was the first good idea she'd had. The mood Candy was in, Bette was lucky that she didn't tear her limb from limb.

'*At Home With The Careless* is all about family values in a modern setting,' Nick said, like he was reciting facts from a press release. 'The footage is safest with me. It's not in anybody's best interests to do anything rash that might impact on the viewing figures.'

Candy felt like throwing up all over his stupid, pretentious shoes. 'You really are an absolute bastard, aren't you?' she asked rhetorically, but she already knew it was going to be impossible to get a rise out of the reptilian Nick. 'Congratulations, Bette, you really know how to pick them.'

It was an exit line because if Candy stayed there, sharing oxygen with the two of them a second longer, she'd totally explode.

But she hadn't even taken two steps out of the door when Bette caught up with her. 'Sweetie, I know this is a bit of a shock, but you can't just go storming off like this.' Bette tried to touch Candy, hug her, but Candy slapped her hands away.

'Leave me alone,' she snapped. 'You make me sick and I can't stand to be around you.'

Since when did Bette ever listen to a single thing that Candy said? 'Look, I know it all seems like the end of the world right now, but you'll see that it's for the best. David and I, we love each other, but we're not *in* love with each other, baby. And I have needs . . .'

'Oh my God! Will you please stop talking?'

'Candy does have a point, darling,' said a crisp voice behind them, and Candy whirled round to see Mimi standing there, swathed in a fur coat and her ubiquitous dark glasses.

'Did you know about this?' she demanded.

'Candy kinda walked in on me and Nick,' Bette hastily explained, and the solemnity of the occasion merited the removal of Mimi's shades.

'Oh dear,' Mimi said succinctly. 'I knew this wouldn't end well.'

It stood to reason that Mimi and Bette were in cahoots about this – they went back a long way. Even further back than Bette and David. 'I'm sorry that my colossal upset is such an inconvenience to everyone,' Candy sniped. 'Is there anyone, apart from me, who doesn't know?'

Mimi and Bette exchanged a look that Candy longed to rip off their faces. 'Well, David does and he said that he was cool with it. But Reed doesn't know,' Bette said urgently. 'I didn't want to bother him, with the engagement and the movie and everything.'

'How very noble of you,' Candy sneered, because she couldn't lose the attitude for one moment. The attitude was all that was between her and the floor, where she wanted to lie in a sobbing heap.

Mimi took Candy's arm and pulled her into an alcove

where they wouldn't attract quite so much attention from the hospital staff. 'Amusing as your hissy fits are, Candy, you need to put this one on hold and help us come up with a plan B.'

'What do you mean?' Candy asked sullenly, because she was more than the sum of her hissy fits and she had a right to be pissed as hell.

'We're halfway through filming the current series and it's too much strain on David. I really thought he was cool with everything,' Bette blurted out, like she actually gave a damn. 'Filming for hours on end, and he really needs some time and space to get well . . .'

'. . . and not have you and that . . . that creep rubbing your sordid affair in his face,' Candy finished for her. 'Well, what do you want me to do about it?'

'If you came home,' Bette began carefully. 'Had more camera time, like you used to, it would take the pressure off of everyone. And then we can come up with a proper solution for the next series.'

The next series? Candy felt exhausted at the mere thought of it. Yeah, the show had saved their flagging fortunes, but it had also destroyed them in the process. Not that they weren't all a little broken to start off with.

'I don't even want to do another series, neither does David, and I don't care if this series gets pulled halfway through,' Candy said hotly because it was the truth. 'You signed the contract, not me, so your boyfriend can take *you* to court. In the eyes of the law, I'm still a minor.'

Even Mimi managed to crack a facial expression after

that bombshell. 'You can't,' she said firmly. 'Not if you want to keep all your endorsements – and what about David, Candy? He needs you right now. Any more upsets and I dread to think what he might do.'

It was meant to be the winning argument that would bring Candy back on side. But she was done being the designated adult while Bette and David lived out their teen psycho-dramas and expected everyone else to deal.

No,' she said, shaking her head. 'Screw this, I'm going home.'

Candy didn't go home. Mainly because there were camera crews camped around the block. Kris had already booked her a junior suite at Hotel Gansevoort, and the manager met her at the goods entrance and personally escorted her through the kitchen so she could go up in the service elevator.

She wasn't expecting to sleep, but the moment Candy's head touched the extravagantly plush pillow she was comatose.

Twelve hours of sleep got rid of the dark circles under her eyes, but it did nothing to put Candy in a better mood. She'd had two seconds of well-rested bliss when she first woke up, and then the events of the last forty-eight hours all rushed in, clamouring to be heard.

About the only good thing was a message from Reed on her voicemail, when she checked her iPhone on the way to the hospital.

'Why didn't you call me?' he demanded. '*The Sun* started

ringing at four in the morning, your phone was off and then two hours later there you are on the news, heading to the airport with a police escort.' Then he sighed. A long, heartfelt sigh, which Candy didn't know how to decipher. 'You really don't get the brother/sister thing, do you?' Reed murmured. 'It means that we can throw horrible accusations around and even try to kill each other, but we're still brother and sister. And that means that we're there for each other when the going gets really rough. It's a pretty cool arrangement.'

Candy nodded in agreement. It really was. 'I'm going to LA tonight but please call me. And if you need me to come to New York, you know I will. You only have to ask. OK, then. We'll speak soon. And I love you, Cands.'

There was absolutely no way she was calling Reed, Candy thought as she tried to swallow past the lump in her throat. The moment she heard his throaty purr, she'd be bawling her eyes out. She had to . . . No, she could get through this on her own.

Although when she came out of the hospital elevator and saw Bette and Mimi waiting for her with approving smiles, Candy wanted to run in the opposite direction. Reed had been right when he said that being part of a family was for keeps. No matter how pissed she was at her parents, they were still family. Though she wished they were more like Alfie's family, but that was asking for the impossible.

'Good girl,' Mimi noted. 'Bette and David both need you, Candy. You're the glue that holds the Careless clan together.'

Candy had been compared to many things in her time, but never a tube of Bostik. She pulled a face as she let Mimi and Bette tug her down the corridor towards David's room.

'We're going to have a little summit with David,' Mimi explained smoothly. 'See how we're going to fit his recovery around the shooting schedule.'

'OK, but that should be between the three of us. Like, immediate family only,' Candy pointed out because there was stuff she wanted to say to her so-called primary care-givers. 'And actually, Mimi, you're not. No offence.'

'I'm your agent,' Mimi said implacably, as if that settled it. It didn't, but as she opened the door to David's room, Nick de Laurentis was already striding purposefully towards them and maybe Mimi's presence might be helpful.

Then again, maybe not. 'I'm not going to rehab and I'm not going to finish the series,' David gritted out again, curiously dignified in his patterned hospital gown.

'But you promised!' Bette pleaded, finally inching forward from the far corner of the room so she could perch on the bed. All the better to give David her best wounded stare. 'It's what we both wanted.'

'No, it's what you wanted, and I'm done with trying to make you happy because, baby, it's an impossible task. You'll never be happy, Bette. You always want what you haven't got.'

Candy felt strangely detached from the surroundings as

she sprawled in an easy chair. It was like watching an episode of *At Home With The Careless* and at the eleventh hour, David would cave and Bette would have her way, whether it was getting another mange-ridden cat or going to Reykjavik for Christmas or David being sent to Utah to do the twelve steps.

'Sweetie,' Bette cooed, covering David's pale hand with her own. 'You know I care about you and I want you to get well again and—'

'The only thing you care about is trying to resurrect your flagging career and clinging on to the last vestiges of youth,' David flung back caustically, snatching his hand away. 'It's the only reason you're shtupping him.'

'No, David, not the only reason,' Nick de Laurentis said coolly as he lounged against the wall. 'But let's not go off-message.'

'Y'know, maybe you two should have some alone time,' Candy said, standing up and hoping that Mimi and that bastard in the suit would take the hint. They didn't, and all of a sudden she had her parents' undivided attention. Which was a novel experience.

'Candy,' Bette sighed. 'Please try and talk to your father.'

'Well, there has to be a cool rehab place somewhere,' Candy hedged. 'One that isn't all hand-holding and singing "Kumbayah" . . .'

'Do you want to know where Bette was when you were flu-ridden?' David barked. 'She was holed up in Maui with him . . .'

It wasn't a newsflash. Candy had worked that out all by

herself, but it still hurt that Bette had been so busy arranging her secret shag-a-thon that even her only daughter was on the No Contact list. And then she felt another, bigger pang because this completely gross affair with Nick de Laurentis might actually be a permanent thing.

But Bette was blushing, which had to be a first. 'You've never minded before,' she hissed furtively, like everyone else in the room couldn't hear.

'Because they were just flings, one-night stands with pretty boys so you could kid yourself that you still had it,' David said savagely and it was like he'd had a total personality do-over. Sweet, gentle, befuddled David had left the building. 'Guess you finally decided to upgrade.'

'Why don't I take Candy off to get some coffee?' Mimi suggested calmly from the sidelines.

Candy was already halfway to the door without a backward glance when Bette's voice hauled her back.

'Well, no wonder I look for love with other people,' she suddenly screamed in a register Candy didn't know she could achieve. 'The only thing you love is drugs. When I first met you I thought you were dangerous and exciting, but now you're just a worn-out cliché. I've been propping you up for years!'

'Not propping, darling, sucking me dry!' David shouted back. 'I should have sent you back to Long Island a week after you decided to move in with me.'

'I wish you had.'

Mimi's hand was suddenly on Candy's shoulder, propelling her firmly towards the door as her face started to crumple. If Bette had gone back to Long Island, then Candy wouldn't have existed. There'd be a world without Candy Careless in it. And neither Bette nor David seemed that cut up about it.

'Candy, sweetie, he's probably got a tonne of drugs still coursing through his veins, and Bette's upset,' Mimi said soothingly as she shut the door firmly behind them. But the door wasn't thick enough to muffle the sounds of fighting.

'Oh God, they hate each other!' Candy moaned, cannoning off the wall when Mimi took her hand away. 'How can that be possible? They're meant to be the poster children for love against all the odds. And she's been having affairs and he's let her . . . It's beyond revolting.'

'Relationships are complicated,' Mimi muttered, and she should have known. She'd been married four times and was currently living with a Swiss banker called Gustav. 'Sometimes the people you love aren't necessarily the people who are the best for you.'

'I swear, I'm staying single for ever,' Candy vowed. Mimi simply smiled and arched a disbelieving eyebrow. 'I mean it. Seems to me that love is just an excuse to pull out someone's heart and grind it to dust.'

They turned a corner and, by unspoken agreement, came to a halt. Candy slid down the wall until she was sitting on the floor and hugging her knees. 'Tell me it was just an argument, Mimi,' she said softly. 'And they'll forgive each other for the drugs and the screwing around and we'll go back to being a slightly dysfunctional family again.'

Mimi didn't say anything for quite a while. Then she reached down and patted Candy's cheek in a very unMimi-like gesture. 'Stay here and I'll come and get you when things have calmed down.'

Half an hour later when Candy walked back into the room, David was white-faced and thin-lipped with anger while Bette was staring out of the window, her fingers drumming impatiently on the sill.

'It's all been decided,' Mimi explained briskly, like their heart-to-heart earlier had never happened. 'Candy will move back to New York . . .'

'Just hang on a second, you can't just announce something like that without even discussing it with me, and expect it to be cool.'

Nick de Laurentis straightened his tie. 'You're still under contract for another two months. Her birthday's on February fourteenth, right, Mimi?'

Mimi nodded and tried to stretch her mouth into a comforting smile. 'It's two months out of your entire life, Candy. That's really not such a big deal, is it?'

Actually, it really was. Candy cast a look at David and Bette, who were both trapped in their own, quietly furious worlds. 'Well, are either of you going to say anything?'

Bette turned and stabbed a rigid finger in David's direction. 'I will not be in the same room as that man without you there to act as a buffer,' she ground out. 'You should have heard the things he said to me.'

'Truth hurts, doesn't it, darling?' David purred. He shot an angry look at Nick de Laurentis, who smiled thinly.

'That bastard's threatening to sue me if I quit. He's had my wife and now he wants my bank account too. And if I have to see this mess through to the end, then you're going to be there to make sure I don't end up strangling your darling mother. Fun times, eh, baby girl?'

It hadn't been an argument before. It had been the irrevocable breakdown of her parent's marriage, which seemed like it had been crumbling for months anyway. And they wanted Candy there to witness it going through its final death throes? Not fucking likely . . .

Chapter Twenty-Eight

Candy had been back in London for two days and trapped in the flat the entire time as there were still hordes of paparazzi camped outside.

Mimi and Bette had been phoning hourly but Candy let the calls roll over to voicemail, and Nick de Laurentis had had a lawyer's letter delivered ordering her back to New York ready to start filming, which had sent the news crews outside into an orgiastic frenzy. The only person she hadn't heard from was her dad. She knew that he'd left the hospital because she'd seen it on the news, but he was annoyingly silent. Or maybe he'd been shipped off to rehab, and Candy remembered from last time that they weren't allowed to contact the outside world for the first two weeks.

But the outside world was completely overrated. And even though Candy was under virtual house arrest, she was kinda glad that she didn't have to go outside. London was cold and grey and wet, and had seemed like that for weeks, and as long as she could find a supermarket that would deliver and the TV was still working, there didn't seem to be much reason to ever set foot outside again. Especially as there was an Alfie somewhere in London that she might bump into. *Urgh*, so not going there.

It was just too much to deal with. And there was tonnes

of stuff on the Sky+ box that she'd never got round to watching.

Candy was interrupted three hours into her non-stop *Supernatural* marathon by the doorbell ringing. And ringing. And ringing. Which was odd, because the paparazzi had stopped doing that after Candy had opened the living-room window and chucked a bucket of cold water over them.

Candy climbed off the sofa, put her biggest dark glasses on, and opened the window. 'Quit ringing the bell, or I'm calling the cops,' she screamed.

There was the usual motley crowd of rat-faced guys in puffa jackets and woolly hats, all drinking coffee from Al's Turkish café on the corner. And there was also a ragged-looking guy wearing jeans and a sweater who made Candy nearly fall out of the window in shock.

'Do you think you could come down and answer the door?' he called up. 'I'm in the midst of a major crisis and I'd rather not shout out the details, thank you very much.'

And spitting out every single permutation of swearwords that she knew, Candy went downstairs to let Alfie in.

'Jeans,' was all Candy could say as Alfie fought his way to the open door. 'You're wearing jeans.'

'Yes, on the weekends, I wear jeans,' Alfie panted because he was carrying a heavy box. 'Don't just stand there, move!'

Candy told herself that it was only because Alfie had caught her off-guard that she stepped aside without an argument, but when three guys tried to follow him in, she

258

yelped in alarm and tried to block their way.

'This sewing machine weighs a bloody tonne,' one of them complained, which was odd and random.

'They're with me.' Alfie called over his shoulder as he climbed the stairs.

'Who are your mates, Candy? You dating any of them?' one of the photographers called out as the last boy, carrying several garment bags and boxes, squeezed into the hall.

The photographer actually dared to wedge his foot in the open door. 'Piss off,' Candy squealed and took great delight in shoving the door as hard as she could so the man had no choice but to jump back while his foot was still attached to his ankle. Then she looked helplessly up the stairs after the boys, who seemed to be carrying the contents of a haberdashery shop between them.

As for Alfie? In jeans! Why was he constantly sending Candy into a headspin? She could know him for a couple of centuries and he'd still be able to surprise her.

Candy trudged up the stairs, painfully aware of her ragged hair, bare face and . . .

'Why are you still wearing your pyjamas?' Alfie asked as Candy stepped through the door. 'It's afternoon, Candy! And why have they got pumpkins all over them?'

'Because I bought them last Halloween,' Candy explained absently, and then she crossed her arms over her chest and tried to glare. It wasn't her best effort. 'How dare you barge in like this?'

'I'm Ravi,' one of the boys said, on his knees as he plugged in the sewing machine. 'Alfie's cousin.'

'I'm Khalid, Alfie's cousin's best mate.'

'And I'm Ben, no relation. Alfie and I were at college together,' the last one said, throwing a box down on the coffee table. 'Can I have your autograph for my mum?'

If there weren't pins on the floor, because there were always pins on the floor, Candy would have stamped her foot. She tried again. 'What are you doing here?'

'I have a fashion show on Monday, it's Saturday afternoon, everything is half finished and I had it on good authority from Pretty, who's been glued to *MTV News*, that you have nothing on right now,' Alfie said lightly enough, but there was a bite to his voice which might have been annoyance that Candy had been non-wordy, though it was more likely panic.

'What fashion show? What's going on?' Candy growled, and she didn't appreciate the three-way smirking action from Alfie's mates like she was being small and irritable on purpose.

Alfie waved a vague hand about. 'I've been working on my own line, I'm sure I told you.'

'No, it didn't come up,' Candy gritted, because, actually Alfie never, ever volunteered anything in the way of personal and useful information.

'Well, I'm telling you now and as I always help you out of tight spots, I thought you could return the favour.'

'What do you mean by *always*?' Candy snapped. 'Stop making out like I'm some kind of needy damsel in distress.'

Alfie smiled obliquely, which was really annoying. 'Well, maybe not damsel, but you're constantly in distress. There was the time I got you some food at that exhibition before you fainted, and there was the time you were ill and I made you soup and you threw up all over me, and you didn't know how to do pin tucks until I showed you.'

Candy screwed up her fists into tiny, impotent weapons. 'Stop twisting things around to make out like you're some knight in a bespoke suit, because not even!'

Ravi coughed pointedly. 'Do you two want to be alone?' he asked drily, and he kind of had a point because Alfie and Candy were bickering like an old married couple, and Candy hadn't had so much fun since . . . well, she could hardly remember when.

'You should probably get washed and dressed,' Alfie advised calmly. 'And stick the kettle on. I hope you have plenty of food because we're going to have to work round the clock.'

'I still haven't said that I'm going to help you,' Candy grumbled, already heading towards the bathroom. Then she had a thought that merited sticking her head around the doorway again. 'There's no food. I've been living on rice cakes and peanut butter, which leaves a really gross gritty aftertaste, so could someone go to the supermarket?'

An hour later, Candy was sitting cross-legged on the living-room floor dressed in jeans and a cute little jumper Conceptua had knitted, her hair pulled back in two bunches. Putting on make-up would have been way too obvious, but at least she was clean.

Ben, Ravi and Khalid had left, but they had gone on a

mercy dash to Sainsbury's first to purchase emergency supplies of chocolate HobNobs, Diet Coke, Hula Hoops and some ready meals. Alfie had also insisted on some fruit and salad, because he said he didn't intend to get rickets over the weekend.

And now it was just the two of them. Candy guessed they were going to have The Big Talk™, but Alfie simply started to unpack garments from a plastic storage container.

Candy stared in awe as he produced little black dresses with linings and trims made from stinging pinks and oranges. Nipped-in jackets lined in brilliant reds and yellows, and skirts teamed with fine little knits in acid greens and electric blues. She'd have worn every single piece, and Candy was pretty discerning when it came to matters of fashion.

'They're beautiful,' she breathed reverently, holding up a high-waisted, grey pencil skirt shot through with pink glittery thread. If anyone else had tried it, it would have come across as tacky, but Alfie's designs were so subtle and his tailoring so expert that it worked. It shouldn't have done, but it so did.

Alfie looked pleased. 'You inspired the collection,' he admitted casually. 'That day we ended up in Dalston and you wanted to go into the sari shop. And when you complained about how uncomfortable your dress was at the exhibition, it made me think about construction in a different way.'

Now it was Candy's turn to pink up. She'd never inspired anyone in a positive way before. Though after they'd broken up, Jacob had written a song called 'Absurd Media Creation'. 'For real?' she asked doubtfully.

'For real,' Alfie confirmed. 'And you wear a lot of vintage, and so I started to think about looking at vintage clothes with a modern perspective and a cultural twist, but without going down the whole Bollywood route . . .'

'Because it's so five years ago,' Candy finished for him. There were so many things she wanted to say to Alfie, but she decided to start with the most urgent. 'So what needs doing first?' Everything else could wait until later.

Chapter Twenty-Nine

It turned out that the most mundane, mind-numbing sewing really helped to take Candy's mind off things. It was quite hard to angst about her parent's marriage disappearing down the crapper when she was sewing on buttons, and over-locking seams, and knowing full well that Alfie would make her do them again if they didn't come up to scratch.

They kept the conversation light and inconsequential. What Candy had done in Shanghai, the latest in the Tanner family saga, gossip from Nico's – and that kept Candy's mind off things too. Because she'd forgotten how funny Alfie could be. Not just funny peculiar but funny ha-ha too, with a sense of humour as dry as a pickled gherkin. He'd drawl out some acid observation and Candy would snort with laughter. And if Candy didn't get to say what she wanted to say, which mostly started with, 'Look, I'm sorry' and 'What the hell is up with you sometimes?' then that was OK because she wouldn't have swapped this easy banter for all the couture gowns in Paris.

It was well past midnight and Candy had little white spots dancing in front of her eyes as she delicately and painstakingly sewed minute pink beads on to a dress. She groaned in appreciation as she stretched her tired muscles. Alfie looked up and smiled in sympathy.

'I feel like I have a lead weight tied to the back of my neck,' he said, shifting so his back rested against the sofa. 'And I think my fingers are about to seize up.'

Candy glanced over at the to-do pile, which didn't seem any smaller even though they'd been working steadily for the last nine hours. 'Shall we take a food break? Get our energy levels back up?'

Alfie nodded. 'I Just want to finish this seam. Why don't you go and put the kettle on?'

'Jesus, Alfie, how much tea do you drink in one day?' Candy mocked. 'I think you have Darjeeling running through your veins instead of blood.'

Candy was dunking the teabag eleven times, just as Alfie liked it, when her phone rang. It was the phone that had replaced the phone that had just been replaced because the press had managed to trace the number. Only five people had her new number and Reed was the only one that she wanted to talk to.

For a second she debated switching it off, but since Alfie had been here, Candy felt less bruised. Stronger. Able to deal with whatever crap was about to be thrown at her.

'Hi,' she said unenthusiastically.

'Candy? It's Nick de Laurentis here.'

She should have stood by her first instinct and not answered. 'What the hell do you want?'

'You in New York by Tuesday morning at the latest,' he supplied silkily. 'We need to start filming again and both your mother and father are refusing to get in front of the cameras without you there.'

'That's not my problem,' she hissed furiously, one eye on the open door in case Alfie suddenly appeared. 'I told you already, if they're not together any more then I'm not going to be part of some bullshit happy families conspiracy. Cancel the fucking show already!'

'Now, Candy, you know I can't do that, dear,' he said condescendingly, like she was eight and refusing to eat all her greens. 'There are contracts in place, syndication deals, I won't bore you with all the details. Suffice to say, that Bette and David are on board and you need to jump on too.'

'Don't have to do shit,' Candy snapped, and damn, her voice was starting to tremble though she wouldn't give him the satisfaction of making her cry. 'I never signed a contract, so you can sue my mom instead.'

'You really do think I'm a bastard, don't you?' he chuckled. 'I wouldn't sue Bette obviously, but David did have a clause in his contract about staying drug and alcohol free. It would be a terrible pity if someone just happened to leak his medical records to *The New York Post*.'

'You wouldn't fucking dare!' Candy gasped.

'Just try me, kid,' Nick de Laurentis challenged grimly. 'I want your ass back in New York on Tuesday.'

He hung up and Candy realized that she'd been making tea on auto-pilot, so she had two mugs the perfect shade of American tan tights in front of her, and that Alfie was standing in the doorway, though Candy didn't know how long he'd been there.

He gave her a thoughtful look. 'Are you all right?'

It was the first time that anyone had asked Candy that in a long, long time and it very nearly broke her. She didn't answer immediately, it took a few moments before she said, 'I'm fine,' in a voice that was just about steady.

As Candy handed Alfie his tea, he gave her a sidelong glance like he didn't think she was at all fine, but he didn't say anything, just followed her back into the living room.

The easy chit chat of before was gone. Candy couldn't trust herself to speak, and all the bad shit and worry was back in her head and chasing around in endless circles. 'Are you sure you're all right, Candy?' Alfie asked softly.

She shook her head swiftly.

'Is that a yes or a no.'

'It's a "I don't want to talk about it",' Candy rasped. 'Can't talk about it.'

Alfie actually put down the dress he was working on. 'If you wanted to tell me, then it would be in the strictest confidence,' he said carefully. 'I wouldn't be on the phone to the Sunday papers. Just so you know.'

And that reminded Candy of the other thing that she really wished she could stop thinking about. 'I'm sorry,' she blurted out. 'For what I said after we . . . after that time when . . . I'm sorry I implied that you were the kind of person who'd do a kiss and tell. And I'm sorry that I said you were gay and wouldn't leave it be. I do that all the time. I run my mouth off and I never know when to stop.'

Tears were plopping on to the glass coffee table now, too many of them to rub away with her fingers. So Candy put her hands over her face to see if she could stem the flow that way instead. It didn't work so well and Alfie was sliding across the floor to rest one hand on her shoulder. He didn't do anything else, but his warm hand comforted her, anchored her, so she didn't feel like she was still freefalling.

'I keep calling you a freak,' Candy mumbled quietly so Alfie had to lean in close to catch each breathless word. 'But really I'm the freak. I never fitted it anywhere in my life and being famous has just made it worse. Like, my immense freakdom can't even be contained by my immense celebrity. And you're not a freak, Alfie.' It suddenly seemed very important that he knew that.

Alfie's hand resting on Candy's shoulder became an arm that pulled her closer, so he could give her a prolonged, if awkward, hug. 'Well, actually I think I am a freak,' he whispered in her ear. 'But I've learnt to embrace my freakdom. Maybe you should try it.'

'You're really not a freak,' Candy protested. 'I'm way more of a freak than you with my freaky family and my stupid freaky lifestyle. I should have the word tattooed on my forehead.'

'Only you would actually start getting competitive about which one of us was the biggest freak,' Alfie said, but he didn't sound as if he minded that much.

'What happened in Milan?' Candy asked, though when she'd first opened her mouth it was to find out why the kissing had gone from wonderful to weird in the time it took for a box of pins to fall on the floor. But she wasn't altogether sure that she wanted to know the answer.

Alfie wriggled away from Candy so he could rest his back against the sofa again, but before she could start to feel completely rejected, he coaxed her over so they were sitting side by side. 'It was such a great opportunity,' he mused. 'But I hated it from the moment I got there. It was so disorganized and everyone rolled in for work when they felt like it and it was all long lunches and air kissing and I felt like I wasn't learning anything. Also, everyone wore loafers and white jeans.'

It sounded like Alfie's very own personal hell. And Candy could empathize. 'People who wear white jeans and loafers should be shot,' she said sourly, because she had a strong feeling that Nick de Laurentis wore white jeans and loafers when he was poncing about the Hamptons in summer. 'Especially if they're not wearing socks.'

'Amen to that,' Alfie murmured. 'But it wasn't just that. I missed my family. Dreadfully. I know it's not cool to admit that, but there you are.'

'I think it's cool,' Candy argued, daring to rest her arm against Alfie's and wondering if he'd notice. 'Your family's so great. Like, you actually seem to get on.' And it was on the tip of her tongue to tell Alfie all about her white picket fence and home-baked apple pie fantasy, but she clamped her mouth shut just in time.

'What were you about to say?' Alfie asked curiously. 'You do that a lot. I can tell you're on the verge of spitting something out and then you go all silent and cross-eyed.'

'I do not go cross-eyed,' Candy snapped reflexively. But it was true. There were so many things she wanted to ask

Alfie. Like, f'rinstance: 'Do you regret kissing me?'

The moment that the words left her mouth, Candy wished she had a handy time machine so she could travel back five seconds and keep her piehole closed.

Now it was Alfie's turn to not say anything, but look as if the effort was killing him. Great. Way to kick her already bruised ego.

'You're six years younger than me,' Alfie muttered, as if that had anything to do with anything. 'And you don't even like me . . .'

'Are you kidding me?' Candy spluttered. 'I've had this totally debilitating crush on you ever since you looked after me when I was ill.' Her face was so red it had to be visible from Mars. 'God, I swear I have Tourette's.'

'Well, you didn't act like you had a crush on me,' Alfie pointed out. 'Quite the opposite.' He moved a fraction of an inch so they weren't touching any more and Candy didn't know whether she wanted to hit him or hug him.

'That's because I thought you were gay!' she practically screamed. And it was so ridiculously melodramatic, like every single other thing in her life, that she started to laugh. It was hard to hear anything over her own giggles as she mopped at the tears that were streaming down her face, but then Alfie said, 'You win, you're definitely a much bigger freak than I am,' and he sounded so put out about it that it just made Candy howl that bit harder.

Alfie probably only kissed Candy to shut her up, but as soon as his lips descended, Candy felt as if everything that had happened between this time and the last time didn't matter. Life could simply be divided into kissing Alfie and not kissing Alfie.

It was a lot like coming home. This time, they knew how to arrange their lips and their limbs for optimum comfort. Alfie knew that when he stroked his thumbs into the hollows under Candy's ears, it made her wriggle. And Candy knew that Alfie made an almost-purring sound in the back of his throat when she lightly scratched the back of his neck.

They weren't kisses that were going to lead anywhere. It was late and they were both stupid with tiredness and they both knew that shucking off their clothes and getting seriously horizontal would be madness when there were still so many things unsaid between them. Besides, there were pins and needles and sharp-bladed instruments all over the floor and Candy, for one, didn't fancy getting pierced in unpleasant places.

The kisses got shorter and shorter, until Candy was just resting her head against Alfie's cheek. His arms tightened around her and, for someone so bony, he made a very comfortable leaning post. 'You know my offer still stands any time,' he whispered in her ear. 'You can tell me anything and it stays with me.'

'I know,' Candy whispered back, reaching up to press her lips against the corner of his mouth. 'But don't get mad at me if I can't.'

Alfie didn't say anything, but he worked Candy's hair loose from its bunches and stroked soothing circles on her aching scalp, so maybe he understood. 'Don't go to sleep, we still have tonnes of work to do, if we want to stay on schedule.'

Candy yawned and snuggled closer. Alfie smelt really good, like tea and spices and tailor's chalk. 'In a minute,' she mumbled, stifling another yawn. 'Another minute won't hurt.'

Chapter Thirty

Candy blearily opened her eyes as Alfie sat up, yawned and dislodged her from where she'd been doing a good impersonation of his very own eiderdown. 'I heard the street door,' he grunted. 'What time is it? Why is it daylight?'

Candy squinted at the clock on the DVD player. 'Because it's ten in the morning and we've been asleep for hours.' She struggled upright on legs that didn't feel one hundred per cent steady and gingerly touched her hair. It felt very *sprouty* and she had that slightly skanky feeling that she always got when she'd gone to sleep with her clothes on.

'Oh no,' Alfie groaned. 'How can it be ten o'clock? How could we have slept so long?' He was really big with the rhetorical questions first thing in the morning. And if there was going to be a repeat of what happened last time . . . there were pins on the carpet that he could start picking up any second now.

But Alfie blearily smiled at Candy, and his hair was more rumpled than she'd ever seen it, and he had a faint dusting of stubble, which made him look both cute and dangerous. That flipping feeling was her heart doing a few somersaults. 'I'm going to start again,' he said with a rueful grin. 'Good morning, Candy.'

'Morning, Alfie.' Candy looked down at him knowingly. 'I'll put the kettle on, shall I?'

But before Candy could get to the kitchen, a key turned in the lock and Hadley's head peered cautiously round the front door. 'Oh, hi Candy,' she said tentatively. 'Do you mind if I come in?'

Candy quickly checked for possible signs of late-night debauchery and nodded just as tentatively. Had Hadley and Reed split up? That would be good on one level – not so good if Hadley was planning on moving back in.

Hadley didn't have suitcases with her though, just a couple of bulging supermarket bags. 'It took me fifteen minutes to get through the door. Honestly, I never thought I'd say this, but British paparazzi make the guys in LA look like princes.'

Candy raised her eyebrows and tried to angle her body so that Hadley couldn't see through her into the living room. Though she couldn't really imagine Alfie hiding behind the couch. 'Yup, hence the hostage situation.'

'That's why I brought supplies,' Hadley said, holding up the bags. 'I got soup, because it's super-nutritious and you can just nuke it in the microwave. Diet Coke, wheatgrass juice, soy milk, rice cakes . . .' If Ben, Ravi and Khalid hadn't already done the supermarket thing, Candy would have starved for sure if it were left to Hadley.

Hadley was still delving. 'I also got you those Thai spicy bites that you like and chocolate HobNobs.' She gave Candy another wary look. 'I know you like the milk chocolate ones but I got the dark chocolate ones because they're much better for you. Oooh! And the new *Vogue Italia*, it has a shoe supplement.'

Candy blinked slowly. Actually Hadley's shopping hadn't totally sucked and she'd remembered three of Candy's all-time favourite things. Which was thoughtful and touching, especially as Candy really didn't deserve anything approaching kindness from Hadley. 'Um, thanks,' Candy muttered, like the ungrateful wretch that she really and truly was.

'No problem. Reed's worried about you.' Hadley looked torn, like she wanted to get out of Candy's immediate vicinity before things inevitably got nasty, but she had to make sure that Candy hadn't slit her wrists in a warm bath because Reed might be quite pissed about that. 'Are you all right, Candy? Like, really all right?' Hadley was a much better actress than Candy had ever given her credit for – she sounded like she almost cared.

'It'd be nice to get some fresh air, but apart from that I'm just peachy,' Candy assured her.

'Hmmm.' Hadley tilted her head and gave Candy a sceptical look. 'Well, you don't . . . Oh, who are *you*?' she squeaked at the exact moment that Candy felt two hands descend on her shoulders.

'I'm Alfie,' he said equably. 'Who are you?'

Hadley looked faintly disgruntled, like Alfie was purposely not getting a clue because he thought he was too cool to recognize ex-child stars. 'Hadders, he really doesn't know who you are,' Candy interjected. 'He's lousy on popular culture. Thinks Cobra Starship are something to do with NASA.'

'I'm Hadley. I'm a very well-known celebrity,' Hadley explained without even a drop of irony. 'And I'm engaged to Reed, Candy's half-brother.'

Candy desperately wished she could see Alfie's face, though she could feel his fingers flexing frantically. 'I'm Alfie. I'm an obscure fashion designer,' he deadpanned. 'And . . . Candy and I? Colleagues?' he asked Candy, like he wasn't sure if he was on- or off-message.

'Friends,' Candy stated firmly. 'Close friends?'

'Oh, I think so, don't you?' And then Alfie did the unthinkable and placed a brief kiss on the top of Candy's head as he shunted her out of the way. 'I suppose I'll have to put the kettle on myself.'

'What's going on?' Hadley demanded in a stage-whisper. 'Did he stay the night?' She looked over Candy's shoulder into the lounge, which resembled *Project Runway* midway through a challenge. 'Something's not right here, I'm very sensitive to these things. Oooh! That dress would look perfect on me!'

Hadley pushed Candy out of the way so she could get to the object of her affections, one of the black dresses lined with sari fabric, and Candy thanked God that Hadley was, like, the poster girl for ADD. Candy's mental health was completely forgotten as Hadley picked up half-finished garments and squawked excitedly.

'She's like a great big, hysterical puppy,' Alfie decided, coming up behind Candy again. 'Do you think she'd like a cuppa?'

It looked like Hadley wasn't going anywhere. 'She'll

have either a green tea or a Chai latte,' Candy sighed.

When Alfie and Candy walked back into the living room, Hadley had one of the pencil skirts on over her skinny jeans and offered there and then to buy the entire collection. 'Like, seriously,' she said, rummaging in her Balenciaga bag. 'Do you take American Express?'

Alfie was staring at Hadley like she was a fat guy in a Santa outfit. 'You want to buy them?' he asked incredulously. 'All of them?'

'Yuh-huh! Every single piece here makes me look like I have actual curves,' Hadley enthused. 'And if you could make me this dress in white instead of black, then it would totally rip up the red carpet.'

Every time Hadley opened her mouth, it made Candy like her just a little bit more. 'These aren't for sale right now, Hads,' Candy said gently. 'Alfie's showing them on Monday night then he'll make up everything for you in the right size. But he's not cheap.'

Hadley nodded. 'I don't really like cheap,' she confessed. 'It usually brings me out in a nasty rash.'

Candy let herself take a breath out. Hadley had been successfully diverted from asking any awkward questions and now the three of them were happily chattering away about all things fashion. Candy picked up the skirt she'd been working on the night before, retrieved her threaded needle from the pincushion on the coffee table and started attaching the pink beads again.

'. . . the weird thing is that I just can't wear green on screen,' Hadley was telling Alfie, who she'd mistaken for a rapt audience. Candy decided that rapt was actually poleaxed. You didn't meet many girls like Hadley in Dalston. 'It completely washes me out, but off-screen, it really brings out the blue in my eyes.'

Alfie launched into a long, technical speech about exactly why that was, but Candy could see him casting anxious glances at the huge amount of fabric that still needed magic dust sprinkled all over it.

'Hadders, it was really sweet of you to come round, it really was.' Man, she sucked at sincerity, even when she was giving it her all. 'But me and Alfie have got a tonne of alterations to do . . .' Candy let her voice tail off to see if Hadley would change the habits of a lifetime and actually get a clue.

And yes, she was standing up. 'OK,' Hadley said brightly. 'Alfie, I was serious about buying the collection and I really need that pencil skirt as soon as it comes off the runway. Let me give you my digits.'

Candy was very proud of Alfie as he calmly took Hadley's measurements and jotted down a few notes, like selling his entire collection to a well-known celebrity was an everyday occurrence. Then Candy walked Hadley to the front door just to be polite and possibly so she could say thank you.

They were almost home and dry when Hadley clapped her hand to her forehead. 'Oh, there's something I forgot,' she squeaked. 'Something in the bathroom.' And she grabbed Candy's wrist and hauled her down the hall before Candy could protest.

The moment that the door shut behind them, Hadley let go of Candy and folded her arms. 'I know that we're not BFF but Reed asked me to check up on you,' she said with a grim determination that was just a little scary. 'He's all freaking out because he's worried about you and I wasn't sure if Alfie knows the score. He's a civilian, right?'

Maybe the one good thing about this whole ungodly situation was that Candy and Reed were friends again. But she'd managed all those years without Reed, and he had his own stuff going on – Candy couldn't expect him to babysit her for ever. 'I am fine, Hads, really,' she said.

'Well, you don't look fine,' Hadley said baldly. 'I always think you can tell what's going on with someone by the way their hair's holding up, and yours is looking really limp and lifeless.'

Candy tried to fluff her hair defensively. 'I had these stupid bunches in and then I slept funny and—'

'Reed told me what's going on with your folks,' Hadley said gently, sitting down on the edge of the tub. 'I've never liked Nick de Laurentis. He was assistant producer on *Hadley's House*, you know. I didn't trust him then and I was only nine.'

If Candy had been Hadley, she wouldn't have been able to resist digging the knife in and then giving it a few extra turns just for the sheer hell of it. But it had already been established that Hadley might actually be the better person here. 'There's nothing going on with my folks,' was all that Candy could think of to say.

'Oh, Candy, he *knows*. Not just about Bette and Nick, who've been seen together loads of times, but about your dad ODing, too. He's not stupid and he's really worried about you and I'm meant to report back. With bulletpoints,' Hadley stated, then she squared her shoulders. 'Look, we're not friends, so maybe it'd be easier to talk to me, because you don't care whether I'm judging you or not.' There was a brief pause. 'Which I wouldn't, by the way.'

Considering that logic was never Hadley's strong suit, what she was saying did make sense. Sort of. Candy shrugged. 'It's complicated.' But actually it wasn't. As Candy haltingly began to explain the events leading up to the hideous dilemma she found herself in, the facts were simple. She was being forced to play the grown-up because neither of her parents were cut out for that role. And much as she'd like to bail on them, she couldn't. When all was said and done, and you took David's drugginess and Bette's sluttiness out of the equation, they were still family. And families looked out for each other.

'So what are you going to do?' Hadley asked when Candy had got to the end of her tale of woe and despair.

'I'm going back to New York on Tuesday,' Candy replied. 'What else can I do? My dad needs me and I don't want him melting down on camera because I'm not there. Then when the series is over, I'll make him go to rehab and persuade Bette that we're done being America's First Family of Dysfunction.'

Hadley pursed her lips. 'You know, you could just cut them loose,' she suggested casually, like it wasn't the most

282

callous thing in the world ever. 'Sometimes you have to do what's right for you and stop worrying about everyone else. Doesn't make you a bad person, it just makes you mistress of your own destiny.'

Hadley was making sense again, which was starting to seriously freak Candy out. But not as much as the realization that Hadley totally got it. She *understood*. When it came to unhappy families, Hadley had seen it, done it and probably sold the film rights to the highest bidder. Her father had embezzled all the money she'd earned from a childhood spent on studio lots and her mother had rejected her when puberty had hit and Hadley's career had petered out. Compared to the Harlows, Bette and David were practically paragons of parental virtue.

'I know I should, Hadders, but I just can't,' Candy mumbled, fiddling with her toothbrush, then her toothpaste and finally her floss sticks until Hadley reached over to still her fidgeting hands.

'You're such a fake, Candy,' she said indignantly. 'You make out like you're a bad-ass, when really you're just a nice family-orientated girl.'

'I am not! Take that back right the hell now,' Candy hissed.

Hadley had the nerve to stick out her tongue. 'Shan't,' she smirked. Then her expression turned serious. 'I'm starting to get the whole dealio between you and Reed though. Not that it excuses the way you acted – you totally hurt my feelings.'

At least they were back on more familiar territory.

'Oh, whatever, Hadley. You're way tougher than you pretend. And you won in the end, so don't start giving me a hard time.'

'It wasn't a competition,' Hadley said stiffly. 'And we could have still been friends. Like, friends are the new family.'

Candy wondered whether Hadley had read that in a magazine or found it in a fortune cookie. It was just the kind of half-baked bullshit that always got a rise out of her. 'God, I hope not,' she drawled. 'Otherwise I'm doubly screwed.'

'You're so impossible,' Hadley lamented, as Candy moved towards the door. 'Have you got a copy of your contract for the show?'

Way to change the subject. 'Yeah, but the Fierce lawyer looked at it and he said that there was nothing doing.'

Hadley gave Candy a pitying look. 'Of course he said that. If you pull out the show, Fierce lose their commission. Like, duh!'

Candy could really have done without the condescension or the scathing comments when she eventually unearthed her crumpled legal documents from under her bed. Hadley took them from her between thumb and finger like they needed to be disinfected.

'I guess I should get going now,' she said. 'I think my work here is done. Bye, Alfie,' she added as she swanned past the living room on her way to the front door. 'I'll speak to you soon,' she said to Candy. 'But you could, like, call me if you needed to talk.'

And before Candy could spit out her usual piss and vinegar to show Hadley that she wasn't completely whipped, the other girl hugged her.

It was even worse than Alfie's hugs, which were markedly improving each time. Hadley hugged and flinched away from the body contact at the same time because her weirdy upbringing had left her with a severe case of cuddle deficiency syndrome. So Candy hugged her even harder and planted a big, sloppy kiss on Hadley's cheek for good measure.

'Thanks, Hadders,' she said, and actually meant it, when the other girl had managed to worm her way free. 'It really helped talking to you, not that I would ever admit that in front of witnesses.'

'I'm *so* telling Reed about you,' Hadley muttered darkly, as she opened the door. 'And I'm telling him you have a man stashed in here!'

And Hadley giggled all the way down the stairs, so Candy hoped that it was just her lame idea of a joke.

'That girl has got serious humour issues,' she announced as she walked back into the lounge, where Alfie was industriously beavering away on his sewing machine.

He looked up briefly and gave her a vague smile. 'Everything OK?'

'I guess,' Candy said tracing a pattern with her toe on the carpet. Was he talking about what had happened last night? Or did he mean the stuff that she wasn't ready to tell him? Or did he mean was she ever going to stop procrastinating and get back to work?

'Good. Can you finish up the pink beadwork and then start pressing cuffs and hems?'

Obviously he meant C.

Chapter Thirty-One

They worked mostly in silence for the rest of the day, apart from regular trips to the kitchen to stock up on tea, Diet Coke and chocolate HobNobs.

Unbelievably, it wasn't quite ten o'clock when Candy sewed on the last button. Five minutes later, Alfie finished the last seam and sat back with a satisfied grin.

'I never thought we'd get everything done,' he admitted ruefully. 'I thought we'd have to pull another all-nighter.'

Candy decided not to point out that yesterday's all-nighter had turned into sleeping in each other's arms, so she just pretended to shudder at the thought. 'That would suck,' she mumbled.

'There's just one last thing to do,' Alfie said, dropping to his knees and hunting through the debris on the floor. 'We still need to stitch in the labels.'

Candy stared at her fingers, which were a scratched-up, faintly bloody mess from all the times she'd cut and nicked herself. At one painful point during the afternoon, she'd managed to stab the sewing machine needle right through her finger. It had been the only time that they'd rowed, because Alfie had shouted at her and said that if she bled on the dress she was working on, he'd kill her. Candy had decided not to take it personally.

Now she sighed. 'Let's get them done super quick. And then, like, do you want to have a shower or are you going to head home . . . ?' All the things that had been put to one side while they worked were now making their presence felt.

Alfie sifted through the labels: elegant grey satin squares with *Alfie Tanner* embroidered on them in silver. 'I have to be up early tomorrow to take all the clothes to the venue and get them fitted on the models.'

Candy took the labels that Alfie was offering her. 'Seems silly to have to call a cab, cart the clothes home and then do it all again tomorrow. More chance for things to get creased, buttons to fall off, skirts go missing . . .' She didn't need to continue because Alfie was already looking bilious.

'I thought we'd be working right up until tomorrow morning, so I did bring a suit with me,' he confessed guiltily, like Candy should be surprised.

'Well, stay here then. There are three spare rooms and a sofa.' Candy might be an iconoclastic, popular culture anti-heroine but she wasn't going to third base with Alfie until they'd been dating for at least a month. Jeez, she was turning into Hadley. 'I think there's even clean sheets in the linen cupboard.'

That sealed the deal. 'OK,' Alfie nodded, carefully threading a needle. Candy always marvelled at how he could talk with sharp implements in his mouth. Once, she'd seen him drink a cup of tea while he had pins pursed between his lips. 'So what are you going to wear tomorrow night?'

Candy raised her eyebrows. 'I don't know. Whatever's not in the washing machine, I guess.'

Alfie gave her an offended look. 'You could wear the dress I made you, which you haven't even thanked me for by the way.'

'Alfie, you know I was dragged up and raised by wolves and all that shit,' Candy tried to mollify him. 'I loved the dress and it fitted perfectly. I don't even know how you figured out my measurements.'

It was Alfie's turn to raise his eyebrows. 'Don't you?'

'You've been checking me out?!'

'Well, yes, when I wasn't pretending to be gay,' Alfie said, as dry as a jar of olives. 'So you'll wear the dress at the show?'

He thought she was going to the show? Shit!

'I can't go,' Candy said helplessly. 'I mean, I want to, but I can't even get out of the front door to buy a pint of milk.' Alfie wasn't exactly making encouraging noises but Candy soldiered on. 'And the minute I do leave, they'll follow and, like, it was bad enough outside The Ivy that time. Now it will be like that, but to the power of a gazillion.'

'But I need you there,' Alfie stated simply, like that should be enough to change her mind. 'You can't let me down like this.'

'I'm not letting you down,' Candy huffed. 'You don't know what the press are like. They totally have their knives out for my family and the last thing you need is a lot of negative publicity by association. I'm thinking of you!'

'How very noble of you,' Alfie said sourly, and really he was the most temperamental person she'd ever met. His entire mood could change in the blink of an eye. 'Silly really, to think that you might be there to support me.'

If it were anyone else but Alfie trying to guilt-trip her, Candy would have slapped them upside their thick heads. And the fact that she wasn't was quite a surprise. 'I *want* to be there,' she wheedled, looking at Alfie from under her lashes in a way that was meant to be beguiling but probably looked retarded. 'Anyway, I have to go back to New York super early on Tuesday morning so I can't really stay out late on Monday.'

That was a proper excuse. That was a Get Out of Jail Free card. Transatlantic travel was a bulletproof explanation.

Alfie's fingers stilled. 'You're just leaving, after everything, after all this . . .' He sounded completely flat. 'When were you going to tell me?'

'Soon,' Candy lied, because she'd been hoping it wouldn't come up. If she didn't think about it, then she didn't have to deal with it. 'I have to go, it's all part of the thing that I can't talk about.'

'I knew it. I bloody knew it,' Alfie said softly, as if he were talking to himself. 'I knew it was a mistake getting involved with someone like you.'

'Someone like me?' Candy echoed. 'What the hell is that meant to mean?' She was certain there was a crack coming about people being famous just for being famous and having no discernible talent.

'You thrive on drama, Candy.' Alfie put down his sewing because obviously lecturing her on the error of her ways was far more important. 'I don't know what's going on because you haven't deigned to tell me, but I'm a hundred per cent certain that you've turned a slightly unpleasant situation into a three-act play—'

'I so haven't—'

'With a sub-plot and walk-on characters,' Alfie continued, warming to his theme as he got up so he could pace. 'You can't even walk down the street without it turning into a piece of performance art.'

'Oh my God!' Candy gritted. 'Have you even looked in a mirror lately? You dress like someone from a black-and-white movie.' She scrambled to her feet so she could halt Alfie in his tracks and grab his hands, but when she tried to entwine their fingers so they could kiss and make up, he pulled away from her. 'Look, Alfie, if it was any other time, I'd be there. Jesus, my dad's been in hospital and my mom's being even more crazy than usual. I kinda think that takes precedence.'

Alfie threw his hands up in despair. 'There's always going to be something that takes precedence because we all have drab little lives compared to you. You're the most self-involved person I've ever met and Christ knows I've had to fit enough models! It's a Candy Careless world and the rest of us just live in it,' he finished bitterly. 'Well, I don't need this!'

It was unbelievable. Alfie was the one boy in the world who was turned off by Candy's celebrity, rather than trying to hitch a ride off the back of it. Which should have been comforting. Except, it was the most infuriating thing ever, and he'd completely misjudged her. How many other famous people would have spent the last thirty-six hours hand-sewing and making cups of tea? Would Paris Hilton even know what to do with a tea bag? Hadley couldn't even use a microwave! Candy had tried being reasonable, which was always an effort, and now she was done.

'Get out!' she shrieked at a pitch only audible to bats. 'I never want to see you again!'

'Gladly,' Alfie hissed. 'I wouldn't want to contaminate your rarefied air with my civilian ways.' And with his nose in the air, he stalked majestically out of the flat.

Ten seconds later, there was a knock on the door. Candy yanked the door open, not even a little bit surprised to see Alfie standing there, still looking furious but embarrassed too. And so he should be; it was the most lame storming off that she'd ever witnessed.

'Yeah?' she demanded belligerently.

'I left the clothes here,' he said stiffly. 'I'll send Ravi and Ben round.'

'Whatever,' Candy spat, like she was far too important to be concerned with Alfie's courier needs. But she stood aside to let him in.

'So, I need your phone number to arrange a time to come and pick them up. If I'm allowed to have your phone number, not having a primetime TV show or a number one album,' Alfie remarked snidely, scooping up his bag and shoving a few things in it.

'Well, it's not like I can go anywhere,' Candy reminded him. 'I do happen to be trapped in this lousy apartment.'

'Just give me your bloody number and stop being so dramatic. God, I'm sure the Royal Shakespeare Company already have you on speed dial for next time they need a Lady Macbeth.'

Even when he was angry, Alfie was funny. OK, funny in a mean way, but Candy still wanted to pause the fight so she could snort with laughter. Instead she gave Alfie the most haughty look she could muster. 'Just take your stuff and leave,' she said icily. 'And you can't have my number. My agent says I'm not allowed to give it out to just anybody.'

Mimi had said no such thing, but it made Alfie give one last outraged sniff, before he walked out again. This time he slammed the door behind him so hard that Candy's teeth rattled.

Chapter Thirty-Two

It was a very cranky Candy who finally surfaced on Monday morning. She was a teenager – being able to sleep on a dime was meant to be part of the package; a compensation for being a slave to her hormones. Insomnia was not meant to be part of the deal.

It didn't help that everywhere she went in the flat, Alfie's presence was now indelibly imprinted. The bathroom smelt of his aftershave, and he'd even left a small tub of Aveda moisturiser behind because he was a total metrosexual (which explained why his skin had felt so soft when she'd rubbed her cheek against his).

The kitchen was witness to the hundred cups of tea that he'd drunk and the plain chocolate HobNobs he'd bravely volunteered to eat because Candy preferred the milk ones, and the lounge . . . it took Candy five attempts to enter because it wasn't the living room any more but Alfie's workroom.

Candy desultorily folded the finished clothes and put them in the plastic dustbags that Alfie had left, because she was actually a very caring girl. The TV was stuck on *E!News* as the remote control had gone AWOL. Candy watched with one eye and listened with one ear, pausing only to witness the pretty that was Justin Timberlake turning up for some red carpet event. After she'd finished boxing everything up, she'd start on her packing.

'. . . witnesses say the fight erupted out of nowhere when David Careless picked up a bowl of fries and threw them across the room.'

OK, that got her attention. Candy looked up to see grainy cellphone footage of her parents having a ferocious row in some dimly lit restaurant. The picture was low res, but she could see Bette's platinum blonde head bobbing in agitation as David gestured wildly with his hands.

'No one knows what the fight was about,' chirped the cheery-looking newsreader. 'But with David's recent hospitalization and daughter, Candy, living in London, is the strain getting too much for showbiz's oddest couple?'

That was a really good question. Candy waited for the guilt to kick in; on average it took about ten seconds. But a minute later and all that she felt was the same sick, sad feeling in her stomach that she'd managed to find a well-dressed, articulate boyfriend, whose kisses made her completely undone, and lost him in the space of forty-eight hours. On the bright side, at least it put the whole parental thing into perspective.

Finally, Candy was all packed. Really, she should phone someone and let them know that she was coming. Then again, let Nick de Laurentis and Mimi, who hadn't exactly stuck up for her, worry that Candy might be a no-show. Certainly she wasn't fingering the buttons of her iPhone because she wanted to call Alfie and wish him luck. Not even!

It was a shock when her phone did actually start to ring.

Candy's heart leapt all the way up her throat for a second, but it was only Hadley.

'Hey, how are you?' Candy asked fairly pleasantly.

'I'm fine. How are *you*?' Hadley cooed. 'I guess you've seen the news. I don't know what your parents are playing at. Haven't their publicists told them about damage control?'

'Hey, why live your life in private when you can do it in public?' Candy sniped. 'Welcome to the family.'

She heard Hadley gulp. 'Well, I won't keep you,' she said hurriedly, like she was in a rush to maybe call off the engagement. 'Just I spoke to my legal guy and he said there's nothing doing with the contract. It's, like, loophole-free. And now with your parents rowing in public, they'll pressure you even harder to come back and save the show.'

Candy sighed at the thought of going back to that apartment . . . Even though the walls had been knocked out it was still pretty small for three people at daggers drawn. Though maybe Bette would shack up with Nick de Laurentis, which meant that Candy would be on constant watch to make sure that David wasn't getting high. Big whoop. 'Well, thanks for trying, Hadders.'

'Look on the bright side,' Hadley tweeted. 'You've still got the fashion thing and you've got Alfie. It's not all bad.'

But it was all bad because she didn't have Alfie. Not any more. Then, to her horror, Candy started to cry. At least it wasn't *in front of* Hadley, but that didn't seem like much comfort right then.

'Candy, you're crying! What's the matter?' Hadley gasped. 'You'll see Alfie at the show and then you can apologize for whatever you've done wrong. Did you swear at him? I bet you did!'

It was so typical of Hadley to automatically think that Candy was at fault. She knew her so well. 'I'm not going to the show,' Candy sputtered. 'I've going to NYC tomorrow morning and there's photographers outside.'

'Pffft! Never thought you'd be scared of a few tubby guys with Nikons,' Hadley sniffed. It occurred to Candy that all the sympathy and advice could just be a front and that actually Hadley was enjoying the opportunity to lord it over her. 'I'm really getting to see another side of you, Candy.'

'I wasn't mean to Alfie,' Candy whined. There was a deafening silence from the other end of the line. 'I wasn't! He didn't even ask me if I was coming to the show, he just assumed—'

'When you assume you make an ass out of u and me . . .'

'My God, Hadley, quit being such a dick!' Candy growled. 'And he called me a drama queen and said that I was totally self-involved, which I'm not, I just have a lot going on right now.'

'Well, you do,' Hadley conceded. 'It does seem a bit unreasonable of him when he knows that you're being bullied by lawyers and parents and scary industry types—'

'No, he doesn't, I didn't tell him,' Candy interrupted impatiently. 'You were right, he's a civilian – he just wouldn't get it.'

'God, you really don't deserve a boy like that, Candy. I bet you *were* mean to him and said loads of mean things that you can't even remember saying, because it's what you do,' Hadley concluded with a tiny, heartfelt sniff. 'I had to have back-to-back sessions with my therapist when you started calling me Sadley.'

It was definitely Dump On Candy day. 'OK, I'm a terrible, evil person,' Candy snapped. 'I got the memo. I'll go back to New York, and you and Alfie and Laura and all the other people who hate me for being such a douche won't have to deal with me any more.'

'Oh, stop being such a pity queen,' Hadley said tetchily. 'You still have time to make up with Alfie, though he may just tell you to screw off.'

It was the rudest thing Candy had ever heard Hadley say, which was mildly diverting for all of five seconds. But then they could get back to talking about Candy. 'He won't want me there,' she moaned. 'Not after the argument, and anyway he won't notice me because there'll be all the clothes that need his attention, and he'll need to fit them, and he's way controlling about that kind of thing – and shit, he'll be fitting them on models. There'll be a tonne of models there and I'll be the shortest, roundest girl in the room and he won't even notice me.'

'But then he'll look up and see you,' Hadley sighed dreamily. 'Like, everyone else will just melt away and all you'll be able to see is each other. And Alfie will be in a tux, and you'll have a sparkly blue dress on and a big white flower in your hair, and he'll walk up to you with, like, this burning gaze and he'll take you in his arms and kiss you. You'll swoon and he'll stop you from falling and—'

'Hadley, what the fuck are you talking about?' Candy snarled, because she'd been right there until the sparkly blue dress and then she'd realized Hadley was in her own world. Or that she'd inhaled too much hairspray.

'Sorry,' Hadley giggled. 'I was borrowing heavily from my Orlando Bloom fantasy, which was before I met Reed, FYI. What I'm saying is that you won't know what happens unless you find Alfie and tell him how you feel. And if you're there to actually help him fit the models, then added bonus.'

Candy was already halfway to the bathroom and trying to remember if she'd put the hot water on. 'OK, yeah, screw it, I'm going,' she decided. 'I can't believe I've just taken relationship advice from you.'

'And I can't believe I just offered it,' Hadley said drily in a very unHadleylike way. 'Still, we are almost sisters and now you owe me, which I'm totally going to remember when it comes to my bridesmaids' dresses.'

'You know, Hadley, you're a total bitch,' Candy grudgingly offered. 'Respect.'

'Remind Alfie that I've got dibs on the pencil skirt,' Hadley said. 'And don't worry about the other stuff. I have a feeling that everything is going to work out just fine.'

Candy didn't, but she let Hadley cling to her Pollyanna illusions. She had two hours to make herself look so drop-dead, knock-out, catch-your-breath gorgeous that Alfie would drop to his knees to kiss the hem of her dress. Well, he probably wouldn't, but it was a nice idea.

And two hours and seven minutes later, when Ravi and Ben shouted up from the street, Candy was slicking on her Ruby Woo lipstick. She was wearing the dress Alfie had made for her (which was so cunningly constructed that she didn't need to wear her gutbuster underpants to yank in her belly), a pair of killer heels and a slightly anxious smile.

Candy hoped that she looked like a young Elizabeth Taylor or a less skanky Dita Von Teese. Neither of whom had ever probably had to travel in a bashed-up white Transit van or help load it while hordes of camera-wielding scum tried to take her picture.

'You got a new job then, Candy?' one wag guffawed.

Candy ignored them in favour of telling Ravi that there was no way she was travelling in the back of the van and he could just damn well budge up and make room for her on the front seat.

And then to a chorus of motorbikes revving up to follow them and the blinding flash of cameras, Candy hitched up the skirt of her dress so she could climb up into the van, and wondered if this was the worst idea she'd ever had.

She'd find out soon enough.

Chapter Thirty-Three

They were already running late and now they had a convoy of motorcycles driving alongside them, though Ben took that as a challenge to go through as many red lights as possible.

Candy was not amused, especially as she was trying to put on a last coat of mascara. 'For Christ's sake,' she snapped as Ben took a corner too fast. 'I nearly poked my eye out.'

'I think we lost the tail,' Ravi said excitedly, peering out of the window.

'We're not in an episode of *Law and Order*,' Candy sighed, but it was no use. The pair of them were thoroughly over-excited at their heroic tactics in rescuing Candy from the clutches of the tabloid press and the prospect of seeing models in various states of undress. Which was a surprise. Candy had imagined Alfie's friends to be a bit more poncy. Possibly they'd sit around eating smelly cheeses and watching black-and-white films with subtitles. Not Ben going into raptures about possibly seeing: 'Tits. Naked tits. Naked model tits. Doesn't get much better than that!'

He sounded so happy that Candy didn't have the heart to point out that most models she knew (apart from Laura) were pretty short-changed in the breast department. 'Does Alfie know the sordid reason why you're helping him?' she asked drily.

They giggled like naughty schoolboys. 'He thinks we're doing it for twenty quid and some of his mum's onion bhajis,' Ravi choked out, as Candy clung to the door handle while they took another really sharp turn.

Eventually they pulled up outside an old church in Shoreditch. Candy turned to the boys with a confused look. 'Alfie's doing a fashion show in a place of worship? Don't think that would even happen in New York.'

'They're turning it into luxury flats,' Ben explained, opening the door and jumping out. 'The property developers said it would be OK as long as Alfie didn't send any birds down the runway in their skivvies.'

Candy thought of Alfie's elegant clothes and decided that there was nothing there that even God could disapprove of. She took the hand that Ben was offering so he could gently lift her down, then they started unloading the clothes. Or Ravi and Ben unloaded, and Candy scolded them for dragging the clothes bags on the ground as they walked around to the church hall, which was being used as the dressing room.

Candy paused at the entrance. The last time she'd seen Alfie they'd said horrible words. *He'd* said horrible words to her, so why was she standing here, shivering her butt off in his fancy dress, when she was probably the last person he wanted to see?

'Shift your arse, Candy,' Ben bellowed behind her, and before she could think about it, Candy was taking the three steps that led over the threshold and into a place where pandemonium reigned.

There were no topless models because they were all huddled in their thick coats shivering at the lack of heating. Candy watched in dismay as goosebumps popped their way along her arms while Ravi and Ben dumped their piles on an empty table.

'Don't just heap them like that,' she complained, grabbing a dress. 'Go and hang them up. You can match the outfit to the rail – see, it's all on that list pinned up over there.'

They didn't look too happy about being bossed about, but Candy gave them her most baleful glare, the one that promised a world of pain, so they did what they were told.

At least she had something to do now: carefully taking off the plastic wrappers and checking for damage before hanging up clothes. Candy had even bought a little sewing case and a stylist's kit . . .

'What are you doing here?'

Alfie didn't sound very pleased to see her, so Hadley's eyes-meeting-across-a-crowded-room fantasy had been bullshit. But then, he didn't sound like he was about to call Security and have her thrown out either.

'Nice to see you too,' Candy snapped, whirling around. And it *was* nice to see him again, especially as he was suited and booted. But he had that tight little furrow between his eyebrows and his lips were pinched.

'Don't start . . . Saskia! Where is the DJ?' he suddenly shouted at someone across the room. Really shouted, so that Candy thought her eardrums might never recover.

The effortlessly pretty girl he'd had lunch with that day

hurried over. 'This is a bloody nightmare. Apparently the caretaker's in the pub and he forgot to put the heating on and people are starting to arrive and we're still dusting the pews.'

'But I need you to get the models in hair and make-up,' Alfie growled. 'I have to sort out the clothes and I still need to do the running order and five of the girls haven't even turned up yet.'

Maybe Alfie's pained expression had nothing to do with Candy. Which was something of a blow to her ego, but she'd probably recover.

'I could do the model wrangling,' she offered, with a casual shrug. 'I've been backstage at loads of shows. The running order's up – have you got the model cards?'

Saskia's eyes had widened in shocked recognition when Candy first opened her mouth, but now she was eagerly opening a folder and rifling through comp cards. 'You're a life saver,' she gasped. 'These are the models. I've got their mobile numbers and Alfie did sketches to show hair and make-up.'

'Cool,' Candy said, taking it all from her. 'Why don't you get Ben and Ravi to hunt down the caretaker instead of standing around trying to chat up models? And I'm Candy, by the way.'

'Saskia – I was at college with Alfie and I'm dating his brother Sanjay, otherwise I would not be here,' Saskia gritted, her green eyes flashing. She really was extraordinarily beautiful. And dating a Tanner who was not Alfie, which automatically made Candy like her a little bit.

'And if you shout at me again, Alfie, I'm telling your mum,' she added before she hurried off.

Alfie shuffled his feet. The threat of his mother's wrath had momentarily calmed him down. Candy rummaged in her bag. 'Sewing kit,' she said, handing it to him. 'Go and sort out the clothes and stop bitching at people who are trying to help you.'

'OK,' he muttered, then had the nerve to arch an eyebrow at her. 'You're really enjoying this, aren't you?'

Candy didn't even have to think about it. 'Yup,' she said smugly. 'And you'll never be able to call me a drama queen again because actually being mouthy and bossy are good qualities to have in a crisis.'

There was a little stand-off that lasted all of five seconds before Alfie found a smile and bent down to kiss her cheek. 'I'm glad you're here,' he murmured in her ear, but then she was forgotten and he was striding towards the clothes rails.

A ragged cheer went up when the heating finally came on with a dreadful clanging noise. By then Candy was boiling hot and red-cheeked from running around after various models, who all needed a good slap.

'I work for free,' one Polish girl wailed mournfully. 'But is too cold.'

'Rubbish,' Candy said stoutly. 'What are you going to do when you have to shoot swimwear in the middle of a blizzard? You have to suffer for beauty!'

Eventually, all the girls were lined up. Candy had

carefully peeked through the gauzy white curtains into the cavernous interior of the church. Thankfully, the altar and all the godly stuff had been removed and more white gauze had been hung everywhere. Candy could see the team from Nico's sitting right at the front, as well as several fashion editors and the entire Tanner clan.

'Remember: elegant, strong, sexy walks,' Alfie ordered the models who were all chattering excitedly. 'Don't do any of that prancing stuff.'

Candy busied herself removing invisible pieces of fluff from the outfits with a roll of sticky tape from her bag. 'Remember not to smile, but don't look bitchy,' she added. 'Walk strong.'

Saskia looked at her watch and smiled as the DJ played the right tune at exactly the right time. She consulted her clipboard. 'Ludmilla, on my count. One, two, three . . . GO!'

As each model stepped out on to the runway – or the tiled path running down the centre of the church, if you were going to get technical about it – Candy felt as proud as any mother seeing her children off to big school for the first time. Alfie was visibly shaking and staring at a spot on the floor, but Candy peeked out again.

'They're all smiling,' she informed Alfie. 'And that woman from *The Guardian* is making loads of notes. Oh, they're all clapping the pencil skirt . . .'

'Stop it,' he begged, clapping his hands over his ears. 'What was I thinking when I decided to do my own line with no backing, no business plan, no idea of what I'm doing?'

Saskia shared an exasperated look with Candy. 'Oh do, shut up, Alfie,' she snapped, as the models returned from the runway and gathered around them. 'You have to do the victory lap now, so get your lanky arse out there.'

Candy looked at Saskia with something approaching awe. She was like the older sister that Candy didn't even know she'd wanted. 'C'mon, Alfie,' she cajoled as the first girl stepped back out into the church. 'You *have* to go out.'

Alfie shut his eyes. 'I don't have to. I prefer to be a shadowy figure in the background'

'If it's good enough for Marc Jacobs, then it's good enough for you,' Candy bit out, giving Alfie's sleeve a tug in the direction of the curtain. 'Go! Scoot! Begone!'

'OK, but you're coming with me,' Alfie gulped and, before Candy could protest, he was marching out, her hand tucked securely in his as they followed the last model between the pews.

Candy knew a second of sheer embarrassment because she'd taken her shoes off ages ago and forgotten to put them back on again and she could see people smiling at the difference in their heights. But then she also saw that people were getting to their feet and clapping Alfie, and he was letting her share a tiny bit of his triumph. A triumph he'd earned not because he had connections, or some sort of nebulous fame, but because he really did make the most kick-ass clothes.

Alfie squeezed Candy's fingers tightly as they got to the end of the walkway and he gave a stiff little bow to even more applause. On the way back up the church, he let go of her hand so he could wrap an arm round her shoulder. 'I wouldn't have had a show without you,' he shouted over the roar of the crowd.

They stepped through the curtain, back into the dressing room, and were suddenly enveloped in a scrum of well-wishers, various Tanners of assorted sizes and some very strangely-dressed hipsters who had been at St Martin's with Alfie.

Chapter Thirty-Four

It wasn't often that Candy had to watch from the sidelines, but it was impossible to get near Alfie. Not when he was having business cards pressed on him from all sides.

Candy busied herself making sure that the models didn't just drop their clothes on the floor and leave them there. Or worse, stuff them into their bags. She knew all their little tricks. Irina had once walked out of a shoot with a fur coat, though her booker had made her return it.

Soon everything was back on the rails and Candy accepted a plastic cup of champagne from Nico, who was putting a brave face on the fact that his right-hand man was destined for better things.

'I taught him everything he knows,' Nico insisted loudly, casting an anxious glance in Alfie's direction. 'He's talking to a major venture capitalist. I bet he hands his notice in tomorrow.'

'Alfie's not going to do anything rash,' Candy said, smiling as Eddie Tanner clapped his son on the back. 'And you'll find another obsessive compulsive junior designer in a nanosecond.'

'Not like Alfie,' Nico said mournfully. 'And you buggered off pretty sharpish too. Creative Director for Le Sac so I hear . . .'

'Yeah, for as long as my face is plastered all over the TV

and the tabloids,' Candy said defensively. She knew that as soon as she quit the show she could kiss goodbye to her Creative Directorship, which was one of the few by-products of her celebrity that she was actually proud of.

Nico gave her a thoughtful look. 'You shouldn't sell yourself short,' he told Candy. 'Orders are up two hundred per cent for the bags you worked on. Sure, you need technical training but you have a strong instinct for fashion, and you actually have a point of view. If you decide to go to college in London and you want some more hands-on experience, give me a call.'

'For real?' Candy gasped. How whacked was it that she was so thrilled to be offered unpaid work if she could actually find a place at a fashion college? She was a totes crap celebrity.

'For real,' Nico promised, raising his plastic cup at someone on the other side of the room. 'You know where to find me.'

For the rest of the evening, Candy became an honorary Tanner. Turned out that once you came through for one of them, the others accepted you without question. Though Pretty seemed to think that meant that she had a guaranteed place to stay if she ever made it to New York.

'I'll be no trouble at all,' she insisted. 'And we can order Chinese takeaway in those cute little cartons they have in the movies.'

Candy could see Alfie fighting his way through the crowd towards her, and not a moment too soon.

'I'm not sure that your mom would be too happy about

you going to New York,' she prevaricated. 'And my parents' place is too small for guests.'

Before Pretty could protest, Alfie butted in. 'Do you want to cadge a lift home with Ravi and Ben?' Candy's heart sank just a little bit. If she went home now, there wasn't much time for a proper goodbye. 'They said they'll take us as far as Euston.'

There were nudges and theatrical winks from the peanut gallery as Candy tried not to grin like a moron, especially when Alfie casually took her hand. Getting out of the church hall took for ever. Mostly because Eddie and Meera wouldn't stop jawing on about how proud of Alfie they were, and would Candy like some leftovers to take home with her, and what a pity it was that she was flying back to New York tomorrow because they wanted her to come round for Sunday lunch.

Then she had to listen to a blow-by-blow account of all the half-glimpses of naked model breasts Ravi and Ben had witnessed, and even though it was a freezing cold night, Candy was relieved to be dropped off a mile from home.

'Alone at last,' she said to Alfie, as they started walking up Eversholt Street towards Camden.

He frowned as he looked at her. 'It's December and you decided to come out without a coat?'

Candy shivered as soon as he said it. 'None of them worked with my outfit,' she said through chattering teeth. 'Anyway, it's not *that* cold.'

Alfie was already whipping off his wool overcoat. 'It's just as well for you that I always wear a suit jacket,' he said, wrapping the coat around Candy. It swamped her, dragging on the frosty ground as she took a few steps. 'It doesn't matter,' Alfie said. 'It's just clothes.'

'Are you sure you're feeling all right?' Candy asked sweetly, as she huddled into the borrowed coat. 'I think you might be going down with a fever.'

But Alfie just grinned and put an arm around her so they could huddle together for warmth. Candy watched her breath crystallize in front of her and hoped that the kebab shop at the top of the high street was still open because she really needed some chips. She was just about to share this startling revelation with Alfie when he cleared his throat.

'You're still going to New York tomorrow then?' he asked hesitantly.

Candy's shoulders slumped. 'I'm contractually obligated to,' she admitted. 'My parents currently can't stand to be in the same room as each other, let alone have a TV crew following their every move, so I've got to go back and run interference.'

She could just see it now. The three of them sitting round the cluttered table in the kitchen and David spitting out, 'Candy, ask your mother if she's seen my new issue of *Rolling Stone*?' And Bette would reply, 'Tell your father that I have a date with Nick de Laurentis and I have better things to do than look for his silly music magazines.'

'I thought they had a good marriage,' Alfie ventured. 'They seemed pretty happy when I met them.'

Candy snorted. 'Yeah, well what we both failed to realize was that my mom was screwing someone else and my dad was back on the drugs. He ODed last week – that's the real reason he was in hospital.'

There! She'd said it, and to a civilian too, who wouldn't possibly understand because he had a family who were normal. Well, not normal, but together. And they did proper family things like have Sunday lunch and turn out to support each other, even if there wasn't a TV crew to record every last telegenic moment. And Alfie wouldn't get it because he didn't do drama or chaos and Candy didn't do anything else.

'All happy families are the same, but every unhappy family is unhappy in its own way,' Alfie said suddenly.

'What the . . . ?'

'It's a Tolstoy quote, it's from the beginning of *Anna Karenina*,' Alfie informed her just a little too smugly. 'It seems appropriate to your situation. Families can be a pain in the arse but that's better than having no family.'

'I guess,' Candy said grudgingly. 'I'd rather have your family though. Do you think your parents would like to adopt me?'

Alfie didn't look convinced. 'You'd have to stop swearing, learn how to make chapattis and remember the names of all my cousins before they'd sign anything.' They came to a halt, as they waited for a light to turn red. 'How long will you be away?'

'Should take two months to wrap the season, then I'm eighteen and I'm done. I'm not going to sign a new contract,' Candy said fervently. 'And I've got enough money in the bank to live on for ever, as long as I don't

315

start splashing out on private jets and shit.'

They started to cross the road, Candy veering sharply to the left in the direction of the kebab shop, whose window was glowing merrily in the distance. 'I'll wait for you,' Alfie said quietly, so Candy had to strain to hear him over the rumble of the traffic. 'If you want me to.'

'Yeah, I do,' Candy said, risking a glance at the deadly serious expression on Alfie's face.

He shot her one of those smiles that turned Candy's heart inside out and back to front. 'Well, that's settled then.' He let go of her hand. 'God, I'm starving! That kebab shop looks open. Do you want to get some chips?'

They were dipping their hands into a scalding hot bag of chips, dripping with salt and vinegar, when something wet landed on Candy's face. She squinted up at the sky to see big, fat, white flakes slowly start to drift down from the heavens.

'It's snowing,' she squealed excitedly, because snow was still as magical to her now as it was when she was a little kid. It was just white powder, but it covered the grey, grimy world and made everything look shiny and new. And now that she was actually outside, she noticed there were tonnes of fairy lights strung from the lampposts because it was almost Christmas. Not that Candy was going to get what she wanted from Santa because she'd been a way naughty girl this year.

Alfie pulled up the collar of his jacket and grimaced. 'It looks pretty now, but tomorrow it will be all grey and slushy,' he groused.

Candy punched him on the arm. 'Don't be such a buzzkill,' she laughed, tilting her head back so she could catch snowflakes on her tongue. 'If it was snowing really heavily, I'd *so* put some down the back of your neck.'

Alfie's eyebrows shot up. 'That's fighting talk,' he warned.

Candy shrugged. 'You think I wouldn't?' She threw a chip at him as a snowball substitute, then shrieked as he came at her with a mock growl.

The chips fell to the snow-covered ground as Alfie picked Candy up and whirled her around so fast that the neon shop signs, Christmas decorations and car headlights blurred around her. 'Stop! Stop!' Candy begged, clutching tight on to Alfie's shoulders. 'You're making me dizzy.'

But then she decided that it was the look in Alfie's eyes that was making her giddy and short of breath. She didn't think that anyone had ever looked at her like that before: tender, amused, maybe a little bit exasperated. She cupped Alfie's face in her cold hands, as woolly gloves definitely hadn't gone with her outfit either, and kissed him.

Then there was a lot of kissing. So much kissing that Candy wasn't exactly sure how they managed to get to Bayham Street with all the kissing and stroking and pulling at each other.

It took five goes before she successfully inserted her key in the lock, and getting up two flights of stairs was very hard when Alfie kept stopping to press Candy against the wall and kiss her so hard that she swore she might have stopped breathing a couple of times.

'Do you want me to come in?' Alfie asked, nuzzling

Candy's ear as they reached her landing.

Candy once more struggled with her key. 'I'll kill you if you duck out on me now,' she giggled. She had plans for Alfie, which consisted of going to third base for definite.

'In that case, I'd better stay,' Alfie decided, blowing a raspberry against the back of Candy's neck, which just made Candy giggle even harder. Alfie did playful? Who knew?

The door finally opened and Candy and Alfie fell into the flat, banging against the coat rack and sending Candy into a fresh fit of giggles. 'Get the kettle on,' Alfie demanded. 'I kiss better with a hot drink inside me.'

'Sir, yes sir,' Candy snapped, though a little part of her couldn't believe how sappy she was being. Well, she'd cringe about that on the flight back to New York tomorrow. 'Shall we kiss a bit more while we're waiting for it to boil?'

Alfie laughed as he straightened the coat rack and looked all set to agree with Candy's cunning plan – when there was a muted giggle *and* a pointed cough from the lounge.

'That all sounds great,' said a voice from the living room. 'But we'd like a word with you first.'

The smile was instantly wiped off Candy's face as if someone had taken an eraser to her mouth. She shot an agonized look at Alfie, who was staring transfixed through the open doorway of the lounge. 'Well . . .' he mumbled.

Candy peered over his shoulder to see Irina, Hadley and Laura sitting on the sofa like three not very wise monkeys.

Chapter Thirty-Five

The three of them needed to stop paying rent and appearing at really inopportune moments, Candy thought, her back stiffening as she prepared to go on the defensive.

'What are you doing here?' she asked angrily, Alfie's hand on her arm the only thing stopping her from rushing in and trying to bodily eject them from the flat.

'Waiting for you,' Irina drawled, giving Alfie a heavy-lidded appraisal, before turning to Hadley, who was smiling brightly though the occasion really didn't warrant it. 'Is this the boy?'

'It is. Isn't he adorable? Alfie, this is Laura and Irina, both successful models with many advertising campaigns between them,' Hadley said, standing up and gesturing at Laura and Irina like she was the hostess of *Wheel of Fortune*. Hadley prided herself on her introductions, though Candy couldn't imagine why. 'Laura, Irina, this is Alfie, he's a genius fashion designer and he's Candy's special friend,' she added unnecessarily, even throwing in some air quotes.

Laura gave Alfie a careful little wave. 'Hey,' she said. 'You work with Nico Lonsdale, right? I think I met you at a fitting once?'

Alfie nodded dopily. Not dopcy as in he was in the presence of tall, leggy models and couldn't believe his luck.

More like dopey because he already had an image in his head of Laura and Irina swaying down the runway in his designs. Candy could just tell. 'Pleased to meet you all,' he said when he finally found his voice, then he did a complicated step and shuffle so he was standing behind Candy like she was a human shield. He gave Candy's shoulder a quick squeeze. 'I'll be in the kitchen if you need me.'

The door slammed behind him before Candy had time to haul him back so he didn't leave her alone with three girls who each had a valid reason for wanting her dead. Not that she was going down without a fight.

'You know, for three people who are earning a gazillion dollars between you and have other places to live, you sure do like to come back here a lot,' she sniped, leaning against the doorjamb, in case she needed to make a quick getaway. 'Whatever. I officially don't care.'

And with that she made to leave and barricade herself in her room with Alfie, though Candy didn't feel like she wanted to set up home on third base any more.

But Candy wasn't even halfway out of the room when Irina suddenly picked her up and plonked her down on the sideboard. 'You move from there, I smack you,' she told Candy cheerfully, fencing the smaller girl in with freakishly long arms.

People taking gross advantage of Candy's lack of inches was a surefire way to make Candy mad. Once in eighth grade, one of the basketball team had lifted her up on to a cupboard in one of the classrooms and it had been too high

320

for her to jump down. Candy could still remember the cheek-burning humiliation when she'd had to offer one of the Maths geeks $10 to bring her a chair. Now she settled for trying to kick Irina in the shins and spitting, 'How fucking dare you?' at her.

'Oh for crying out loud, Candy, why do you always have to be like this?' Laura burst out. 'You're impossible!'

Actually, Candy was kinda proud of that. Better to be impossible than a wussy girl who'd turned her back on her mates as soon as a boy came along. All three of them had perfect new lives and perfect new boyfriends who adored them unconditionally, even though Candy knew that each of them had their own flaws, from leaving soap scum round the bath to putting half-eaten apples back in the fridge.

'Why are you even here?' she demanded, wriggling against Irina's firm grip and getting an insolent grin back in return, which just made her madder. 'Not like I care! I'm going back to New York in the morning and when I come back I'll be eighteen and I won't be living in this shithole!'

Hadley clapped her hands in glee. 'But you're not! You won't,' she cried unintelligibly.

Laura wound a lock of shiny brown hair around her finger. 'Well, actually she might have to, because I'm rapidly going off the idea,' she said sourly, which didn't clue Candy in as to what the hell was actually going on.

'But you have to, you promised,' Hadley pouted.

'Ja, don't be such a pussy,' Irina spat at Laura. 'Is shitty to go back on your word when you agree to stuff.'

At least, Irina and Laura would never be BFF; that was

something. 'Did you guys happen to do a whole bunch of mind-altering drugs on the way here?' Candy enquired archly. 'And I am going to New York, Hadley. I have a big, long contract in my suitcase says so.'

'You're not,' Hadley repeated, and she still wasn't making any sense, plus it was getting seriously irritating. 'We're moving back in so you can stay here and take part in a new one-season only reality show . . .'

'Nick de Laurentis wants to call it *At Home With the Fashionistas*,' Laura explained helpfully. 'Fierce spoke to him this afternoon. Says if we agree to do it, then he'll release your parents from their contracts.'

Candy scrutinized the potted plant in the corner for a hidden camera because they had to be *Punk*ing her. 'I don't believe you,' she mumbled. 'He was clear – couldn't wait to film the death scenes of my parents' marriage . . . Oh shit!' She scrubbed the back of her hand over her eyes, which were starting to leak.

'Oh, Candy, don't cry.' Hadley hurried over to try and give Candy one of her sub-standard hugs. It occurred to Candy that Hadley was enjoying this way too much.

'Don't touch me!' she hissed, twisting frantically to try and evade both Irina's grip and Hadley's hands of doom.

Irina finally stepped back and shrugged volubly. 'Well, gratitude is too much to expect. I almost forget how noisy you are.'

Hadley's face crumpled slightly. 'Come on, guys, we're all going off-message here,' she said, but her perkiness had dissolved, which Candy was truly thankful for. She gave

Candy a serious dose of puppy-dog eyes. 'Aren't you even a little bit pleased?'

Candy tried to ease herself down from the sideboard without tearing her dress. 'No, because you lot are totally playing me. I'm not sure how, but you are.'

'You know how some people are passive aggressive?' Laura remarked, crossing both her legs and her eyes. 'Well, you're aggressive aggressive.'

'All three of you hate me,' Candy burst out. 'Well, maybe Hadley doesn't – but why would you give up your privacy and move back in *here* just to help me out? Believe me, if I was in your shoes, I wouldn't.' If Candy was in their shoes, possibly she wouldn't just blurt out her thoughts without filtering them first.

'Oh, Candy, I don't hate you,' Laura snapped. 'You really piss me off a lot of the time, but you've been there for me when I hit absolutely rock bottom and I figured that I should return the favour. Though I'm having serious second thoughts.'

'And I not hate you either,' Irina assured Candy. 'Sometimes I dislike you most intensely, but I'm helping you out because I have a heart.'

Candy wasn't buying that for a second and neither was Laura because she snorted in disbelief. 'Yeah, whatever.'

'OK, Javier said it was the right thing to do and also I want to be on TV,' Irina admitted without an ounce of shame. 'You all been on TV, is not fair.'

'And I'm doing it because we're almost sisters,' Hadley reminded Candy, with that little glint in her eyes that could be mistaken for fervour though Candy was convinced it was vengeance. Why else would she keep bringing up the S-word?

'Well, thanks then, I guess,' Candy muttered after a moment's uncomfortable silence. God, she really was an ungrateful bitch. She tried again. 'Seriously, thank you.' But already she was worrying about payback, and she didn't have to wait long.

'There are conditions,' Laura stated firmly. 'I'm not being filmed without make-up on, or in my underwear, or any other states of undress.'

'I want one of the big rooms,' Hadley butted in. 'And I have to be scripted. I'm much funnier when someone else is writing my words.'

'You not having my room, have hers,' Irina bit out, pointing at Candy. 'She the one who owes you big. Me? I want top billing.'

'No way am I moving out of my room,' Candy hissed. 'Look, this will never work if you're going to use it as a stick to beat me down all the time. I said stuff. You said stuff. We all said stuff. But we either build a bridge and get over it or this is a pretty crappy idea.'

'You want to go back to New York then?' Laura asked with narrowed eyes.

Candy thought of Alfie, who was cowering in the kitchen, or more likely with his ear pressed to the door. And then she thought of New York, which had lost a lot of its glitter mostly because it didn't have an Alfie in it. Plus it came with the added bonus of her parents who seemed to be gearing up for a really ugly divorce. 'God, no,' she sighed. 'I really, really don't.'

Hadley's hands fluttered. 'Candy's right. We have to stop arguing so much, if there are going to be TV cameras about.'

'I not see why,' Irina sniffed. 'The more we argue, the more we get good ratings.' She smiled dreamily. 'Maybe I get my own spin-off show.'

Laura and Hadley were now glaring at Irina for her plans to steal their TV thunder with some blatant camera-hogging, and Candy was still their least favourite person in the world. But in the oddest way, she'd missed them. She'd even missed the constant bickering, though not as much as she'd missed the freakish times when they'd all been getting on and would gather in the front room to eat Thai takeout and watch a DVD together. Though usually they'd ended up bitching about the characters' clothes.

But Irina was right. That wouldn't make such compelling TV as the other ninety per cent of the time when they were hurling abuse at each other.

'You know we don't have to actually live here,' Candy explained kindly. 'We can just come back on the days we're filming.'

She was met with blank stares. 'I didn't know reality TV worked like that,' Laura frowned. 'When I was on *Make Me A Model*, there was always a camera focussing in on my open pores.'

'It's not reality TV, Laura. It's a reality-based, genre-defining dramedy,' Candy drawled and, though the effort nearly killed her, she managed to keep a straight face.

Laura simply looked relieved. 'Thank God for that,' she sighed, stretching her long legs out. 'It's so poky in here. And Danny was being all weird that he'd end up on TV if he came round. He might be getting a transfer deal to AC Milan but you absolutely can't tell anyone.'

'Like we even care about that ball-kicker,' Irina barked. 'Javier's shooting for French *Vogue*.'

'Well, Reed's movie is going to be premiered at Cannes,' Hadley said hotly. 'And he's lovely and we're going to get married. So there!'

Candy rolled her eyes because no way was she joining in. Alfie wasn't her boyfriend. Not officially. They were, like, pre-dating. And footballers, film directors and fashion photographers kind of trumped him at the moment, and if he was listening at the door, she didn't want him to get an inferiority complex. She was all heart.

As Laura and Irina began to snap and snarl, the kitchen door slowly opened and Alfie's head emerged. 'Pssst!' he hissed at Candy. 'I've drunk my tea, I've done the washing up, I rearranged your kitchen cupboards, but I couldn't face doing the fridge. May I please come out now?'

'. . . you always be fat to me,' Irina was shouting. 'Even when you in a size six, like that would ever happen.'

'And you'll always be a foul-mouthed, skanky bitch who by rights shouldn't even be modelling incontinence pants,' Laura shouted right back.

'Don't you remember that being in a negative environment makes me break out,' Hadley whined in the background.

'Are you sure you want to?' Candy asked Alfie, with a brief gesture over her shoulder. 'They could be at it for hours.'

Alfie held a steaming mug aloft. 'I made you tea. Why don't I watch you drink it in your room?'

As a plan, it got Candy's vote. 'But you know I don't like tea,' she said to Alfie, once they were in her room with the door firmly shut.

Alfie sat down on the bed, picked up the mug from the nightstand and took a sip like it was nectar of the gods and not a really piss-poor substitute for a good cup of coffee. 'Well, you'll have to learn to like it if you're staying in London,' he said, lifting up his arm so Candy could snuggle against his side.

'You heard then?'

'It was hard not to. I don't think the conversation ever went below a few thousand decibels,' Alfie said drily. 'The neighbours banged on the ceiling at one point, but none of you seemed to hear.'

'Are you pleased that I'm staying?' Candy asked, slightly nervous of the answer, because if Alfie had been planning to change his number and his identity while she was in New York, then she'd really screwed up his plan.

But Alfie calmly took another sip of his tea before replying. 'Yes,' he said firmly. 'Now you can come to my mum's for lunch on Sunday.'

And then he kissed her.

Epilogue

Alfie was coming down the stairs as Candy raced up them, and only an adroit side-step on his part stopped them colliding.

'Late,' he said succinctly, looking at his watch.

'My tutor wanted to talk about my second year module after class and the traffic was ungodly,' Candy complained, reaching up to kiss him on the cheek. Then she stepped back and opened her coat for Alfie's inspection.

He was all fashion designer and not much of a boyfriend as he ran a professional eye over the black lace mini-dress he'd made her the night before. Candy tugged at the oyster silk under-dress. 'One of the armpits is weird. Doesn't fall right,' she complained. 'You puckered the seam.'

'In the face of extreme provocation,' Alfie reminded her. 'You were kissing my ear, if I remember rightly.'

'Sucks to be you,' Candy said with just a small side order of huff. 'I thought you liked it when I kissed your ear.'

'I do,' Alfie protested, as he ruffled her hair. 'But it's dangerous when I'm operating a sewing machine.' He paused. 'Oh! Of course, it's Wednesday. I should have known.'

Candy frowned. 'What happens on Wednesdays?'

'You have pattern-making as your last class and it always makes you cranky.'

'You got that right,' Candy sighed. 'My skirt pattern sucked like nothing else. My tutor said it would make a better doily than a circle skirt. And really I do love the dress. See, I'm wearing it with my favourite tights.'

This time when Alfie looked at her legs, it was with a boyfriendly leer. 'Very nice,' he said blandly. 'But I think your exceptional lateness was just a cunning ruse to stick me with most of the fetching and carrying.'

'As if!' Candy gasped indignantly. Then she grinned. 'So are you nearly done?'

Alfie rolled his eyes. 'Almost, but there's lots of crap under your bed that you can sort out. And someone from Fierce called and said the flat has to be clear in an hour. Absolutely clear, they were very sure about that.'

'Oh, what*ever*,' Candy drawled. 'Like, they have any power over me.'

'Well, I'm telling you to finish packing because I can not listen to Irina and Laura screaming at each other for much longer without killing one of them,' Alfie said, picking up the boxes that he'd put on the stairs. 'Get to it, young lady!'

Candy saluted smartly, but Alfie was already disappearing down the stairs. And he was right, because she could hear the sounds of disagreement getting louder and louder as she got closer to the second floor.

'I don't know how that Lanvin dress got into my case,' Laura was insisting without much conviction.

'I do. Your fat fingers put it there,' Irina growled.

'But Irina, you keep taking my pink Juicy Couture lounge suit when you think I'm not looking,' Hadley added. 'Why can't you just get one of your own?'

Candy pushed the door open and was met with a scene of utter chaos. Even when they'd been filming *At Home With the Fashionistas*, there'd never been so many people crammed into such a small space. There was Laura, Irina and Hadley really not doing much in the way of packing but lots in the way of arguing. Reed was glued to his BlackBerry, but turned and waved at Candy. There were boyfriends and friends of boyfriends (including two Premier League footballers) actually doing the heavy lifting as well as the professional movers Hadley had hired, and Sophie and Saskia, who were in the kitchen methodically eating their way through the food that was left in the fridge.

'OK, you know we're meant to be out of here in an hour,' Candy said by way of a greeting, as she dropped her book bag on the floor.

'You haven't exactly been helping, Candy,' Laura moaned. 'I cancelled a job today, so why didn't you just skive off college?'

Candy shrugged. 'I have my end-of-term exams coming up.'

'You're such a brainache,' Irina scoffed. 'And that hair still look like shit. Why have you not grown it out yet?'

The day that they'd wrapped filming on *At Home With the Fashionistas*, Candy had had all her hair chopped off into a really short pixie crop and dyed red. Now very few people recognized Candy until she opened her mouth and they heard her speak. And even then, she'd cut way back on

331

the swearing, so it was only the American accent that gave her away.

'I think you mean brainiac,' Candy told Irina sweetly, because she was also trying really hard not to get a rise out of people, which she missed because it was fun. 'I'm going to finish up my room. See you in a few.'

The three of them were back to arguing about clothes-stealing within a nanosecond and, pausing to give Dean Speed a wide berth and a dirty look (which he returned with interest), Candy headed for her room.

When she'd left this morning it was still a cluttered mess: clothes piled up everywhere, bags and shoes spilling out of her cupboard, and make-up, magazines and sewing accessories littered over every spare surface. Now it was almost an empty space, apart from a few last boxes that Alfie hadn't yet transferred to Ravi's van.

With a deep sigh, Candy sank to her knees and started rooting under her bed. Mostly, it was junk. Old fashion magazines with the pages she wanted to keep already ripped out, a box of press cuttings that could go straight in the bin, and a crate full of the Le Sac bag samples, which had never made it into production because Candy had quit the business called show and, just as she'd predicted, all her endorsements had dried up like water hitting a hot griddle.

There was also a photo from the LA premiere of Reed's film. They'd all flown out, courtesy of the TV network, and Candy stared at the photo of the four of them taken on the red carpet. All of them were wearing specially designed Alfie Tanner dresses: Irina in a red strapless number, Hadley in a draped white Grecian gown, Laura wearing a corseted black dress and Candy in a very short Kelly green frock. Candy remembered how Laura, Irina and Hadley had jostled for prime position in front of the cameras until they'd finally realized that pushing and shoving at each other wasn't the right image. Then they'd linked arms and posed prettily, each of them making little adjustments so the cameras got their best sides. They didn't look quite real – all gussied up in their best frocks and party make-up like they could only exist in the pages of a magazine.

It was weird that the three of them had become even more famous. And not just because the one and only season of *At Home With the Fashionistas* had been a break-out success. Irina was making £10,000 a day and moving to New York to present some horrific rap show on MTV. Laura was the new face of TopShop and was following Danny to Milan, and Hadley had just signed on to do the new Spielberg movie. Hadley and Reed had had the longest engagement in the world, but the inevitable was scheduled for late September and Candy still wasn't used to the idea or that happy about it. At least she could listen to Hadley bleating on about centrepieces without visibly flinching. But no way in hell was she wearing a buttercup-yellow bridesmaid's dress.

And Candy? Was currently finishing up her first year as a fashion student, wasn't the face of anything and didn't miss it. She'd bought a small house in Stoke Newington overlooking Clissold Park, just round the corner from Alfie, which she was going to share with Saskia and Sophie (who'd lost the attitude once Nico promoted her and she started dating Ben). Candy did her own laundry, could cook a mean chilli, and the highlight of her week was going to the Tanners' for Sunday lunch.

Only last Sunday she'd heard Meera say to Eddie as she helped to clear the table, 'I didn't think Candy was right for our Alfie, but I'm grown very fond of her especially now she doesn't swear so much. She really feels like one of the family.'

'And she's a good little grafter too,' Eddie had agreed. 'Not afraid to get her hands dirty, and she's made Alfie loosen up too.'

It had meant more to Candy than all the column inches and endorsement deals that she'd had when she was the Eleventh Most Famous Person in the World. Besides, she'd never live it down at college if her picture were still plastered all over the papers.

Now, she stuffed the premiere photo in one of the boxes, threw a handful of rubbish into a garbage bag, then plugged in the vacuum cleaner so she could suck up all the bits of fluff coating the carpet. Alfie came in just as Candy was merrily listening to the tinkle of pins being sucked up the hose.

'You missed a bit,' Alfie remarked pointing in the far corner. 'And you're going to break the hoover if you don't pick up the pins first.'

Candy smiled beatifically. 'Bothered. Not like we're getting the security deposit back. I smashed a picture within the first five minutes of arriving here, y'know.'

Alfie didn't look that surprised, as he hoisted up the last of the boxes. 'But you'll miss living here, won't you?'

'Not even! There was never enough hot water and the fridge was way too small for four and I couldn't sleep at night because lots of drunk people liked to walk down our street at three in the morning,' Candy ranted. 'Though it was cool to be so near the big Sainsbury's.'

'But you'll miss your friends,' Alfie insisted, because he was now used to Candy's rants and never gave them his full attention.

And yeah, she probably would, because they were actually all friends again. Kinda. Sort of. They'd bonded together against a common foe – the TV crew who were always trying to sneak up on them when they were in their underwear or catch them fighting.

Laura obviously felt the same because as Alfie and Candy entered the lounge, she was in floods of tears and trying to hug Irina and Hadley. 'I'm really going to miss you guys,' she sobbed. 'God, I can't believe I'm going to miss Irina.'

Irina looked unimpressed, but she gave Laura's back a surreptitious pat. 'I not really miss you. But I guess we say hello when you're in New York.'

'You're both being really silly,' Hadley said, offering Laura a tissue from her bag. 'You'll see each other at the fittings for your bridesmaid dresses and Candy's going to have a housewarming party . . .'

'Am not!' Candy snapped, coming to a grinding halt, much to Alfie's consternation, because he groaned in a long-suffering way. 'I've just had the floorboards painted white and I don't want a whole bunch of people coming round and trashing the place.'

Alfie had the audacity to lift his leg and gently nudge Candy's ass with his foot to get her heading towards the door again. 'She's having a house party,' he gritted. 'She'll text you. For God's sake, Candy, will you move? I'm parked on a yellow line.'

. 'OK, OK, I'm coming,' Candy grumbled as she heard Irina hiss gleefully to Hadley, 'She so whipped. I never thought I'd see the day.'

Because Alfie was carrying all the boxes, Candy managed an airy wave. 'Later, losers!' she drawled, following Alfie out the door and down the stairs. 'I didn't say I was going to have a housewarming, Alfie!'

'My mother's already started cooking for it, so you'd better have one if you know what's good for you,' Alfie replied cheerfully.

Candy wisely refrained from saying anything, especially as Alfie hadn't realized that he was doing all the carrying and she just had her handbag. Their progress was hampered by two rangy blonde girls, each carrying several large bags, suddenly charging up the stairs.

'Watch it!' one of them snarled in an Australian accent as they were forced to slow down to let Alfie and Candy past without potential bone breakage.

'Watch it yourself!' Candy snarled back, as the one behind shrank away from her with an apologetic smile. . They were twins. Tall, skinny, blonde twins. There should be a law against that, Candy thought as she started walking again.

Their voices drifted down the stairwell. 'Megan, you were so rude! And we're early. Really early.'

'I already told you: we had to get here first to bags the biggest rooms. Besides, I'm not letting anyone push us around.'

'The new girls,' Candy grinned at Alfie as they stepped out on to the street. 'They try any of that attitude on Irina and she'll throw them out of the window.'

Alfie put the boxes in the back of the van as a taxi drew up and deposited another lanky teenage girl and two dumpy, harassed-looking parental units gasping at how much it had cost to drive them from Euston station. 'Oh yes, looks like the next generation has just arrived,' Alfie said, holding the passenger door open for Candy.

She waved at the open front door as Alfie started the engine. 'Bye-bye Bayham Street,' she sing-songed. 'It was kinda nice knowing you.'

Candy smiled as Alfie pulled out into the road. The past was over and done with, the present was full of possibilities, and the future blazed away in front of her.

Fashion Glossary

What's With All the High-Falutin Fashion Speak in this Book?

Atelier
French for workshop, often used to describe a fashion designer's studio. They love their French, do the fashion folk.

Baste
Nothing to do with turkeys, but to do with using large stitches to temporarily join pieces of fabric together, which can be easily removed.

Dart
Darts are V-shaped tucks in a pattern to make it fit better. For instance, bust darts give fullness to a dress, whereas darts at the hip and waist will take away fullness. You especially tend to find darts in vintage clothing.

Directional
Just a high-falutin way of saying that something or someone is 'fashion forwards', or wearing the trends before they happen.

Draping

Some designers rarely work from patterns but drape their material on a form and design that way instead. Draping is also an important part of the design process to see how different fabrics fall.

Dress Form

This is a padded mannequin (usually just of a torso and hips) that designers use to fit their designs. Forms come in different sizes and are an essential tool for any designer.

Gather

This is a way of pulling fabric together (such as in a skirt) to create fullness.

Georgette

A lightweight, sheer fabric usually made of silk, which gives a crêpe finish. Often used for swanky designer dresses.

Grey Gardens

This is a seminal US Seventies documentary about Little Edie and Big Edie, an eccentric mother and daughter fallen on hard times, who lived in a crumbling house with a gazillion cats. Little Edie's penchant for turbans, wearing upside-down dresses as skirts, and leopard print has turned her into a fashion icon for the likes of Marc Jacobs. A film starring Drew Barrymore is out in 2008.

Grosgrain

A very heavy silk with horizontal ribbing. It's often used for ribbons.

Muslin

A cheap, rough material, which is used by designers to make trial garments so they can see how effective their pattern is. (Muslin squares also make ace facecloths!)

On Trend

Just a really fashion way to say that a designer's collection or a piece of clothing is very of the moment because it's working some of the season's biggest trends in colour or cut.

Organza

A thin, sheer silk, usually with a silvery sheen, which is often used for evening wear.

Overlock

A useful stitch used for seams that prevents fraying, especially when using stretchy fabric.

Pantone

A coded colour system used by the design and fashion industries. A Pantone book is a huge directory of numbered colour strips (like paint swatches) so there can be no confusion over the shades used in the design process.

Pinking Shears
These are dress-making scissors with crinkly edges so they don't fray the fabric they're cutting.

Pressing
Not the same as ironing! Pressing is an important part of making clothes; once sewn, seams need to be pressed to make sure that they're not puckered or crooked.

Ragpicking
Those sneaky fashion designers employ people to source really good vintage pieces which they'll re-interpret or remix for their own collections. But don't tell anyone.

Rickrack
The cutest trim in the world! It's a flat, wavy braid that should be added to as many things as possible.

Seam Allowance
It's really technical but this is the little bit of fabric between the cut edge of the garment and the seam line.

Tacking
See **Basteing**

Top Stitch
A row of stitching, visible on the finished product. Particularly used on accessories like handbags.